When I went back to read the story of Abraham and Sarah after reading Barren, the story really came to life! I could imagine them as real people with real thoughts and emotions instead of just historical facts. I would recommend Barren to anyone.
-Stephanie Weaver, Operations & Academic Administration for Whole Word Institute

Great story! I enjoyed it and long for more.
-Camille Elliott, Insurance Agent

I'm typically a Sci Fi/Fantasy fiction reader, but Barren was a great read!!!!! I'm ready for book two.
-Robb Bossley, Operations Manager

Once I picked up this book, I couldn't put it down. It grabbed my attention from the very beginning, and I couldn't wait to see what happened next. Great read, and I'm looking forward to the next book.
-Erin Levesque, Elementary School Paraprofessional

I found this to be a theologically-rich, thoughtful, and imaginative re-telling inspired by the story of Sarah in Genesis! The author's deep knowledge of the Word of God and of the ancient Near-Eastern world of the Patriarchs is evident in her writing. Yet, she pens with such creativity and flair. By placing familiar biblical themes in a contemporary setting, the author invites us to grapple with grief, faith, identity, and the longing for motherhood in a deeply personal and refreshing way. The emotional journey of the protagonist feels sincere and realistic, and the steady-paced narrative gently reminds readers that, like in the original Genesis story, God's purposes often unfold through seasons of waiting and trust.
-Christian Book Excellence Awards

BARREN

A CONTEMPORARY STORY OF SARAI

ELIZABETH SIMON

LIZARD BOOKS, LLC

BARREN

Book Cover by NeatDesign

First edition 2025

The Scriptures quoted are from the NET Bible® https://netbible.com copyright ©1996, 2019 used with permission from Biblical Studies Press, L.L.C. All rights reserved.

Publisher's Cataloging-in-Publication Data

Names: Simon, Elizabeth, author.

Title: Barren : a contemporary story of Sarai / Elizabeth Simon.

Description: Port Charlotte, FL: Lizard Books LLC, 2025.

Identifiers: ISBN: 979-8-9927467-1-6 (hardcover) | 979-8-9927467-0-9 (paperback)

Subjects: LCSH Sarai (Biblical figure)--Fiction. | Abraham (Biblical patriarch)--Fiction. | Native Americans--Fiction. | Christian fiction. | BISAC FICTION / Christian / Contemporary | FICTION / Christian / Biblical | FICTION / Women

Classification: LCC PS3619 .I66 B37 2025 | DDC 813.6--dc23

To my loving husband, who has always supported me throughout this journey.

AUTHOR'S NOTE

Genesis has always been my favorite book of the Bible. Since I started studying it through the BEMA podcast and The Bible Project, I've read it over fifty times. What really fascinates me is how we often treat these stories like fairy tales—something we hear without really thinking about. The "lullaby" effect kicks in, and we know the stories so well that we don't stop to consider the strange, sometimes unsettling details. But when you take a step back, some of these stories are pretty bizarre. For example, why wasn't Eve freaked out when a snake started talking to her? I know I'd be terrified if an animal suddenly spoke to me. And think about Abram—his decision to leave his family and go to a new land was a huge deal. Do we really understand how massive that was? Or what about when Abraham almost sacrificed Isaac? Did Isaac just calmly walk down that mountain afterward, like nothing happened?

The Bible was written to a specific group of people (the Jews) by a specific group of people (the Jews) in a specific cultural context. But in modern American Christianity, we often try to make the Bible fit our culture instead of understanding the culture in which it was written. This can lead us to misunderstand what the Bible is actually trying to tell us, compared to what God originally intended. And sadly, many people don't care that we're misinterpreting it. They just accept whatever they've been taught, without questioning the ideas passed down by well-meaning but misguided pastors across America.

One day, I started thinking—or maybe it was God putting this on my heart—about how these strange stories would play out if they happened today. Could they even happen in modern America? Take Sarai, for example. What if she had to marry her uncle after her father died? Could that happen today? I looked it up, and it turns out, in all fifty states, it's illegal for an uncle to marry his niece—except in one case. In some Native American tribes, where they are sovereign nations apart from the United States, and customs and traditions are different, an uncle could marry his niece.

That got me thinking about whether it's even possible to adapt these stories for the modern world. Just like the example with the marriage custom, I had to reimagine many parts of these ancient stories to make them fit into today's American society. This made me realize that God knew exactly what He was doing when He chose the time and place for His story to unfold. While I could manipulate the details to make them fit today, things were a lot simpler in the time and place where God's nation was born.

Another thing that struck me while reading these stories is something we don't often think about. We focus so much on the "heroes"—the patriarchs like Abraham, Isaac, and Jacob—but we forget about the people they hurt along the way. Take Sarai, a young girl who lost her father and was given in marriage to Abram. What about Hagar, who was forced to have sexual relations with someone just because she happened to be there? Or Eliezer, who would've inherited Abraham's wealth if Isaac and Ishmael hadn't been born? And Leah, the sister with "weak eyes," who was never truly loved by her husband. What were their thoughts and feelings as these events unfolded?

In *Barren*, the first story in the *Margins of Genesis* series, the focus is on the thoughts and feelings of Sarah, or "Princess," as she's called. In future stories, I'll dive deeper into the lives of other characters, like Hagar in *Rejected*, Isaac in *Distressed* when he's almost sacrificed by his father, Eliezer in *Faithful* as he searches for a wife for Isaac, Rebekah in *Misunderstood*, and Leah in *Unloved*.

I want to make it clear that these stories are works of fiction. They aren't meant to be exact retellings of the Bible, nor are they inspired or scriptural. They're just stories—fiction based on the basic plot of the Bible. My hope is that when you read them, you'll start to think differently about the real Bible stories and the people behind them.

ONE

"Princess. Michaela. Wake up!" Someone was calling my name, pulling me from a dream. I groaned and rolled over causing the old bunk bed to squeak under the shift in weight. It couldn't be morning yet, but I saw light from behind my closed eyelids. Someone shook my shoulder, and I opened my eyes to see Grandad's worried face. His face was blotchy, and his eyes were red, as if he'd been crying. I had never seen Grandad cry before in all my life. Something was very wrong.

"Girls, get up!" he urged, his voice filled with worry.

I sat up, confused. "What's wrong?"

"There's been an accident. We need to get to the hospital right away."

"What?" Michaela and I exclaimed together, now fully awake.

"Louis is already out front. Get dressed quickly and meet us outside. Your parents were in a car accident."

I quickly jumped down from the top bunk, nearly knocking over my sister Michaela, whom we called Mickie, as I scrambled to get ready. After slipping on our fur-lined buckskin coats, we met my brother Louis outside our creaky, double-wide trailer. We all jumped into Grandad's beat up, old station wagon, knocking snow off the bottom of our winter moccasins.

Grandad drove us over the bumpy gravel roads that crisscrossed in grids throughout our Native American reservation, or Rez as we called it. His car was barely holding together as he zipped around the curves. I clung to the door handle, my knuckles white.

We flew past our school that held classes from kindergarten through twelfth grade. The reservation's general store and the lake were a blur as we soared past them, gravel skidding off the side of the narrow road as we rounded the corners.

On the south side of the Rez, the casino was the only building with any paved roads leading up to it. The car finally hit the smooth pavement as we passed the casino, and Grandad slowed down slightly to avoid the ice. We were finally off the reservation, and Grandad drove the other hour to the hospital. I held on tightly as we swerved through the narrow, winding roads.

When Grandad parked in the small hospital parking lot, we all jumped out. I hadn't realized I was holding my breath until I let out a deep sigh of relief, grateful to be done with that ride. I stepped onto the parking lot, and a gust of wind whipped my long, dark hair across my eyes. I quickly pulled it back so I could see, securing it with a hair tie from my wrist, and dashed after my family toward the emergency room.

As we raced in, everything felt like it was moving in slow motion. The empty waiting room was small, with the check-in desk taking up most of the space. An ambulance was parked outside the double entrance doors to the right, its flashing lights casting red and white light on the walls. There was a single door on the other wall to the left of the front desk leading deeper into the emergency room. A heavyset blond woman with a worried expression sat at the desk, trying to look busy while avoiding my gaze. Her gloomy look filled my head with terrible thoughts.

Grandad ordered Louis, Mickie, and me to stay in the waiting room and went to find out what was going on. My heart was racing, and I wrung my hands in my lap, as I sat stiffly in the gray and red pleather chair against the wall. I attempted to clear my throat, but my mouth was too dry, and I stifled a cough. Mickie had beads of sweat on her forehead, and she was squirming in her seat. Louis sat completely still, back straight.

Grandad returned, his face pale. He motioned for us to follow him. We walked through the door to the left of the desk and down a hall. I knew it was bad when everyone looked at us with sad recognition. Some gently touched his arm as he passed, like they were saying, "Sorry.".

Grandad paused in the hallway and turned to address us. "Kids, the accident was serious," he said. "Their truck hit a patch of black ice and skidded off the road, wrapping around a tree."

"Are they going to be okay?" Louis asked.

Grandad's eyes slid away. "No," he said softly. "Your dad was killed instantly."

The room seemed to spin, and darkness threatened to engulf me. I felt numb and reached out to steady myself against the wall, grabbing onto Mickie's arm with my other hand. She was crying softly beside me, and she pulled me into a hug. *Daddy is dead?* It couldn't be true. I was Daddy's girl. *How can I live without him?* Tears streamed down my face as I sobbed uncontrollably against Mickie's shoulder, the grief gripping me. Louis stood with his mouth agape and face pale.

"What about Mom?" Mickie said with a trembling voice.

"Your mom is alive, but she's on life support. We can see her now, but be prepared, there will be a lot of tubes. And you might not even be able to touch her," Grandad gently explained. We nodded and followed him down the hallway and into the elevator. He pressed the button for the second floor, and we waited, the sound of soft sobs filling the tight space.

He led us through the double doors leading to the short corridor of the intensive care unit. The smell of antiseptic engulfed me, making my stomach turn.

I could barely see through my tears as we went down the hall, turned the corner, and arrived at Mom's room. Grandad was right; a snarl of tubes were everywhere, and monitors beeped all around her. Her neck was in a brace, her face was covered in bandages tinged with seeping blood, and she had a breathing tube in her mouth. Dark purple bruises lined the skin of her arms, the only skin visible due to all the bandages and tubes. She looked so still, almost peaceful, except for the slight rise and fall of her chest, thanks to the ventilator.

"Her heartbeat is very weak. I don't know how much longer she can hold on," Grandad said, his voice breaking as he looked at the heart rate monitor. "She can't breathe on her own."

Fresh tears spilled from my eyes as I gazed at her battered face. I touched her hand, which was lying still by her side above the bedsheets. This felt like a nightmare I couldn't wake up from. Touching Mom's hand injected some reality into this terrifying situation.

"Mom, can you hear me?" I whispered through my sobs. There was no response. Not even a flicker of movement from her or the beeping monitors.

"Mom, we're all here," Mickie said, her voice trembling. "We love you. You can get through this." If anyone could get her to react, it would be Mickie. Mickie had always been Momma's girl, making Mom beyond proud with every new accomplishment. Still, there was no change. She held Mom's hand, squeezing it gently, hoping for any reaction. But nothing happened.

Louis stood back, watching us quietly. It was clear he handled grief differently than I did, or maybe he hadn't gotten over the shock and processed what was happening in front of him yet. He seemed to still be in denial.

"What happens now?" Louis asked, breaking the silence. He looked at Grandad.

"We wait to see if she improves. They're going to run more tests to check her brain and see how badly her organs have been damaged. The next forty-eight hours are crucial." Grandad was clearly trying to be hopeful, but the worry in his eyes betrayed his real feelings. "They'll only allow one of you to stay in here at a time," Grandad added.

"I'd like to stay first, if that's okay," Mickie said, wiping away fresh tears.

Grandad nodded, and he led Louis and me out the door and to a smaller waiting room nearby. "I'm going to make some calls," he said, hugging us before leaving us.

I went to Louis and hugged him tightly as more tears flowed down my cheeks. I could feel him quietly sobbing into my hair, his grief mixing with mine. He held onto me and swayed back and forth, rocking me in his arms as I sobbed into his shirt. My tears flowed until none were left.

Worries flashed in my mind like lightning in a storm. *What if Mom isn't okay?* I tried to push that thought away. Mom just had to get better so life could go on for all of us...but without Daddy. More tears fell. Louis and I broke apart and sank exhausted into the small waiting room's uncomfortable chairs, letting our sorrow wash over us.

Two

Two days ago, a late September snow covered the ground in a layer of soft powder. It clung to the brightly colored leaves, making the reservation look like a winter wonderland. Although it was still autumn, the chill of winter was in the air. I took a deep breath, threw my arms wide, and spun around, soaking it all in. The cold air smelled crisp and clean, stinging my lungs as I breathed in.

This was my favorite time of year. School was back in session, and the trees were bursting with color. I had turned sixteen the week before, so this was the start of a brand-new year for me.

I could hear Mom and Daddy in our back shed cleaning and butchering Daddy's latest catch. I walked across the wide wooden porch and down the stairs of our trailer, passing by two tall spruce trees standing guard on either side of the steps. The trees offered shade during hot northern Minnesota summers, since air conditioning was a luxury we didn't have for the house. Only the back shed at the far end of the lot, which was used to hang and prepare Daddy's meat and fish, had air conditioning.

I went around the back of our home and popped my head in the shed to see if Mom wanted to make dinner with me. "Mom, did you see? It snowed," I said excitedly. "Can we make venison stew?" I suggested to Mom as the two of us left the shed and sloshed through the wet snow to the back door of the trailer.

"That sounds like a great idea, Princess!" Mom said, opening the back door and following me into the kitchen.

Princess was my Indian name, given to me in a naming ceremony shortly after I was born. We all had Indian names, but most of the tribe used their given name. For some reason, Daddy liked my Indian name better than my given name, Isabelle, so the whole family called me Princess.

"I'm so proud of you for all you've learned. You've really taken initiative around here lately."

I blushed at Mom's compliment and pulled out the recipe book Mom had given me for my birthday last week. I pointed to one of the little tips she had inked into the margin to ask her about it, then pulled potatoes and spices from the cupboards and meat and vegetables from the refrigerator.

Men and women had distinct gender roles in our tribe. The women took care of the kids, gathered berries, cooked, trapped small animals like rabbits, and made clothes and other things to sell at the reservation's general store. Since I turned thirteen, cooking had been my job, and I found that making dinner was one of the few things I was good at. Since I felt being a mom was my calling in life, I embraced the homemaker mentality.

Mom and I chatted as I browned the ground venison and she chopped the onion and mixed in the spices. She diced up a few potatoes and squash while I shucked a corn cob. The sun was setting by the time we had dinner simmering, and the savory smells filled the kitchen. Mom was an amazing cook and patiently taught me everything she knew about cooking in the kitchen and over an open fire. The time I spent with Mom cooking and helping with family chores was so special to me.

When the timer dinged, I carefully lifted the bubbling pot off the stove and set it on the counter next to the oven. Opening the back door, I called to Daddy through the crisp, wintry air, "Dinner's almost ready, Daddy!" I saw him wave back through the shed window. Mom grabbed the fry bread from the pantry, and we lined up the stew and fry bread, plates, bowls, and cutlery on the laminate countertop next to the refrigerator.

"This looks amazing, Princess!" Daddy said, breathing in the smells of the stew as he walked in the door and spotted our buffet line. "I didn't know I was in for such a treat."

I couldn't help but feel proud. Daddy always knew how to make me feel special.

Mickie and Louis joined my parents and me in the kitchen, and the five of us scooped stew into our chipped plastic bowls and carried them to the wobbly table in the small dining room off the kitchen. We chatted and laughed as we ate, and I felt so lucky to have my family around me. Sure, we disagreed sometimes, but we got along better than most.

"Your mom and I are going to the Twins baseball game tomorrow in Minneapolis," Daddy said, wiping his mouth with a paper napkin. "They're close to making the playoffs, and this could be the game that gets them in."

Cable television was still a new thing on the reservation, and Daddy had signed up for the service as soon as it was available. It was the one thing he splurged on. Now, when he wasn't out hunting or fishing, he loved to relax with the family and watch sports on our old, battered television.

"That sounds fun, Dad," Louis said, pulling his long, wavy hair back into a ponytail to keep it from falling into his soup. Like all the Native boys, Louis had learned to hunt, farm, and fish, but he'd chosen to work at the casino, which was the economic core of our reservation and managed by my uncle Nate. Louis liked watching baseball at the sports bar in the casino when he wasn't busy working.

"Are you staying overnight? It's a long drive, isn't it?" Mickie asked before shoving another heaping spoonful into her mouth, a bit of stew slopping down her chin into her napkin in her lap.

"No, we're driving back after the game. I need to be at the market in town Saturday morning to sell the new catch," Daddy said. He was the oldest of his brothers and stayed true to his Native roots. He was a man of the land, spending most of his time fishing in Zaagaigan Lake on the Rez and hunting in the thick woods around us. He sold the strings of deer, bear, and moose to our neighbors, and every Saturday morning, he loaded up his old Ford pickup truck with extra meat from the deep freezer and drove to Oodena, the closest town, to sell it at the farmer's market. Mom used the hides from the animals to fashion coats, leggings, robes, and hats.

"I got one of the lead roles in our school play!" Mickie announced, changing the subject. "We're doing Cow Pie Bingo, and I'm Scout!" My sister was the talented one in the family. She got straight As, played on the high school basketball team, and often took the lead in drama productions. Everyone loved her, and I looked up to her, wishing I could be more like her. But while I worked hard for my Bs, school didn't seem that important to me. I dreamed of being a wife and mother someday.

"Oh, that's wonderful, honey!" Mom said, her eyes lighting up with pride. Mom loved seeing Mickie perform. She was so great on the stage, shining brighter than the stage lights and transforming into her character as if she had been born to act.

Ugh, why does she have to be so perfect? I thought and immediately felt guilty.

I swallowed my jealousy, patted Mickie on the shoulder, and tried to sound happy for her. "Great job, sis! Everyone wanted that part!"

Louis chimed in, nudging me on the arm with his elbow. "You didn't get the part of Maybelle, did you, Princess?" he said, joking about the part of the cow that walks around the field pooping during the bingo game.

I gave Louis a mean look.

"Louis," Daddy warned in a stern voice.

"I didn't try out," I said through clenched teeth.

"Geez, I was just joking," Louis said under his breath, becoming overly interested in his stew.

"Daddy, can you help me with my math homework after dinner?" I asked. "I don't get polynomials."

"Of course, honey," Daddy replied.

After dinner, Louis cleared the plates while Mickie did the dishes. Daddy and I sat together, ready to tackle my math homework. Polynomials were tough, but having him there made it easier. Daddy always made me smile, even when algebra felt like a puzzle.

And now...Daddy was gone.

***

Uncle Abe burst into the small waiting room in ICU, rushing over to us. "I came as soon as I heard. Oh, Louis! Princess!"

We stood from our chairs, and he wrapped us in a tight embrace, his eyes shining with unshed tears.

"What did they do to deserve this?" I demanded. "What have we done to turn the spirits against us?" I sobbed.

Most of the tribe believed in the spirit world, that there was spiritual power in all living things. We believed in a higher power that created the world, and we believed in Mother Earth and the spirits of the rain and the lake. Uncle Abe was the only one in the tribe who believed in one god whom he called Jehovah and said had created the world and everything in it. He didn't believe in other gods or spirits that controlled our destiny.

"Honey, there are no spirits against you," Uncle Abe said softly. "Jehovah has a plan, even in all of this pain. We can't see the bigger picture right now, it looks terrible and scary, but Jehovah will work all things out for good. We have to hold onto hope."

I pushed him away, wrapping my arms tightly around myself. "How can you say that?" I snapped, my voice trembling with anger. "There's nothing good about this!"

"Oh, sweetheart," Uncle Abe said gently, reaching out to touch my shoulder. I pulled away from his touch as if he had burned me and turned away, resisting his hopeful comments. "I know it's terrible. I don't understand it either. He was my brother," Uncle Abe pleaded. "We never can see the good future when we're in the middle of the crisis. But we have to keep faith, even in this darkness."

He tried to touch my shoulder again, to comfort me, but I was too lost in my own pain to respond. *How can Uncle Abe say these crazy things! I need my daddy! What kind of god would allow this to happen to our family? Doesn't He understand the pain, the grief, the misery?* I thought of Mom and how we could lose her, too.

***

After school yesterday, I was in the middle of making dinner when the old, corded phone in the kitchen rang. "Hello?" I said into the phone when I picked it up.

"Hi, Princess." It was Uncle Abe, and my stomach flipped in anticipation. Mom and Daddy wouldn't be home from Minneapolis until late, so Uncle Abe said he was coming by for dinner. We didn't need a babysitter, but it was always great to have family around, and Uncle Abe was my favorite uncle.

Rich and smart, Uncle Abe owned his own business. He lived on the nicer side of the reservation near the lake and casino and worked from his home. His company had been successful over the past year, but he didn't let his success go to his head.

"Sure. There's plenty of food for you. Come on over," I said. After hanging up the phone, I continued making the rice and fish and added an extra fish filet to the pan.

I few minutes later as I was finishing dinner, there was a knock at the front door. I dashed to be the first to answer it.

"Hello, Princess!" Uncle Abe exclaimed, pulling me into a warm hug. His long, dark hair was pulled back into a ponytail, giving him a distinguished and handsome look.

Louis walked up behind me and gave Uncle Abe a side hug. "You know you're always welcome here," Louis said, smiling and pushing his dark, wavy hair out of his face and back behind his ear.

Uncle Abe, Louis, and I walked back into the kitchen where Mickie joined us. We filled our plates with food then moved to the dining room to eat. After dinner, we all went into the living room and sat on the rumpled couch in front of the old television to watch a movie together. Being the youngest, I sat on the worn carpeted floor between Uncle Abe's and Mickie's legs since there wasn't enough room for all four of us on the couch. I was nearly dozing off, leaning against Uncle Abe's leg, when the movie ended. I was too sleepy to stay up any later, so I hugged Uncle Abe, said goodnight to Mickie and Louis, and headed to my room.

I shared a room with Mickie, and all three of us kids shared a washroom. Our bunkbed fit snugly along one side of the small room, and our matching dressers lined the other side. I climbed up on the top bunk and snuggled into my thick blanket. As I was drifting off to sleep, I heard the front door close behind Uncle Abe as he left to go home.

That was the last thing I heard before Grandad woke us up with the terrible news about the accident.

***

Pain shot through my stomach, snapping me out of my thoughts and back to the present. I looked around in panic through my tear-filled eyes for a washroom. This pain wasn't new for me, nor did it have to do with my grief. For years, I'd had debilitating cramping and diarrhea the week leading up to and during my monthly periods, which we called "moons." I didn't have long to find a washroom before disaster would strike.

I rushed out of the waiting room and asked the nurse where the nearest washroom was. Luckily, it was right down the hall, and I made it in time.

The stomach pain continued as I walked back into the waiting room. Grandad was in there with Uncle Abe and Mickie. Louis must have been with Mom because he was nowhere to be found. Grandad noticed my pale face and the way I was holding my stomach and looked at me with concern.

"Is everything okay, Princess?" he asked, worry in his eyes.

"I'm fine," I mumbled back. Grandad handed me a water bottle that he must have gotten from the break room or vending machine, and I gulped it down. My head throbbed from dehydration, from the crying and now the diarrhea. The water made me feel a little better. The pain in my stomach was still there, though, and I wanted to curl up somewhere quiet, but I couldn't do that here.

"You left pretty quickly," Uncle Abe noted.

"It's nothing. Really. Just my monthly moon," I replied, trying to sound casual. I pressed my arm against my stomach, trying to ease the pain without drawing attention. I didn't know why Grandad and Uncle Abe were making such a big fuss. The monthly moon often came with cramps, showing its power.

Grandad kept watching me closely as I sat there hoping the pain would fade. Instead, after about thirty minutes of pure agony, I felt another wave hit me and bolted out of my chair and back out the door.

When I came back, it looked like Grandad and Mickie had been deep in conversation, but they fell silent on seeing me. Louis had returned from Mom's room and was sitting with Uncle Abe. His eyes looked red from crying.

"Did you find out more about Mom?" I asked.

Grandad shook his head. "She's still undergoing tests. We'll know more soon. It will be your turn to see her once she's back in her room."

I nodded, still pressing one arm against my stomach, trying to look normal. I wondered what tests they could do in this small, ill-equipped hospital. For the first time in my life, I wished we lived closer to the big city.

After about an hour, a nurse entered and said it was my turn to see Mom. As I walked out the door, Grandad followed me, watching me closely. I tried to act as normal as possible, standing straight and hiding my stomach pain. He went to talk to one of the doctors who was standing near the nurses' station as I went in to see Mom.

Mom lay there, still and quiet, surrounded by tubes and steadily beeping monitors. I couldn't help it; my tears spilled over. I wiped them away with the back of my hand. "Mom?

Can you hear me?" I pleaded with her, taking her hand in mine. I rubbed it gently with my thumb, massaging it, as if I could massage the life back into her. She made no sound, made no movement, gave no indication she could hear me at all.

"Mom, if you can hear me, I love you." I swallowed hard against the lump in my throat. "Please come back to us," I begged, my tears falling onto her hand. "We can't do this without you."

But she continued to lie as silent and still as a statue. If it hadn't been for the bandages on her face and head, it would have looked like she was sleeping. *Is it my imagination or is the heart monitor beeping slower than before? Is she giving up?*

I couldn't let myself think like that. Losing her would be too unbearable. I forgot about my stomach pain because my heart ached so much. I started talking to Mom as if it were a normal day. "Mom, I had a math test today. It was awful as usual, but I think I passed. At lunch, Megis told us all about her vacation she's going to take over winter break. She's going off the reservation to the big city! Isn't that fun? Then in PE, I finally nailed my back handspring." I babbled on, hoping that acting like she was conscious might somehow bring her back.

The beeping of the monitors, which had been slow but steady as I was talking to her, seemed to slow down even further. I paused to look at them but had no idea what all the lights and numbers meant. She didn't look any different, and none of the doctors or nurses seemed to notice the slowing monitors or be concerned enough to check on her. I continued to talk to her, hoping the slowing down of the beeping wasn't a problem.

I talked for what felt like an eternity while the beeping continued to get slower and slower until an alarm sounded. The monitors flatlined with a long, piercing noise.

"Mom! No!" I screamed. "Someone, come quick!"

The nurses were already rushing in, pushing me aside as they lowered the bedrail and started CPR. I struggled against them, calling out to her in panic. *This can't be happening! Mom, no! You're supposed to get better!* I became dizzy, as darkness crept in from the edges of my vision, and everything went black.

THREE

I woke up on a bed, fully dressed, feeling disoriented. The ceiling loomed higher than it did over my bunk at home, and the walls were stark white. A television hung on the wall in front of me next to a row of tan cabinets, which were hanging on the wall over a counter with a sink. I realized I was in a hospital bed. The sun had risen, and sunlight streamed through a large glass window. Uncle Abe sat beside me in a gray chair, his eyes puffy and red.

My memories flooded back. "Mom!" I screamed, bolting upright. "Uncle Abe, please tell me she's okay!" I swung my legs over the bed, staring at him.

"Princess, I'm afraid she's not," he said softly, standing up and wrapping his arms around me. "Your mom didn't make it."

Tears spilled down my cheeks as I buried my face in his shoulder. I'd never felt such heartache.

Grandad entered the room and hugged me for a long time in silence. Finally, he pulled up another gray chair beside Uncle Abe and sat. "Princess, I want you to see one of the doctors here."

Wait, why? I'm not sick; I fainted when I heard about Mom. Does he think I need a therapist? I definitely felt like I could use one after everything that had happened in such a short time. Grandad must have seen the confusion on my face as I wiped my tears with the back of my hand and sniffled.

"I was talking to Michaela," Grandad continued. "She mentioned your cramps and stomach issues during your moon. Dr. Johnson is one of the best gynecologists around, and I want you to see her while we're here."

"I'm fine," I protested. "Cramps are normal. Michaela gets them, too." After all that had happened, I wanted to go home and be alone. *How can he be thinking about moon cramps after Mom just died?*

"Honey, Michaela's are normal, but yours seem more...intense. It's important to get checked out," he insisted.

Before I could argue, a woman in a doctor's coat entered, holding an iPad. I looked down at my hands, refusing to look at her, still lost in my grief. Grandad introduced her and stepped out of the room with Uncle Abe, leaving me alone with her. The doctor sat in the chair Grandad had vacated and looked at me with kind eyes.

"I'm sorry for what you're going through," she said gently. "I lost my dad last year, so I understand some of your pain." I wiped my nose and looked down at my hands. "When did you first get your monthly moon, Isabelle?" she asked. Although she wasn't Native, she seemed to know many of our traditions and lingo.

The answer to her question was easy, since coming of age for a woman in our tribe came with a whole ceremony. Our monthly period signified our spiritual power and ability to bring life into the world, so the year after a girl's first moon was celebrated with certain rituals, like using our own special dishes and not eating traditional foods so as not to affect the crops. "I was eight. I got mine a couple years before my sister, and she's a year older than me."

"Have they always been painful?"

"Yes, but I'm used to it. It's almost normal for me now," I admitted. "I thought it meant I had extra spiritual power."

She chuckled. "Maybe that's the case. You do seem like a strong young lady." She paused before continuing. "How long do your moons last?"

"A little over a week, every three weeks. Sometimes I spot in between, but it doesn't hurt as much when that happens."

"Do you have other symptoms with them?"

Embarrassed, I told her about the stomach pain and the diarrhea.

"I'd like to schedule an exam for you in my office downstairs," she said.

"Do I really need one? I've been dealing with this for eight years now, and it hasn't been an issue yet," I protested.

"Because of the diarrhea, I think it's warranted. I'll have my medical scheduler give your grandad a call to get you in as soon as we can." I nodded again. She stood to leave, smiling at me. "It was nice to meet you, Isabelle. I'll see you soon." I smiled back awkwardly, and she turned and left the room.

***

The next day I was back at home when Grandad branded the scissors that cut off Louis, Mickie, and my hair as a sign of our mourning. Our hair hadn't been cut since we were born, as long hair was a sign of spiritual strength in our community. As if our sorrow wasn't embedded deep enough in our mind, now it was physically evident in our looks. We were sure to be the only kids in school with short hair.

Grandad was now our legal guardian, and while I loved him, I missed Daddy deeply. Grandad moved in with us, as he, Uncle Abe, and Uncle Nate made arrangements for the double funeral, which would take place at the powwow the following Friday.

At seventy-five, Grandad was active and sharp. He had worked hard until his late sixties when he had been basically forced into retirement. I never knew my grandmother. She had been forty-eight when she'd died in childbirth with Uncle Nate. Grandad had never remarried after her death, but he had kept himself busy with work. Even after retiring, he kept busy with hobbies, a side job editing a prominent medical journal, and his role as an elder in the tribe's government.

***

The weekend was hard. Grandad, Uncle Abe, and Uncle Nate worked with Louis and some of the other tribal members to build a teepee in our yard from maple and ironwood saplings and string from the bark of the basswood trees around the reservation. Inside the teepee, Mom and Daddy's bodies, dressed in full regalia, would rest in simple oak boxes for the next few days. We built a campfire outside the teepee so visitors could stay warm and so I could make food over the fire for everyone who came to honor my parents. We stayed home from school Monday through Wednesday to help with the guests and attend to the campfire.

Going back to school on Thursday felt like torture. I was on my moon, which meant racing to the washroom between classes and taking Motrin to deal with the cramps and stomach pain. On top of that, all three tribes near our reservation shared the school, and they all knew about the accident. Only about fifty kids from my tribe, the Chaldean Indians, were in school, but from all three tribes combined, there were around four hundred students, and their sympathy only made it harder to cope.

"Hi, Izzy," my friend Megis said when she saw me in the hallway right before lunch. She looked at me with sad eyes and a pitying expression. "How are you feeling?"

Everyone wanted to ask me how I was feeling and if I was okay. She was the fifth person that had said something like this to me. Most people looked at me with sorrow and passed by quickly, not knowing what to say. Both reactions felt like daggers to my heart.

Of course, I'm not okay! My parents are dead! Gone forever! What was I supposed to say? I mumbled I was fine, tried not to make eye contact, and moved along to the next thing in my day...and the next person who asked how I was doing.

I was tired of answering the same questions over and over again and wanted everyone to leave me alone. I sat alone at lunch, as far away from the prying eyes as possible, and kept thinking about the things I'd no longer have: Daddy would no longer help me with math; Daddy could never teach me to drive; Daddy wouldn't give me away at my wedding one day. I held my head high, determined not to cry, but I was dying inside.

***

The bonfires crackled brightly the night of the funeral, filling the air with the warm scent of sage and heating the entire arena. Our school was too small for a football team, so the back field served as the perfect spot for our tribal powwows. We used the powwows for special prayers and ceremonies like weddings, funerals, and coming of age rituals.

In the center of the grassy field was a packed dirt circle, our dance arena. A large grandfather drum sat at its center, with an empty Eagle Staff holder right in front of it. Aside from the popping of the logs on the fire, the arena was quiet now, waiting for the ceremony to start.

Surrounding the dance area, the school's bleachers formed an outer circle, leaving a six-foot-wide entrance in front of the drum. Three flag holders—for our tribal flag, the United States flag, and the Minnesota flag—stood near the entrance during the opening ceremony. On either side of the field, bonfires flickered, casting light and adding a sacred sage scent to the atmosphere as night approached.

Along the front of the field, closest to the school, was a line of vendor booths where tribal members sold crafts, food, clothing, and jewelry. Folks browsed the booths, talking and chatting as they went along. It wouldn't be long before the opening ceremony began.

Uncle Abe and Uncle Nate were drummers in the ceremony while Louis was tonight's youth representative in the honor guard. We were all wearing our traditional powwow attire. The men had already broken out the winter regalia, wearing buckskin shirts and leggings under bustled winter robes with fur-lined moccasins. Their long black hair was tied back in ponytails under rabbit-fur caps.

Grandad and his friends, the oldest members of the tribe who made up our "elders," walked to the front of the arena. Uncle Abe, Uncle Nate, and the other drummers took their places around the drum. The elders offered a blessing to kick off the powwow, and anyone still lingering rushed to their seats. The drummers began warming up as Reu, the master of ceremonies for the night, welcomed everyone and explained the order of events. With the funeral ceremony today, the powwow would focus on the Flag Song, the Honor Song, and the funeral.

The Grand Entry processional started. Grandad carried the Eagle Staff while two of his friends held the United States and Minnesota flags. Louis proudly carried our tribal flag, his chin held high, trying his best not to cry.

Next came the head dancers followed by the other dancers. Fifteen elementary school kids joined in, looking adorable in their regalia as their teacher guided them to stay in line. They marched to the front row of the bleachers to sit until it was their turn to dance.

When the Flag Song began, we all stood in reverence and watched the drum circle perform. The Flag Song was like our national anthem, typically played only on drums, although it had words in our native tongue. Powwows helped us keep our language alive and taught it to the younger generation. We also took Chaldean language classes in school so our native language wasn't lost completely.

Once we sat again, the oldest member of the tribe offered an invocation and performed the smudge to purify the arena. During the smudge ceremony, the elder lit prairie sage in a bowl with a wooden match. The smoke was wafted with a feather around the arena toward the people, cleansing the arena of negative spirits and helping us focus on the celebration.

After the smudge, one of Mom's friends sang the Honor Song to the beating of hand drums while the flags were raised high. This song honored the veterans who served in the American military, and the remaining six veterans stood proudly in the bleachers as the song played. Once it finished, the flag bearers marched to their stands and placed the flags.

Reu introduced the Head Man and Head Woman dancers, the drum groups, the flag bearers, and all the different dance groups, including the elementary school kids. Our family was called to the arena to be blessed, and the caskets were brought in and smudged, too. The dancers performed a traditional funeral dance around the caskets to send my parents off to the next world. Prayers were said before and after the dance. The majority of the powwow focused on us and the untimely loss of two important members of our tribe, preparing their souls for the next life.

The burial ground was across from the school. The processional was the last part of the funeral. The caskets were carried, surrounded by my family, with dancers leading the way. Hand drums played as we walked to the open grave, where Mom's casket was gently lowered on top of Daddy's into the hole that had been dug by Grandad, Uncle Abe, Uncle Nate, and Louis earlier that day. Another smudging ceremony took place at the gravesite, and each member of the tribe put a scoop of dirt into the grave over the caskets. When everyone finished, it was our family's turn to close the grave.

As I placed the last scoop of dirt on their resting place, a heavy sense of finality settled over me. I realized I would never see Daddy again. Silent tears rolled down my cheeks. Mickie held my hand with Louis on her other side as the rest of the tribe started to leave until only the three of us were left. Grandad stood a little way off, patiently allowing us this final moment with our parents.

FOUR

My appointment with Dr. Johnson was the following Tuesday, after my moon ended. I found myself back at the hospital where Mom had taken her last breaths, and memories of that night, a week and a half ago, flooded back. I wished there could be a smudging ceremony for the hospital because it felt like bad spirits were hanging around.

At sixteen, I'd never seen a gynecologist before; my visits were always with a pediatrician, so I had no idea what to expect. I had been embarrassed to talk to Dr. Johnson the day Mom died, but I was doubly embarrassed about the exam. I felt exposed, sitting naked under the paper gown and sheet, waiting in the examination room for Dr. Johnson to arrive. I wished Mom was here to talk about it with me.

I had never had anything in those private places. During our moons, girls were not allowed to do many of the normal activities like swimming, so I hadn't even used a tampon before. The whole exam was embarrassing, awkward, and uncomfortable.

I was irritated at Grandad that I even had to come here. There was nothing wrong with me. Mom never had any problems with the way I reacted to my moons. *What does Grandad know about it? Who does he think he is, stepping in and trying to tell me, a girl, how I should be feeling during my moon? He's never had a moon in his life!*

Dr. Johnson tried her best to make the exam as easy as possible, letting me know exactly what she was doing before she did it. She did a pelvic exam, a Pap smear, and a transvaginal ultrasound. After the ultrasound, she inserted a thin tube into me and moved it back and forth. It was an uncomfortable and painful experience.

When she was done, Dr. Johnson left me in the room to change back into my clothes. Clothed, I sat on the exam table feeling violated. I had never allowed anyone to see those private areas, and now I felt like I had been on display.

She walked back into the room and sat on the chair next to the counter, where she placed her iPad and several pieces of paper. She looked at me and sighed.

"Based on the exam and ultrasound, I have some suspicions about what is causing you all the pain and diarrhea during your periods. I want to do an MRI to be extra sure and to find out exactly where the issues are and to what extent. During the ultrasound, I found several cysts that could become problematic. I suspect you may have endometriosis. I did an endometrial biopsy after I did the ultrasound, so we should know the results of that in a week or so."

I had never heard of such a thing and had no idea what it was, so I sat silently, staring at her and waiting for her to explain.

Seeing my confusion, she continued, "Endometriosis is a condition where tissue that typically lines the inside of the uterus grows where it shouldn't be growing, mainly around the outside of the uterus and other reproductive organs, causing abnormal abdominal pain and sometimes diarrhea before and during your moon. The MRI will help us pinpoint the location and size of the endometriosis growths so we can determine whether or not you will need surgery to remove them."

My heart dropped. *Surgery?* The word made me anxious. I had learned to live with the pain; surely, I could keep managing it. *There's no need for surgery. I can keep taking Pepto Bismol and Motrin, right?*

Seeming to read my mind, Dr. Johnson continued, "While we're waiting for the MRI to be scheduled, I'll prescribe you some hormonal contraceptive pills, which should help a little in decreasing the pain you experience before and during your moon. I've already sent the prescription to the pharmacy, so you should be able to pick it up later today." She handed me the papers she had brought in with her. "This has more information about endometriosis so you're fully informed." She handed me another form. "This is the referral for the MRI. Once we have the MRI results, we'll know more about what needs to be done next. Call the number at the top to schedule the appointment."

She stood and held out her hand. "It was a pleasure seeing you again, Isabelle. You can follow me out to the exit."

I shook her hand and followed her out the door, down the hallway, and to the exit door. Grandad stood when he saw me, and we went out to the car together. I handed him the paperwork. "She said she thinks I have endo…something," I told him glumly.

He took the paperwork. "I had suspected something similar." He saw the referral for the MRI. "We'll get this scheduled as soon as we can."

***

The MRI was scheduled a month out, four hours away in Minneapolis. Our hospital did not have any specialty equipment, so MRIs, CT scans, and similar complex medical tests required travel. I got used to taking my new medicine, and while my next moon still brought pain and discomfort, it was slightly more manageable.

Life went on, even with the ache that lingered in my heart. I kept expecting Mom and Daddy to walk through the door, as if they had just been out running errands. When I made dinner, I still cooked enough for five, forgetting only four of us were eating now. Uncle Abe and Uncle Nate took turns sitting in the empty chair. Small reminders of Mom and Daddy would hit me like a wave, and I often cried myself to sleep. *Will the pain of losing them ever fade?*

I read the papers Dr. Johnson gave me and did my own research on endometriosis. The thought of infertility haunted me. My biggest dream had always been to be a mother. What if that was taken away? Mickie was the smart one, likely headed for college and a bright future. School wasn't my strength—I just wanted to stay home and raise kids. Our tribe needed more kids; it seemed to shrink every year. The idea of not being able to have children was terrifying. *What man will want me if I can't give him a child?*

***

The long drive to the hospital for my MRI was nerve-racking, knowing it was the same road Mom and Daddy had traveled before they'd died. The highway wound through the many lakes Minnesota was famous for. It was early November now, and the road was flanked by dense pine forests, still green against the death of the hardwood trees, most of which were bare for the winter months.

Grandad and I talked about the procedure, and he confirmed what some of my research told me. He explained more about what they would be looking for and how the procedure would help the doctor with a diagnosis. It was nice having a doctor in the family to explain some of these things, but it didn't calm my nerves any. In fact, it made me more scared. What if I did have endometriosis and couldn't have kids of my own?

As we entered Minneapolis, I was in awe. This was my first trip to the big city. Poverty ran thick on the Rez, and while he was alive, Daddy had done his best to show us the work ethic that could keep us above the poverty line. But we couldn't afford to spend money to travel, so my siblings and I had never been off the reservation. I had never seen a skyscraper in person, and as the skyline gradually appeared, I was amazed at the striking blend of sleek modern buildings and historic structures against the midwestern sky. The city's vibrant energy was beyond my wildest imagination.

At the medical center, the radiology technician gave me hospital clothes to change into, and I left my clothes in a locker. He arranged me on the table, gave me a button to push in case of emergency, and hooked me up to the IV to administer the contrast. He provided me with ear protection and slid me into the machine.

In the darkness of the machine, I was thankful I didn't have issues with claustrophobia. I was also glad I had done my research. The procedure itself was strange but not terrifying. I lay still inside the machine, trying to block out the faint humming I could still hear through the ear protection. I could also feel my stomach growling. It was lunchtime, and I hadn't eaten since dinner last night.

I closed my eyes and tried to nap to pass the time, but the noise was too disturbing, even with the ear protection. I started daydreaming about what life might be like if I had my own kids running around the reservation. I refused to believe I wouldn't be able to have children and dreamed of having at least four. I could teach one of my daughters how to cook over the open fire, like Mom had. Maybe my sons would join the hunting band like Daddy. Mom and Daddy's legacy could continue through me, even though they were no longer here. A tear slipped down the side of my face as I thought of them, but I couldn't wipe it away in the confined space. Mom and Daddy would never get to see their grandchildren growing up. My kids would never know their grandparents. The ache in my heart pressed into me, and I didn't know if it would ever go away.

After what felt like forever, the procedure was finally over. As the table slid out of the machine, I felt so free. If only I could be free from the grief I still felt from the loss of Mom and Daddy.

***

My follow-up appointment with Dr. Johnson was the following week. It was quick, and Grandad was by my side. Dr. Johnson asked me about how my medicine was making me feel. She told me the biopsy came back negative for endometritis, but the MRI had different results. Dr. Johnson delivered the news: "You officially have endometriosis, and there are growths we need to address. I'm going to have to recommend surgery to remove them."

FIVE

My surgery was set for about a month and a half later. The day before the surgery, winter had fully arrived. The sky was gray and heavy with clouds, blocking out any sunlight. Snow was piled high outside, turning into gray heaps along the gravel roads that plows tried their best to clear daily. The freezing temperatures forced everyone into heavy fur-trimmed coats or shawls, scarves, gloves, and fur-lined moccasins.

Louis was at work, and Mickie was in the bedroom, lost in her homework. Grandad was in the family room, working on a journal article on his laptop when he suddenly stopped typing and lowered his head into his hands. I could hear him let out a cry of pain. I rushed over, concern written all over my face, and I heard Mickie peek out of her room, listening.

"What's wrong, Grandad?" I asked, worry creeping into my voice.

He waved me back, rubbing his temples. It was evident he was suffering. "I think it's a migraine," he said, his eyes tightly shut as he tried to block out the light.

I quickly flicked off the light switch, grateful the glow from the hallway and the computer screen was enough for us to still see.

I realized I didn't know much about Grandad's health since we'd only lived with him for a few months. "Are migraines common for you?" I asked.

"No, not really. I can't remember the last time I had one," he replied, still rubbing his temples. His hand moved to his thick white hair, searching for some relief. "I'm going to lie down for a bit," he said, standing up slowly and heading to his room.

I returned to the kitchen. The smell of freshly baked bread wafted through the house; it was one of my favorite scents, second only to that of the first snow. My surgery was the next day, so I wanted to enjoy a big meal tonight since I couldn't eat food after midnight before my procedure. The menu included a starter salad, roast venison, glazed carrots, and red potatoes, rounded off with fresh bread.

I heard the front door open and close. Louis must have been home from work. A minute later, he walked into the kitchen, breathing in the delicious aroma of dinner. "That smells amazing, Princess," he said with a grin.

I beamed back at him. "Almost ready," I replied.

He washed his hands and began setting the table. "Where is everyone?" he asked.

"Mickie's doing homework in her room, and Grandad's resting in his," I said. "Can you let them know dinner's ready?" He nodded. "Be quiet with Grandad; he has a migraine."

Louis slipped out to get the others while I cut the roast venison and added the final touches to the carrots and potatoes. I laid the food out on the island counter, buffet-style. Louis returned with Mickie, but Grandad wasn't with them.

"I think Grandad wants to keep sleeping," Louis said.

"I'll check on him after dinner," I assured them.

We filled our plates and headed to the dining table. It still felt strange not having Mom and Daddy at the table. Grandad had taken Daddy's old spot, but tonight it was empty, too. We chatted about our day, Mickie's upcoming test, Uncle Nate's casino, and my surgery tomorrow. I felt grateful for our close family, but a flood of sadness hit me when I thought about Mom and Daddy. I tried to push it away, but it lingered.

After dinner, Mickie cleared the plates, made a plate for Grandad, and put the leftovers away. I went to check on him, bringing his plate of food. He stirred awake and whispered a thank you for the food. He mentioned he'd call one of my uncles to see if they could drive me to the hospital tomorrow in case his headache didn't ease up, so I fetched his phone from the family room.

I sat in a chair across the room while he ate, watching him in the soft light. He didn't look sick, but the weariness in his eyes worried me. Maybe he hadn't slept well, or the migraine was wearing him out. He was in his seventies, after all, and even the strongest people slowed down eventually. Most people his age didn't have nearly the amount of energy he had.

After he finished, I took the tray. "Can I get you anything else, Grandad?"

"A glass of water would be nice," he replied. I took the dishes back to the kitchen and returned with a full cup. He thanked me and said he'd turn in for the night. "See you tomorrow, Princess. Thanks for caring for me."

"Of course! Let me know if you need anything." I gave him a quick kiss on the cheek and left.

About twenty minutes later, there was a knock at the door. I opened it, shocked to find two EMTs standing there, an ambulance parked outside with its lights flashing.

"We got a call about someone having a stroke?" one of them asked.

"What?" I exclaimed.

Louis appeared from nowhere. "It must be Grandad," he said, panic in his eyes.

I led the EMTs back to Grandad's room, my heart racing. Grandad was sitting on the edge of his bed, dressed in the same clothes as earlier. He held his phone in his right hand while his left arm hung limply by his side. The EMTs rushed in, checking him over. It was clear he couldn't move his left side much, and his mouth was lopsided. They strapped him to a stretcher and rolled him outside to the ambulance.

I called Uncle Abe after the ambulance rushed away, and he hurried over to take us to the hospital. It felt like a scene from a movie, and I couldn't shake the déjà vu.

Once we arrived, we waited in the emergency room waiting area, sitting in silence. The same blonde girl that had been there during Mom and Daddy's accident was at the front desk, busy with paperwork. It was just past eight in the evening, and the waiting room was full. I picked at my hangnails, anxiety gnawing at me.

After an hour, someone finally called us back to the room where Grandad was being held temporarily. It was a small room with one bed and a rolling cart with equipment on it near the door. There he was, lying in a hospital gown. The bed was raised so he could sit up and talk to us.

I rushed in, tears welling in my eyes, and hugged him tightly. "I'm so glad you're okay!" I exclaimed. Mickie and Louis followed suit, embracing him.

"Me, too, kids," he replied, but his voice was weak and slurred, coming mostly from one side of his mouth. After a short visit with all of us, Grandad asked to speak to Uncle Abe alone, so we stepped back into the waiting area.

Uncle Abe returned from his room thirty minutes later and drove us home. He told us they suspected Grandad had a clot in an artery in his brain that had caused the stroke. They had treated it with clot-busting medication, but he hadn't improved as much as they had hoped. He was being transferred to the bigger hospital in Minneapolis so they could do more tests and create a rehabilitation plan.

The ride back was quiet, the snow swirling outside the window. I couldn't shake the feeling that our caregivers were being taken away from us one by one. Uncle Abe would be staying to watch over us in Grandad's room—Daddy and Mom's old room—while Grandad was in the hospital. Would he be next?

***

Uncle Abe drove me down to Minneapolis for my surgery the next day. I was grateful he was available since he had a packed work schedule. But he was a family guy first, always there for us when we needed him. That was one of the things I loved about him.

"Are you nervous, Princess?" he asked on the way to the hospital after we had emerged from the winding road onto a straighter highway.

"A little," I admitted. "Actually, more than a little. This could change my whole life, especially if I can't be a mom."

"Your life and identity aren't about what you can produce," Abe said wisely. "It's about the character of your heart."

"Yes, but I don't know what I'd do if I can't be a mom. I don't want to do anything else," I replied. He was right, and I would always value my character, but there was no one I wanted to share that with more than my own children—the babies from my own womb.

Sensing my nerves, Abe spent the rest of the car ride trying to distract me from what was coming. He asked about school, the book I was reading, and the blanket I was weaving. We talked about Mickie's basketball games and the casino. Before I knew it, we were driving around a bend, and the tall buildings came into view on the horizon. The second trip to the city felt like the first. I was just as amazed and intimidated by the sights.

The surgery was only supposed to take two hours, plus recovery time afterward. I left Uncle Abe in the waiting room when they called my name to prep for surgery. I changed into a hospital gown, put my clothes in a bag, and settled into the hospital bed as they hooked me up to an IV. Soon enough, I drifted off to sleep.

When I woke up, I was in a different room. A nurse came over, asking how I felt. I was groggy but otherwise okay. She said it would be another twenty or thirty minutes before I could get up. I had no idea what time it was or how long I'd been out.

After I changed back into my clothes, Uncle Abe came in to help me out of the hospital. I felt tired and a little sore, but they'd given me pain meds to help. He talked to the doctor about how the surgery had gone, but I was still too out of it to hear what was said.

***

I was always the one looking after everyone, so it was hard for me to relax and stop moving around the kitchen when I got home. Thankfully, winter break was about to start. I only had to miss the last day of school before the break to recover from my surgery.

It took me about two days to feel like myself again and to stop relying on pain medicine. During winter break, Uncle Abe and Uncle Nate took us to see Grandad in the hospital in Minneapolis. It was a lot of driving back and forth to the Big City, and it was getting exhausting. For someone who had never been off the reservation before this year, I had seen a lot of the outside world in a short period of time.

Grandad seemed in good spirits. We all crowded around him, sharing stories about our days. Sure, his left side wasn't working, and his mouth drooped slightly, but his mind was still sharp. After a little while, he asked to speak with Uncle Abe and Uncle Nate alone, so the three of us stepped out and sat outside the room by the door. Mickie went to the washroom, and Louis headed off to find a vending machine, leaving me alone.

I knew I shouldn't eavesdrop, but I couldn't help myself. I moved my chair closer to the door.

"Abe, I sold my house and land rights to Eber's grandson who just found out they were pregnant before all this happened," Grandad began, his speech still slurred, making it difficult to understand. "I want you to take the money and buy an RV. We're going on a road trip to Houston, Texas. There's a top-notch stroke rehabilitation center there. It's one of the best in the nation."

"Are you sure you can handle that? That's a long trip," Uncle Nate interrupted. "What if something happens on the way?"

"Given my condition, you might be right," Grandad said, sounding defeated.

"I don't want to think about you not making it to Houston," Uncle Nate continued. "But we need to have a plan for the kids, too. If something were to happen and you weren't here, the state would decide what happens to the kids."

"I can't even imagine what would happen if they ended up in foster care or the boarding school. The system is a nightmare. They're great kids, and it could ruin their lives," Uncle Abe said, worry in his voice.

"I had a friend in high school whose parents died. First his dad's hunting band had gotten attacked by wolves, and his dad didn't survive it. Then his mom, heartbroken over losing him, took her own life. Since there were no 'eligible' foster families on the reservation, he was taken by the government to the boarding school two hours away, and it messed him up. We would write letters back and forth, and he told me horror stories about other kids at the school getting sexually abused. I would die if that happened to the girls," Uncle Nate added, his voice heavy with concern.

"You're right. I never expected a situation like this before they turned eighteen. If I died tonight, the boarding school would probably be their fate," Grandad admitted. "The boarding school is so much worse than you can ever imagine. They take away your heritage and treat you like slaves. You've heard about what happened to me and the other elders in the tribe when they took us all to the boarding schools. It's been hard to regain that culture and heritage they tried to strip us of. We can't let that happen to the girls."

"Louis will be eighteen next month, but the girls have a couple of years left before they're adults. What if we each took one of them in? That way, they wouldn't be left without family," Uncle Abe suggested.

"Split them up? I'm not sure that's a good idea," Grandad replied.

"Look, they're still so young. How would they survive if anything happened to you, Dad? Think about it. They rely on you for everything—food, shelter, money. With the way things are, no eighteen-year-old could survive on minimum wage alone without parents or a husband," Uncle Nate tried to reason with Grandad.

"That's it! It's pretty common in the tribe for uncles to marry their nieces to carry on the family line. We could each marry one of them to ensure they're taken care of. Between us, we can make sure Louis is okay, too—you with your job, Nate, and I can offer a place to stay. That way, they'll be set for the long run," Uncle Abe said.

"Whatever we do, we can't let them end up in the boarding school!" Uncle Nate agreed.

Mickie came back from the washroom and opened her mouth to speak. I quickly shushed her and pointed to the door, moving over so she could listen, too. It was a miracle a nurse hadn't caught us eavesdropping.

"That could be a way to make sure they're cared for," Grandad considered.

"Nate, if we go through with this, who do you want?" Uncle Abe asked.

There was a pause. "Well, Princess is the prettier one, but Michaela is smart. She could achieve whatever she wanted. I bet she could go to college and help grow the casino. We could make it the biggest in the state. Really make a name for ourselves," Uncle Nate said. "Besides, it looks like Princess might have a hard time having kids with her endometriosis."

I winced at the last comment. In our tribe, a woman's power was in her ability to bring life into the world. Whoever got stuck with me would be risking their family line.

Louis returned with snacks from the vending machine. Mickie and I quickly shushed him before he could say anything.

"Okay, then it's settled. I'll take Princess, and you can have Michaela. Louis can live with me and work for you," Uncle Abe declared.

"You're forgetting our trip to Houston," Grandad interjected.

"Right. We can let Louis choose if he wants to stay or go, and I'll take Princess with me to Houston. But we still haven't figured out how you'll get there safely," Uncle Abe said.

"What if I get medically transported like I did here, and you and the kids meet me down there?" Grandad suggested.

"That could work," Uncle Abe agreed. "Let's each figure out our parts of the plan and see how it goes."

I heard footsteps approaching, and we quickly returned to our seats, pretending we hadn't been listening.

Six

Nobody mentioned The Secret Plan after the talk between Grandad, Uncle Abe, and Uncle Nate. Life continued as usual except that Uncle Abe was living with us while Grandad was in the hospital. Grandad had given Uncle Abe a nice RV, so part of The Secret Plan was already in motion.

I was struggling with The Secret Plan, especially the idea of getting married so young and moving away from the reservation.

In our tribe, it was normal to marry as a teenager, especially with so few single people around and the dwindling numbers of members in the tribe. The last four weddings had all been teenage girls marrying guys in their early twenties. Still, I'd been shocked when I'd overheard Grandad, Uncle Abe, and Uncle Nate talking about marriage. I hadn't finished high school yet or even ever had a boyfriend.

But even harder to accept than marriage was the thought of moving away from the reservation. This place was my home, and I couldn't imagine leaving it. Everyone I knew was here, my family was here, and so was my heritage. *What if leaving means losing my identity? What if I don't fit in with the outside world? What if people make fun of me for being different?*

When I'd gone to the hospital in Minneapolis, it had been a huge shock. The city had felt nothing like what I was used to. *Is Texas going to be like that—busy, loud, and crowded?* I was a simple girl living a simple life. *Will I ever fit in? Will this move change who I am?*

I had a lot more questions than answers. I could only hope that by the time The Secret Plan was revealed, things would be clearer.

***

My follow-up appointment with Dr. Johnson was set for the following Monday. Uncle Abe drove me and came into the room with me.

"I have good news and bad news, Isabelle," Dr. Johnson started. "The good news is the surgeon removed all the endometriosis growths during the surgery. With hormone medication, we're hopeful they won't grow back, which means your moons should become normal and much less painful. You likely won't have diarrhea with them anymore."

I couldn't help but smile. "That's great news!"

"More good news: you had a pretty aggressive case for someone so young, but the biopsy came back negative for cancer," Dr. Johnson continued. "The bad news is the growths were large on one of your fallopian tubes, so it's mostly damaged and blocked by scar tissue. This means it'll be extremely hard for you to get pregnant in the future. Your right tube is still functioning, but the left one isn't."

Extremely hard, but possible. That felt manageable. I nodded, but tears stung my eyes. I was being told it might be impossible, or, at least, very difficult to do my job as a woman of maintaining the population of our tribe. I felt useless, worthless.

"So, there's still a chance I can have kids someday?" I asked, wiping my tears with the back of my hand.

"Yes, but it's less likely to happen naturally. If you struggle to get pregnant, you might need fertility treatments, and even that might not work. But you're young, so your body could change between now and then," she assured me.

I took it all in, glancing at Uncle Abe, trying to read his expression, but his face was unreadable. I didn't know what this would mean for The Secret Plan. Surely, he wouldn't want to marry me now. He deserved a family, a wife that could give him children to carry on the family name. I was certainly not the right woman for him. My lower lip began to tremble.

"I'd like to see you for an annual checkup to make sure those growths don't come back," Dr. Johnson said as we walked to the desk to check out.

The receptionist asked if we wanted to schedule my next appointment. Uncle Abe spoke up, glancing at me. "Can we call to schedule later?"

"Of course!" she replied, handing him a card with the doctor's information. "Don't wait too long. The doctor fills up fast."

The car ride home was quiet. I was lost in thought about needing fertility treatment in the future while Uncle Abe was probably contemplating The Secret Plan. When we got home, both Mickie and Louis were there.

"Kids, we need to have a family meeting. Nate will be here in five minutes, and we all need to talk," Uncle Abe announced.

My heart dropped. I hoped this family meeting was more about The Secret Plan than it was about my infertility diagnosis.

Mickie and I had talked about The Secret Plan the night before in bed. She didn't want to move, so she was fine living with Uncle Nate. With a year and a half left of high school, she didn't want to switch schools. We both felt uncertain about the whole marriage idea, but marriage in our tribe wasn't so much about the relationship as it was about the contract to ensure the stability and continuity of the tribe.

We also wondered what Louis would decide. He had only one semester left of high school and a job with Uncle Nate, so it made sense for him to stay. But if he did, and Uncle Abe still wanted me, I'd be the only one leaving. The thought of leaving my sister and brother after what we'd been through this year felt impossible. They were the only ones who understood me.

When Uncle Nate arrived, we gathered around the dining room table.

"Your grandfather is being transferred to a rehabilitation facility in Houston, one of the best stroke centers in the country," Uncle Abe began. "Since my business can be run from anywhere, I plan to move to Texas and set up an office there."

"I'll stay here to look after the tribe," Uncle Nate added. "Our casino can't move as easily as Abe's business. That leaves us to decide what to do with you kids. Now that your grandfather has had a stroke, he isn't going to be able to take care of you. We are concerned that if anything happens to him, you'll end up in the custody of the state and possibly taken away from the tribe. The law states they have to give preference to our tribe, but that doesn't mean the situation would be a good one or that there will be any eligible foster homes within the tribe. If there are no foster families eligible in the tribe, you would be shipped off to boarding school, and you've heard the stories about that."

My mouth went dry. Mickie and Louis had concerned looks on their faces. We had heard The Secret Plan when they'd first talked about it, but having the risks laid out to us made it feel more real.

"Louis, you'll be eighteen next month, so you can choose to stay here with Uncle Nate or come with me to Houston,"

Uncle Abe continued. "You don't have to decide right away, but I'll need to know by the end of the week."

"Our tribe has a long history of ensuring the purity of the lines," Uncle Nate spoke up. "The Chaldean Indians only have about two hundred left in the world, and there aren't many single women. Abe and I are two of the most eligible bachelors in our tribe, especially with my position at the casino and Abe's successful business. But as you have probably noticed, we haven't dated much because there simply aren't a lot of single women in the tribe."

"Tribes are mostly left alone to carry on their traditions when it comes to marriage," Uncle Abe continued. "Our tribe's tradition includes ensuring the purity of the lines, meaning we marry other tribal members. Because we love you as our family and are concerned about your safety, well-being, and your future, we would be honored if you would be joined with us in matrimony."

"Michaela, you're more than halfway through high school and doing great. I thought you could move in with me and stay here," Uncle Nate suggested.

Mickie nodded silently.

"Princess, I'd be honored if you'd come with me to Houston. You just started high school, so the change wouldn't be as hard for you. Plus, you'd be a big help in taking care of Grandad. You're the best cook in the family and good at taking care of us all," Uncle Abe added.

I blushed, feeling special.

"I know this is a lot to think about. Because we love you dearly and we don't want to force you into a situation you don't want to be in, we will give you each until the end of the week to make your decision," Uncle Abe said.

***

That night, Mickie and I lay awake in our bunks and talked to each other about the crazy proposal. While we had known about The Secret Plan, which was now just The Plan, we hadn't been prepared to have to decide like this. It was generous of them to even give us the option to choose whether or not to go along with it.

"No offense, but I am so glad Nate picked me. He is hot and rich, and I've always been an Uncle Nate fan. Not that Uncle Abe isn't attractive and all, but I think Nate is hotter," Mickie said, giggling.

"Maybe this is meant to be because I've always liked Uncle Abe better. He's been my favorite uncle as long as I can remember. He always makes me feel so special," I responded.

Luckily, both Uncle Abe and Uncle Nate weren't much older than us and had been extremely lucky to be as successful as they were. Uncle Nate was only six years older than Mickie, and Uncle Abe was about ten years older than me. They could certainly support each of us and take care of us long-term. And they were both incredibly attractive men. I would have easily picked a man who looked like either of them to date.

"What do you think it'll be like to be married?" Mickie pondered.

"I don't know," I said. "I wish Mom were here to talk to. This is a big change, and she would better prepare us for it."

"No, I mean, what do you think it's like to have sex?"

"Oh, gosh, Mickie!" I exclaimed, embarrassed by the thought. "I don't even want to think about that."

"Really?" she asked. "It was the first thing I thought about when I heard about The Secret Plan. Now I can't get it out of my head. Nate is so strong and sexy. Gosh, to be in his arms...I wonder what it will be like...." she trailed off, staring off into the distance.

I couldn't bring myself to think that way. I was surprised Uncle Abe and Uncle Nate even wanted to marry us. It seemed like we would be more of a burden on them than it was worth, especially me. If they were trying to reproduce and keep the tribe from diminishing, I was the least likely candidate to help with that. Uncle Abe was worth so much more than I could give him. He deserved to have many children. He would be such a wonderful father, as kind and loving as he was.

Being the most eligible bachelors in the tribe, they could have had their pick of the, albeit small, litter. But they'd had a very good point. There weren't many single women in the tribe. I couldn't think of any single women between the ages of eighteen and twenty-four at all.

Three months ago, our family had been intact, and you couldn't have paid me to believe this would be happening to us. Now I had a choice to make that would alter the rest of my life.

***

School wouldn't start again from winter break for another week, and the temperatures had dropped below zero. The deadline to decide what we were going to do creeped closer. Louis was still working at the casino, and Mickie had basketball practice for a few hours most days. I worked in the shed, chopping and grinding the remaining meat Daddy had caught before he'd died. It had been hanging and curing over the past couple of months.

Mickie walked into the shed as I was grinding one of the deer into ground venison. "Have you made a decision yet?" she asked.

"No, not yet," I replied.

"I think I'm going to do it. I've weighed the pros and cons. Nate is a good man. He's good-looking, kind, and well-off. Living with him won't be difficult," Mickie announced.

"But for life? This is a very permanent decision," I said.

"I know. And we're so young. Can we make reasonable decisions about things like this? They have our best interest in mind, Princess. I know they'll take good care of us for life. What chance do we have without them at this point?" Mickie pointed out.

"Yeah, I thought about that. I see you've already dropped the 'uncle,' huh?" I commented.

"Might as well get used to it if I'm going to marry him, right?" she replied.

***

I decided to talk with Uncle Abe before making any decisions. While he was sleeping over at our house to make sure we were all okay and providing transportation for us while Grandad was in the hospital, he went to his house each day to work. I pulled on my warmest coat and moccasins and walked the distance to his house on the other side of the reservation, passing the store and the lake on the way.

Uncle Abe's house was a small, one-story log cabin with a sturdy-looking exterior and a view of the lake in the rear. In front of the cabin were thick log pillars holding up the roof of the porch. It also had a wide back deck on which we could sit and enjoy the view. Sitting beside the cabin was a large white-and-gray RV trailer with black stripes zigzagging across the front.

As I passed by the RV and walked up the front porch steps, I wondered what to say. I didn't have much of a chance to think because Uncle Abe opened the door before I could even knock. "Princess! It's so good to see you!" he said, arms open for a hug. I stepped into his embrace. He smelled of cedar and mint. I breathed deeply, enjoying the earthy scents. "Please come in where it's warmer."

The inside of his house was warm and inviting. There was a small sitting room to the right and a dining room on the left. A hallway led to a larger living room with a picture window overlooking the lake and a fireplace with a fire roaring away. To the left of the living room was the kitchen. Off the living room was another doorway that led to a master bedroom with a washroom, which also had a picture window with a view of the lake. His master bedroom had a nook he used as his office.

I followed him into the kitchen. His home was decorated with tribal artwork and family photographs. Woven rugs lay in each of the rooms, dampening the sound and adding warmth and cultural depth to each room. A large canvas photograph of Grandad, Daddy, Uncle Abe, and Uncle Nate when they were all much younger hung on the wall above the fireplace in the living room.

"Would you like some tea?" he asked, already pulling out the hot kettle and raspberry tea leaves.

"Yes, please. That would be great," I responded. The delay gave me some time to gather my thoughts.

"How about some wojapi?" he asked, pulling a container out of the refrigerator and another out of his pantry. Wojapi was a thick berry sauce made from chokecherries that we ate as a snack or dessert over fry bread. Uncle Abe was known for his radical hospitality and always had food available for guests.

"Yes, please," I said. I loved wojapi, and it would go wonderfully with the raspberry tea.

As he finished making the tea, his cell phone rang. He glanced at it and looked at me. "Do you mind if I take this?"

"Not at all. Please," I said, nodding toward his phone. "I'll be fine waiting here."

He took the call as he moved to his office, and I listened to him talking from the other room without hearing what he was saying. Most people in the tribe stayed on the reservation their whole life. Very few left for college, but Uncle Abe had. After high school, he'd gone to the University of Illinois to study artificial intelligence. He was part of the first graduating class in that program, and he'd returned to the reservation to start his business shortly afterward.

On the phone, Abe sounded professional, authoritative. His company was doing well, but I didn't have much understanding of what he did or what his company did. Artificial intelligence was a mystery to me. I didn't use it, so I didn't know what it was. I'd seen movies with robots, so I always assumed that was what it was all about, but I had never seen Uncle Abe with any robots, so I wasn't sure.

Once he finished his call, Uncle Abe walked back into the living room. "Sorry about the phone call. I wasn't expecting you to come over today. Otherwise, I would have cleared my work calendar."

"Oh, it's no problem. I should have called first. I don't want to interrupt your work," I said shyly.

"Don't worry about it at all," he said. He seemed genuinely happy I was there even though I was clearly interrupting his workday.

I decided it was time to bring up the topic I had come to discuss. "I wanted to talk about your proposal," I replied, my nerves starting to bubble up.

"Absolutely! Let's discuss it," he said kindly. I could see the warmth in his eyes. He was such a family guy. I worried about how he would handle leaving the reservation, especially if we moved to Texas. Sure, Grandad would still be with him, and possibly me and Louis would be with him as well, but like all of us, he was tied to our tribe, our land.

Not knowing where to start, I decided to be honest. "I'm still so young, and I don't know if I'm ready for marriage. I mean, I can see why you and Uncle Nate are thinking this way, and I definitely don't want to end up in foster care or the boarding school if something happens to Grandad. But I'm not sure I'm ready."

"I understand, sweetheart. You're right; you are young for marriage," he began. "You'll make a wonderful wife, just like your mom. You have such a talent for making people feel welcome, and that's one of the things I love about you." I felt my cheeks heat up at his compliment. He continued, "If we got married, we could take things slowly. I know it feels rushed right now, but we can live in a way that makes you comfortable and happy."

"You mean like acting as if we're dating, even though we're married? Like not doing 'married people' things right away?" I asked.

He chuckled, and the lightness in his voice eased my tension. "Exactly! I haven't done any 'married people' things for nearly twenty-six years, so I think I can wait a little longer. We'd still live together, of course, but we don't have to rush into intimacy if you don't want to. The most important thing to me is you feeling cared for and loved," he replied with a smile.

"What if I never feel ready?" I asked, anxiety creeping in.

"If that's the case, we'll deal with it when we get there. I'm not worried about that right now," he said gently.

"But what about my endometriosis? What if I can't have kids?" My head fell, and I wrung my sweaty hands in my lap.

He took one of my hands in his and gently cupped my face with his other hand, making me look into his eyes. "Loving you is more important to me than having kids. If Jehovah wants us to have children, He'll make a way."

He looked sincere, like he cared more about me as a person than having a family. It wasn't about his success or making a name for himself; it was about loving others and honoring his faith. I could see the love shining in his eyes.

"Thanks, Uncle Abe," I said, squeezing his hand. "I feel a lot better now."

"I'm glad you came to talk to me. If we're going to do this, honesty is key," he told me. "It took a lot of courage to ask those tough questions. I'm proud of you. Communication is one of the most important parts of any relationship, and you're doing great."

I beamed. Uncle Abe was amazing. He seemed wise beyond his years. I didn't know many twenty-five-year-olds who understood life the way he did or cared as deeply. Any girl would have been lucky to have him as a husband.

SEVEN

The week had ended, and our deadline was here. Another family meeting was held to talk about what we all had decided. Grandad was being transferred to the Houston facility next Saturday, so the move was going to happen very soon.

Louis spoke first. "I know I only have a semester left of high school, and I already have a job here, so the logical choice would be for me to stay here. But Uncle Nate, you can find other people to work the casino, right?" Uncle Nate nodded. Louis continued, "I can do all my classes online to finish up my schooling, and as the man of my family, I feel like I need to step up and help you take care of Grandad. I'd like to go with you, Uncle Abe, if that's okay."

Uncle Abe smiled. "Of course, you can, Louis. I'd love for you to come with me. That's very responsible of you, son."

It was Mickie's turn, and she looked around the room at each one of us, her eyes landing on Uncle Nate last. "Nate, I'd like to accept your proposal. It would be an honor to be married to you and to help you grow your business in any way I can," she said.

Uncle Nate seemed extremely pleased and excited with her decision.

"I'm also going to accept the proposal," I announced when it was my turn.

Uncle Abe was delighted and gave me one of his famous bear hugs. A small part of me wondered if he regretted the whole situation, and I worried he might someday resent me for it. But despite the circumstances and the fact that this hadn't been what he had envisioned for his future prior to Grandad's stroke, he seemed happy about it.

With two weddings coming up, there was a lot to get done. In our tribe, the wedding ceremony was interwoven with the tribal powwow, like Mom and Daddy's funeral had been. There wasn't too much to prepare, which was lucky for Mickie and me since we were still so young, without incomes, and couldn't do much to prepare ourselves anyway.

Abe needed to head to Houston soon to check on Grandad, so we couldn't wait long. Abe and Nate would tell the elders about the double wedding, and they'd include it in next week's powwow.

I spent the week, our last week of winter break, working on a special blanket. It would be my wedding gift to Abe and would also be used in the blanket ceremony at the wedding. Thankfully, Mom had a few blankets nearly finished when she passed away; it would've taken months for me to finish a new one. Her loom was still set up in the back of the shed. Mickie and I jumped in to add the final touches to two of them.

We also had to figure out what to wear. There wasn't enough time to make any new clothes, so we needed to find our most special dresses. I had a cream-colored dress with blue and red ribbons around the skirt that would work perfectly. Mickie chose her favorite dress, the one she wore when dancing at powwows. It was mostly blue with colorful ribbons along the skirt and sleeves.

The double wedding was all anyone could talk about. When I went to the store for groceries on Tuesday, many of my schoolmates from the other tribes were there. The older girls shot me jealous looks while girls my age congratulated me. They chatted with me about how handsome Abe was and how lucky I was to marry him. Honestly, I couldn't argue. Abe was good-looking, with high cheekbones and a sharp jawline. His chestnut eyes sparkled with depth and warmth. His long, dark hair was often tied back, giving him an effortlessly sophisticated look. He had warm-toned skin and a tall, athletic build that added to his natural charm. His looks, coupled with his successful business, made him one of the most eligible bachelors in the tribe, and soon he would be mine.

I still felt uneasy about the arrangement, mainly because of my endometriosis. The night after the diagnosis, I had cried myself to sleep. The growths and the surgery had left me broken. I couldn't help but worry about what the future held.

I didn't think I was good enough for Abe. Or for any guy, really.

Would he end up resenting me if we went through with the wedding? What if I could never give him a child? He said if Jehovah wanted him to have kids, it would happen. I still had one healthy fallopian tube, so maybe Abe was counting on that. Or maybe Abe didn't even want kids. He was doing well in his business—maybe he'd rather focus on that than start a family. I didn't know what I would do if I wasn't raising children. I could cook and sew, but what good would that do in Houston?

All these thoughts dragged me into a depression. It started to affect my mood around the family, and Abe noticed. On Wednesday night after dinner, while Mickie washed the dishes and Louis went outside to shovel the fresh layer of snow that had fallen earlier, Abe pulled me aside to talk.

"Are you okay, Princess?" he asked. "You aren't acting like yourself."

"I'm sorry." I tried to explain, but no more words came. Instead, my tears began to fall.

"Are you nervous about Friday?" Abe guessed.

I shook my head then nodded my head. I was confused myself, and I couldn't help Abe to understand the problem any more than I understood it myself.

"Talk to me about it. How are you feeling?" Abe coaxed gently. His beautiful chestnut eyes were filled with worry.

"I can't help but feel you're settling for me because of our situation," I said through my sobs. I sniffled and wiped my eyes with the back of my hand. "I don't want you to resent me in the future if you meet some amazing woman who would be perfect for you and who can give you children." There. I had said it.

"Oh, honey," he said softly, his voice filled with love and concern. "Don't think that way." He pulled me into an embrace. "*You* are the amazing woman who is perfect for me. I want to marry you," he insisted. He held me at arm's length and wiped a tear from my cheek. "Jehovah has made you perfect and special, just for me."

"How can you say that, Abe?" I raised my voice, still sobbing. "I'm broken. Barren. I can't give you what you need. I can't give myself what I need."

He hugged me tighter, running his fingers through my hair, his cedar and mint scent filling my nose and calming me. I closed my eyes and melted into his embrace. He spoke softly, his breath warm on my head. "You're the most beautiful woman I know. You're not broken. You are the perfect one for me."

The most beautiful woman he knew? Right now, I felt like a mess. My face was blotchy, and my eyes were red and puffy. I felt even more inadequate, as I couldn't seem to keep myself together around this wonderful, handsome man who was soon to be my husband. How could he want someone like me?

"I've always dreamed of being a wife and mother. Of raising kids," I continued, tears spilling again. "And now, I might not be able to do that. What am I going to do with my life?" I sobbed.

"Sweetheart, you are worth so much more than you give yourself credit for," he continued. "You can't find your value in the things of this world, not even in your ability or inability to give life. You are a part of Jehovah's good creation. You have to believe that," he insisted. "You are valuable because Jehovah loves you, because I love you."

"I love you too, Unc—...Abe," I replied. It was going to take some time to get used to dropping the "uncle" from his name.

"Princess, honey, only Jehovah knows what you and I need. He is all we need. He is enough," Abe said. "He loves us the way we are because He made us that way. If He wants us to have children, it will happen. He is writing the story of the Earth, the world, of us. We may not understand why things happen, especially the bad things that happen to us, but we have to trust His story."

His selflessness struck me. He didn't seem to care one bit about whether or not I could help him carry on the family line. He still wanted me, and that made my heart swell with hope.

***

The rest of the week sped by, and soon it was Friday. I rushed to make food to take to the powwow to share with the tribe. I went with a classic: fried walleye and wild rice.

Grandad was still at the hospital in Minneapolis, but Abe and Nate came over before the powwow. As our guardian, Grandad had given his blessing for both of us to marry and had approved of our wedding. We'd been able to FaceTime with him during the week to show him our dress choices. He was upset he couldn't be here in person but still wanted to see the ceremony. Abe said he would set up a camera to stream the powwow so Grandad could watch.

Abe arrived first, wearing a cream-colored ribbon shirt matching my dress along with a handmade buckskin vest decorated with red and blue beads. He had on buckskin leggings and beaded moccasins with blue and white triangles, symbols of stability and peace in our tribe. It made me feel warm inside, thinking he wanted a long, peaceful marriage with me. He hugged me and kissed my forehead. "I've been looking forward to this day all week, ever since you said yes to my proposal, Princess," he said with a smile that lit up his eyes.

I blushed and smiled back. After our talk, I was still unsure about marrying so young, but I was excited to become his wife and get to know him on a deeper level.

After Abe arrived, Nate knocked at the door. He had found a shirt to match Mickie's dress—blue with colorful ribbons. He also wore a beaded belt with blue and white triangles. He wore leggings with blue beads and fringe and beaded moccasins.

As I finished cooking, we talked about the ceremony. Marriage ceremonies in our tribe were special, and everyone came to witness the joining of the families. I had seen many ceremonies over the years, especially after high school graduation, when graduates often got married right away and celebrated new beginnings and new lives together.

Once the food was ready, Louis washed the dishes while Mickie and I got dressed. We helped each other paint our traditional wedding face paint around our eyes and cheekbones. Since we had cut our hair short when mourning for Daddy and Mom, we pulled the remaining hair we had back to put on our blue-and-white-triangle-patterned beaded headbands, with eagle feathers hanging down near our temples. The rest of our hair fell in short waves down the backs of our necks.

When we were done, we stepped out of our room to find Louis already dressed in his regalia. Abe and Nate had their faces painted, too, and wore eagle feather headdresses. It was time to head to the school, and we stepped out of the house into the frigid darkness of winter. I wrapped a blanket around my shoulders and carried the larger blanket, the union blanket, which I would give to Abe for the blanket ceremony. Mickie, Abe, and Nate each carried their blankets, too, as we walked around the block to the school.

When we arrived at the arena, everyone greeted us with excitement. The fires were blazing on either side of the arena, warming the entire area. I set our fish and rice with the other food that had been brought for the feast after the ceremony. We took seats in the front row of the bleachers to wait for our turn. The elders blessed the arena, and the drummers took their places. Peleg was the emcee and spiritual leader that night. After the Flag Song, invocation, arena smudging, and the Honor Song, they would bring us up for the weddings.

I was too nervous to pay attention to the ceremonies. I was going through the motions I had done week after week for my whole life: stand for the Flag Song, sit for the rest of the ceremony. I barely heard the invocation or the blessing during the smudging. I was sure the Honor Song was beautiful, but I was staring ahead, unfocused. I had participated in ceremonies plenty of times, mostly as a dancer, but I had never been the center of attention like I would be tonight. I was nervous for everyone's eyes to be on me. I wished Daddy could be here to see my wedding, but if he were here, we wouldn't have been having a wedding so soon.

When the Honor Song ended, Peleg called us to the center of the arena. Mickie and I stood on one side, and Abe and Nate stood across from us, with Peleg in the middle. He performed the smudging over Mickie and me first, then over the guys, offering blessings for our future marriages.

Peleg asked everyone in the tribe to form a circle around us. They all left the bleachers, surrounded us on the dirt arena, and held hands to create an unbroken circle of unity. Peleg called upon the four directions and invited the ele-ments—wind, water, earth, and fire—to bless our marriages.

Louis helped wrap each of us in our blankets for the blanket ceremony. I faced Abe. He was wrapped in his blanket while I was wrapped in mine. Mickie stood next to me, facing Nate. Peleg spoke some words in Chaldean, most of which I didn't understand. In English, he asked each bride if we wanted to marry our grooms and live with them for the rest of our lives. One by one, we both said yes. He asked the grooms, and they both said yes, too. We removed our individual blankets, and I stood in Abe's embrace as the larger union blanket wrapped around us, binding us together. I felt his warmth, his breath on my forehead, his cedar and mint smell I loved so much. I had never felt so protected and connected to anyone before.

Once the four of us were wrapped in our two union blan-kets, Peleg said a prayer and announced we were officially married. The two had become one. We removed the blanket together as a couple, and the whole tribe threw corn into the air in our direction, a symbol of fertility. Little did they know no amount of corn could help me. I tried to push the thought out of my head. This was a happy night, and I wouldn't ruin it with thoughts of self-doubt.

The dancers broke the circle and began the wedding dance around us. Abe took my hand, and we listened to the drums and watched the dancers dance a full circle around us. He smiled at me, love shining in his eyes, and we both joined in with the dancers.

EIGHT

After the powwow ended, we gathered our things and walked back to the house. The sky was completely clear. The stars were brighter than usual, shining against the dark backdrop of night. The moon was waning, but it still gave us enough light to see as we walked. I was a married woman now, but I wasn't sure what that meant for us. Abe had promised we'd take it slowly and wouldn't jump into things I wasn't ready for. I felt safe with him, but it was still so new to me. I wished Mom were here to help me navigate these changes.

As we headed back to the house, Abe reached out and took my hand in his, interlacing his fingers with mine. A warm spark shot through me at his touch, like a ray of sunshine in the summertime, warming my whole body. I'd never held hands with a boy before, and it reminded me of how I'd felt during the blanket ceremony with our bodies pressed together and warmth radiating between us. It was thrilling to feel that connection with someone.

This weekend, we needed to pack up the house and winterize it so we could head down to Houston. But tonight, our wedding night, Mickie would stay at Nate's house, and Abe would be here with me. When we arrived at our house, Mickie grabbed her overnight bag and headed off with Nate to hike across the reservation to his house.

In the hallway on the way to the bedrooms, Abe paused and looked into my eyes. He gently took off my headdress and kissed my forehead. "You look beautiful, Princess. I'm the luckiest man alive to have you as my wife," he said, brushing the back of his hand down my cheek. I smiled shyly and hugged him, his rustic scent filling my lungs. I felt so content.

After we broke apart from the embrace, I headed to the washroom to wash off my face paint, shower, and brush my teeth. Louis came in as I was finishing. "Aren't you supposed to be in the other washroom? In Mom and Dad's room where Abe is?"

I spat out the toothpaste. "Well, we're only here for a couple more days anyway," I said, sticking my tongue out at him and giving him a playful punch on the arm. "What does it matter?"

The truth was, I didn't know what I was supposed to do. I didn't know what Abe expected of me. We'd had the talk about not doing "married people" things right away, but did that mean I would still sleep in the same room as him? How slowly did he want to take things?

"Go on," Louis said, shooing me out of the washroom and toward Mom and Daddy's old room.

The door was slightly open, but I knocked anyway. Abe answered, his headdress and face paint gone, but he was still in his wedding regalia. "Come in, Princess. You don't have to knock. This is your room, too, now."

As I looked around the room, tears pricked at my eyes. It felt too soon to accept Mom and Daddy's room belonged to someone else. Both Grandad and Abe had slept here after they'd passed away, and it had felt wrong. While I didn't want to leave the reservation, I was relieved we were leaving this house behind. It was filled with memories, both good and painful, reminding me of the emptiness in my heart.

Abe seemed to read my mind. "It's hard for you to be in here, isn't it?" he said softly, pulling me into a comforting hug and smoothing my hair. "I lost my mom when I was three, and your dad was my brother. I understand that emptiness. It's hard."

I let the tears fall freely as I clung to him. This was supposed to be a happy day, and I felt like I was ruining it.

He held me tighter, rubbing my back. "It's okay. Why don't you sleep in your room until we move into the RV?"

I nodded, trying to regain my composure, the memories still swirling in my mind. "Thank you for understanding," I whispered as I turned and walked back to my room, feeling deflated and grief-stricken. I wondered what Abe thought of me, of the situation. This was not how I had imagined our wedding night would go, and I worried I was already disappointing him.

***

Grandad was getting transported to Houston the next morning, and we were rushing to pack up the house. Everyone agreed Mickie could take whatever furniture and things she wanted since she wasn't leaving the reservation. The rest of us were moving into an RV for a while, so we had to be picky about what we took.

I braided what was left of my hair into a thick plait that hung down the back of my neck, weaving a ribbon through one section. In our tribe, wearing a single braid meant you were married; it symbolized two lives coming together as one. When Abe walked out of the bedroom that morning, he had done the same thing with his hair; his usual ponytail was now a braid hanging down his back. It made me feel happy that he was proudly showing he was married to me, especially after our awkward interaction last night.

Abe took us over to his house to see the RV. It was a travel trailer RV with a queen bed, two twin beds, a convertible dinette that turned into another small bed, a mini kitchen, and a washroom with a standing shower. I was amazed by how nice it was inside. I had no idea you could fit a house into a vehicle that looked like the back half of a bus.

It was tight for three people to live in permanently, but it felt big enough for us. After checking it out, I realized I could only bring clothes and a few kitchen items. We would share the storage cabinets for food, clothes, and personal items.

With that plan in mind, we headed back to the house to pack. Abe hitched up his Jeep to the RV and drove it over to make packing easier for us. Nate and Mickie were responsible for watching over the house while we were gone. The house would be closed up until we got back, and Louis would be its rightful owner as Daddy's heir.

We didn't have a lot to pack. Our life was simple, and we didn't go shopping much. The Rez store only had groceries and toiletries, and Amazon didn't deliver here. Most of our toys from when we were younger had been handmade and bought at powwows, so we didn't have many belongings. Still, it took all day to pack and winterize the house.

***

When we took a break from packing, Abe pulled Louis and me aside. "I enrolled both of you in Texas Online School to finish out this school year. We don't know what's going to happen with Grandad's health in the next few months."

We both nodded.

"I also bought each of you a laptop for school and a cell phone so you can keep in touch with Mickie while you're apart," he continued. "You can set up the laptop at the dining table in the RV while we're on the road."

My eyes widened as he handed us the boxes. These were the most expensive gifts I'd ever received. Our school had a computer lab, but we never used computers in class, mainly because our school was underfunded. We had to take turns in the computer lab to do research, take tests, and write papers. I never imagined I'd have my own laptop. Even during COVID, when schools had been closed and most kids had had to learn from home, the tribe had studied outside in the dance arena because many families didn't have the technology or internet service to learn at home.

I was excited to have a cell phone so Mickie and I could keep up with each other after I left. Cell service in our area had only become available last year.

"Wow, this is amazing, Abe! Thank you!" I said, over-whelmed with gratitude.

"Yeah, thank you, Uncle Abe!" Louis echoed.

We carefully placed our new laptops in the RV and pocketed our cell phones. I gave Abe a hug and got back to packing and cleaning.

***

Mickie and I were in our room, sorting our belongings. "How did it go last night?" she asked casually.

"Ugh, I don't want to talk about it," I replied, feeling sour. I tossed a shirt into the "pack" pile.

"What happened?" Mickie looked up from the box of school papers she was sorting, surprised and confused. She had clearly had a better night than I had.

"I went into Mom and Daddy's room to be with Abe, but when I got there, I felt so sad. It didn't feel right being in there without them, like I didn't belong in there." I fought back tears again.

"Oh, wow. I didn't even think about that," she said. "I wouldn't want to be in there either. It's too soon."

"Can you believe it's only been a little over three months? So much has changed so fast." I stared down at my feet, tracing the circle on the rug with my toe.

Mickie walked over to me and hugged me tightly. "We're in this together," she said softly.

"Sort of...not really. I'll be leaving for Texas tomorrow," I replied, tears welling up again. I angrily wiped them away. "Why am I always crying? I'm such a baby."

"It's okay, sis," Mickie said gently. "Crying is good sometimes. You're not a baby!"

"I'm going to miss you, Mick," I said, pulling her in for another hug. We stayed like that for a while.

"I'll miss you, too," she said as she finally pulled away. "But we have our phones now. You can text me anytime, and we can FaceTime. We'll stay in touch, and you'll be back once Grandad is better."

"Maybe. I hope so. I don't know much about Texas, but it can't be as great as here. I read they don't even get snow!"

***

The trip to Houston would take over twenty-one hours without traffic or breaks. We planned to do it in three days, stopping in Des Moines and Oklahoma for the night along the way. It was a lot of driving, but we didn't want Grandad to be alone in the hospital for too long.

Early Sunday morning, we woke up with the sun and said our goodbyes to Mickie and Nate. They'd be okay without us, but I was going to miss Mickie. She had been my roommate my whole life, and it would feel strange going to bed without her below me in the bottom bunk. So many late-night talks came flooding back to me. She had always been my confidante, mentor, and best friend, helping me through life's ups and downs.

Mickie was taking over Louis's job at the casino when she wasn't busy with schoolwork and extracurriculars. Nate wanted her to learn the business so she could take on more responsibilities once she graduated high school. He dreamed of turning the casino into a destination resort, complete with overnight accommodations and canoe rentals on the lake. He was sure Mickie would play a big role in making that happen.

After saying our goodbyes, we hit the road. Louis and I took turns sitting in the front passenger seat or in the back. I let Louis sit up front first; I had already traveled this road twice for my MRI and surgery, so I figured it was his turn to enjoy the northern Minnesota countryside as we headed south.

The Jeep and RV slowly wound its way through the snowy country roads. The roads were narrow, and the Jeep felt especially long and unsteady with the RV trailer in the back. Abe looked focused, his knuckles white on the steering wheel as he navigated the snowy curves. The Jeep rocked back and forth in the wind, and sitting in the back made my stomach churn. I closed my eyes, trying to fight the nausea, knowing it would only be an hour or two before the road straightened out.

Once the road finally leveled off and the nausea faded, I pulled out my copy of *A Snake Falls to Earth* and started reading to pass the time. Abe and Louis were deep in conversation most of the way, but I was engrossed in the book and not paying much attention. It was slow going on the winter roads, and it took us longer than usual to get to Minneapolis. By the time we finally passed through the city, it was nearly two o'clock.

Abe pulled into a rest area south of the city so we could eat a snack. The rest area was small, with a single building with washrooms on either side, a few vending machines, and a tiny playground. We parked and stepped outside to stretch our legs and use the washrooms. After about thirty minutes, we hit the road again, knowing we still had over three hours to drive before reaching the RV park in Des Moines that Abe had reserved for the night.

NINE

The sun dipped below the horizon with still an hour left before we reached the RV park. We'd planned to get there before sunset, but the snowy roads and our stop at the rest area had delayed us. Abe was driving while I navigated, keeping an eye on the map and the weather updates on my phone as we drove through the flat plains near Des Moines. Louis was sprawled out on the back seat, headphones in, lost in music or a book or whatever he could use to escape the confined space.

The snow was thick and heavy, falling in soft sheets that dusted the world in a blanket of white. It was just below freezing outside, but the cozy warmth of the heater blasting inside the Jeep made the cold feel like a thing of the past. Snow covered the fields, trees, and mountains, and the Jeep with the RV behind it rumbled steadily through it all.

"Tell me about your company. I'm married to you now, so I should at least know what you do," I said to Abe as we navigated through the snowy roads.

"I suppose you should," he said chuckling. "My company develops software for banks and payment processing companies to spot fraudulent activity and to prevent cyberattacks."

I was surprised by this answer. "I thought you worked with artificial intelligence," I wondered aloud.

"Yes, we use AI to identify the fraudulent activity," he replied.

Definitely not robots, as I had thought.

"I started the company with five people, and we have grown to about forty employees now," he continued. "We have three main departments: sales, customer service to handle customer problems with the software, and product technology to build and test the software."

"So, what department do you work in?" I asked.

"I trust my people to run their part of the business. I spend most of my time on phone calls helping them out or traveling to meet with potential investors, trying to get the money to grow the company even more," he said.

"Where do your employees live? Do you have to go see them, too?" I asked, fascinated by the whole concept of his start-up business.

"All my employees work from their homes. We have about ten in Atlanta, eight in Chicago, and five in Houston. The rest are scattered around the country. We come together once a year, but for the most part, they all work from home. There're no offices right now," he explained.

"The company is doing well," he continued. "We now have some of the biggest banks as clients. So, it might be time to set up an actual office soon. I'll probably look for some office space when we get to Houston since I have five folks there already."

It was intimidating to think Abe had built the company from the ground up at twenty-five years old. He was a natural at talking to important people, negotiating deals, and getting the funding he needed to keep the business growing.

As he talked, it was clear he loved his job. His smile was wide, and his eyes lit up with excitement. He didn't care about the money; he wanted to help people, especially those who had been victim to fraud and cyberattacks. I couldn't understand it. I didn't even know what a cyberattack was or what it could do to someone.

We finally pulled into the RV park on the southeast side of the city. Abe went into the office to check us in. It was dinnertime, but the sky was already dark, with no clouds in sight. The stars were bright, glowing. The moon was half full and waxing, but sharing little light with us. I tried to make out anything I could through the darkness.

After checking in, we drove into the park and circled around to our campsite. Abe and Louis got out to figure out the best way to park. The site was a pull-through, so Abe didn't have to unhook the Jeep or back up. Even so, it took a few tries to get the big RV parked right, with Louis outside directing Abe.

Once they finally got it parked, Abe pressed the button for the automatic leveler and grabbed the RV manual to figure out how to hook up the electric, water, and sewer. It was their first time doing this, so it took them a little longer than expected, especially in the dark.

After the electric was hooked up and I could see better inside, I started getting dinner ready. Once the onion, tomatoes, butternut squash, beans, and corn were mixed together with the water in the stockpot, I carried the pot outside to put it over the fire.

When I got to the fire circle, the boys had already finished setting up and were holding a small ceremony, offering thanks to the earth. They'd pulled out a couple of chairs from the storage space and were sitting by the fire. It was freezing out but still warmer than Minnesota. We huddled close to the flames to stay warm while we waited for the stew to cook. I found some big rocks and put them in the fire to heat up so we could use them in our beds later to stay warm.

Once the stew was ready, I took out some fry bread, and we sat to eat. We talked about the trip ahead—how we'd leave at dawn, hoping to make it to Tulsa. As we ate, Abe shared stories of his childhood and stories Grandad had told him about our ancestors.

After we finished eating, I used tongs to pull the hot rocks out of the fire and wrapped them in leather. We covered the firepit with ash and dirt to keep the coals alive but safe. The boys cleaned up outside before going inside for the night while

I put the leftover stew in the fridge and the heated rocks in both Louis's bed and our bed to warm them up. Our first meal as an RVing family had been a success.

We let Louis shower first, and while he showered, I brushed my teeth at the sink in the kitchen while Abe checked his work email on his computer at the dinette. Once Louis finished, and I took my shower. I liked showering at night, washing off the dirt from the day before crawling into bed. Afterward, I rubbed bear grease on my skin to keep it moisturized and warm and dressed in my clothes for the next day.

When I came out of the washroom, Abe was coming back into the RV from doing something outside. He'd already put his computer away and brushed his teeth, so he was ready for bed. Louis had already climbed into the top bunk where he would be sleeping.

Abe walked over to me, pulling me into a hug. I rested my head against his chest and wrapped my arms around him, letting him hold me. I felt safe in his arms. He looked down at me, gently cupping my face in his hand and tilting my head up to meet his chestnut eyes. He smiled, and his smile reached all the way to his eyes.

Abe lowered his head, and his lips gently touched mine. A warm sensation rushed through me, a spark that went straight to my heart. I closed my eyes, savoring the feeling. My heart pounded, and I clung to him, feeling his arms around me, pulling me even closer. A strange feeling washed over me, and I didn't want the kiss to end. This was the first time I had ever kissed a boy, and it sparked a feeling inside me—a deep longing that spread through my whole body.

When he pulled away, I looked up into his eyes, trying to understand what he was thinking, feel what he was feeling. I wanted more, but it didn't seem possible in the tight space we shared with Louis. Abe led me to the bed, and we slipped under the covers, the warmth of his body next to mine, the warm rock between us. He kissed my forehead and gently ran his hand over my hair and down my cheek. He kissed me again on the lips, and the same rush of desire hit me all over again. I closed my eyes, savoring the feeling.

But this time, he didn't linger. He whispered, "Sweet dreams, Princess." He gave me one last squeeze before he rolled over and fell asleep, snoring softly.

I lay there, wide awake, trying to figure out what I was feeling. I ran my finger over my lips, where his kiss had been only moments ago, and thought about him. His breathing was calm and steady as he slept beside me. *How can I make him happy?*

I felt so unsure of myself. Leaving home had been tough. It was the only place I'd ever known, and now life felt different. The sights, the people, the accommodations—they were all new. Still, as I lay next to Abe, I felt a strange peace. No matter where we went, I was happy being there with him.

***

The temperature had dropped below zero by morning, and the wind was blowing hard. When I went to the washroom and flushed the toilet, water overflowed all over the floor. It was so embarrassing. I called Abe in to see what was wrong. He looked at the icy water on the floor and went outside to figure out what had happened.

When Abe came back, he told me we needed to get heat under the holding tank in the RV. He explained he'd drained the black water and flushed the gray water the night before and closed the drain valve to keep the sewer line from freezing. But it had gotten so cold overnight the water in the holding tank had frozen solid. Now he needed to heat it up so the valve would open again.

I unearthed the still-lit coals and put them in a fire horn. I set it under the frozen tank, careful not to get them too close to the RV so I wouldn't accidentally start a fire.

It worked. The heat from the coals melted the ice around the sewer valve, and it freed up. Abe took over from there, and I went inside to clean up the mess from the overflow.

This RV life was harder than it looked. There was way more to think about than we had expected to keep the RV running smoothly, especially in this cold weather.

After Abe took a shower and we were all ready for the new day, Abe and Louis disconnected the lines and put away the RV equipment. We loaded up the RV and hit the road again with eyes on Tulsa. Both Louis and I sat in the back seat so we could work on schoolwork while Abe drove. I pulled out my laptop and logged into the hotspot. Louis and I worked together to figure out how to log into the school portal and get to our new classes.

As we crossed into Missouri, the weather began to turn. The sky, once a soft gray, darkened to a deep, stormy blue. Wind gusts shook the Jeep and the RV behind us, and the temperature dropped even lower. Louis, who had been silent for a while, looked up from his laptop and squinted out the window.

"Think we'll make it to Oklahoma tonight?" he asked.

"We'll make it," Abe said. His voice was steady, but the tension in his shoulders was noticeable. "It's only a little snow. We've got this."

But as the hours wore on, the storm worsened. The snow turned to ice, making the roads slick and treacherous. Abe's knuckles were white as he gripped the wheel, and I could feel the RV swaying awkwardly behind us. Louis, ever the optimist, put away his schoolwork and kept trying to lighten the mood with stories of his time hunting with Daddy, but even his usual bravado couldn't shake the worry in the air.

By the time we reached Kansas City, the RV was sliding dangerously across icy patches of road. Abe pulled off at a truck stop to get gas, and we all agreed to wait out the storm in the RV.

Parked safely at the truck stop, I pulled out some fry bread and wojapi while Louis disappeared into the store for a moment, returning with a small bag of peanuts and a couple bottles of pop. Abe and I sat at the small table while Louis sat on the edge of our bed, eating in silence.

Abe, ever the realist, raised an eyebrow. "We'll get there. One way or another. Even if it does take us an extra day."

"Can we FaceTime with Grandad to see how he's doing?" I asked.

"That's a great idea," Abe said, pulling out his phone.

We chatted with Grandad for a little while before he had to go to physical therapy. He was doing well and settling into the Houston rehab center, but he wouldn't be able to stay in-patient for much longer. We needed to get to Houston so we could take care of him.

It was late, and the RV was getting colder by the minute. Abe pulled out a space heater that easily warmed the small space using the battery bank charged by the solar panels, which also powered the refrigerator. We spent the next few hours huddled together in the warmth of the RV, listening to the wind howl outside. The snow had turned into a full-blown blizzard, and we knew we wouldn't be going anywhere anytime soon.

***

By morning, the snow was less heavy, but it wasn't until around noon that the storm weakened enough for us to continue our journey. We packed up the RV and piled into the Jeep. Abe drove carefully, taking his time on the slick roads, while Louis and I sat in the back of the Jeep, quietly chatting and working on schoolwork. As the sun rose, the landscape began to change. The snow gave way to patches of brown and green, and the air grew warmer, a sign we were finally leaving the brutal cold behind.

By the time we hit the Oklahoma border, the weather had cleared, and the Jeep was full of laughter again. Louis was sitting up front with Abe, both of them talking about what they planned to do when we finally reached Houston. I couldn't help but smile, feeling the weight of the past few days lift from my shoulders.

No matter what came next—whether it was another unexpected storm or challenges at the rehab center in Houston—this trip, this time together, was what we needed. As the miles ticked by and the heat of the southern sun began to warm the Jeep, I realized sometimes the best part of the journey wasn't the destination. It was the time spent together, getting through it all.

TEN

We spent the night at an RV park off the highway in Jenks, Oklahoma. The park was simple, with pull-through sites with full hookups.

Since we were in Indian country, we figured we'd take a little time to explore and see if the Oklahoma reservations were like the ones back home in the Great Lakes. Abe unhooked the Jeep from the RV and made sure the blocks were in place. He hooked up the electricity but decided to wait on the water and sewer connections until we got back. We piled back into the Jeep to meet some of the locals. Abe had called their citizenship office earlier, and they'd agreed to welcome us to their reservation.

We arrived at the banks of the Arkansas River and parked near the designated meeting place. As we got closer, we were greeted by the Muscogee. "Welcome, friends from the north," said Micco, one of the elders of the Muscogee. His voice was calm but strong. "We are honored by your presence in this cold season. Winter has always been a time for gathering and reflection, and we are grateful to host you."

We gathered in a heated tent and were welcomed with a feast. The outside world was still covered in patches of snow, but inside, there was warmth, laughter, and the fragrance of a feast being prepared. Muscogee families had brought food from their land: hearty stews of buffalo and venison, cornbread, and beans. We had brought dried meats and nuts.

The smells of the meal filled my nose, as we began to share our stories seated around a long table. The fire crackled in the center, keeping the cool of the evening at bay. Abe told of the connection between the Chaldean people and the Great Lakes, of the ice that formed on the water in winter and how it reminded us of the need to stay resilient, even in difficult times. Micco spoke of the Muscogee ancestors' journey along the Trail of Tears, of the endurance it had taken to survive the cold and the hardship.

Spending time with the other tribe helped ease some of my homesickness. The feast reminded me of our own powwows back home. The Muscogee weren't our tribe, but they felt more familiar than the other people we had met on this journey so far. I felt a connection with them in a way I hadn't with anyone since we'd started this trip three days ago.

When we got back to the RV at the end of the evening, Abe and Louis hooked up the water and sewer lines so we could shower and get ready for bed. It had been a long day, filled with snowy travel and learning about a new tribe, and I was exhausted. The boys let me go first, so I took a quick shower and got into bed. It wasn't long before I was drifting into a deep, dreamless sleep.

***

We still had at least a day of driving ahead of us before we would reach Houston, but we were already a day behind schedule. We woke up with the sun, like we always did, and started the day by FaceTiming Grandad. We didn't want him to feel lonely in a strange place. He told us, while everyone in Houston had been very kind, they were very different from the people at our hospital up north near the reservation. They didn't understand our traditions and ways. The other day, they'd almost cut his hair while helping him get ready, which would've been devastating for him. It reminded him of his time at the boarding school.

We needed to get there as soon as possible.

Louis and I set up in the back of the Jeep so we could do schoolwork while Abe drove. School was going okay. I had been able to log into my online classes and watch the teacher through Zoom. Louis and I each wore our own headphones so we wouldn't disturb each other. The Zoom call sometimes lagged when we hit dead spots, but if I kept my camera off, I could stay connected through the RV's satellite internet connection.

By one o'clock, we had both finished our schoolwork. We had passed through Dallas, and Abe pulled off at a rest area south of the city. This rest area was way bigger than the one we had stopped at in Minneapolis.

We wandered over to the rest area building, which looked like a building out of a Western movie. It had rustic wooden beams and exposed stonework, a roof that seemed way too high for a washroom, and a giant brass buffalo, its shiny hide branded on one side, standing guard out front like it was the sheriff of the place. I snapped a picture of the buffalo with my phone because, well, it was a giant brass buffalo. Mickie had read that everything was bigger in Texas, and she had definitely been right so far.

Check out our new friend, I texted, sending her the picture.

Where'd you find that?? she replied two seconds later.

At a rest stop in Texas, I texted. *This place is HUGE!*

How's the trip?

Ugh long and slow □ *we still got 3 hrs left.*

Wait weren't you supposed to be there alrdy?

Yeah but we got stuck in a snowstorm

Yikes well stay safe!

I put my phone away and walked down the path into the rest area building. I stepped inside and couldn't help but stop and stare—the atrium was like a museum. The high exposed ceilings gave the place a rustic smell, like freshly cut wood. Right in the middle of the room stood a wooden structure that looked like an old oil well or water pump. An animated plaque nearby came to life, sharing the story of the Navarro County oil boom. Around it, a circle of other plaques told even more about the area's history.

When we were done in the washroom, we met up in the atrium. "Let's go for a walk to stretch our legs a bit," Abe suggested.

Abe slid his hand into mine as we strolled past the playground, and my heart skipped a beat. His hand was warm, and I felt a spark of excitement. I glanced up at him, catching the relaxed smile on his face. I smiled back and gave his hand a gentle squeeze. His grin widened, reaching his eyes, making me feel content and safe.

We kept walking, following the path all the way to the end before turning back. The weather was surprisingly warm, a total change from the freezing cold we'd been stuck in during the last three days of driving. The sun was high overhead, and it felt so nice outside we didn't even need jackets. Sure, the trees were bare, and the grass was brown, but there wasn't a single patch of snow in sight.

When we got back to the RV, I stepped inside to reheat the leftover stew from three nights ago along with some wild rice and served it up. We carried our bowls out to the picnic table under the big pavilion. Sitting there, with the warm air around us and the open sky above, we ate together, soaking in the peace of the moment.

***

With a little more than two and a half hours left to go, we climbed back into the Jeep and headed south again. The land stretched out in every direction, mostly flat, with rolling prairies, farmland, and clusters of trees filling the view. Along the way, we passed grain silos, oil pumps, and even a few wind farms scattered across the horizon. All of this was brand new to me.

The farther south we drove, the more pine trees started to pop up, standing tall against the sky. As we got closer to Houston, the wide-open spaces gave way to bigger highways, heavier traffic, and a different vibe. Industrial buildings and warehouses began to replace the fields while billboards advertising businesses from barbecue restaurants to car dealerships reminded us we were nearing one of the biggest cities in the country.

The rehab center was right in the middle of the city. By the time we reached the outskirts, it was rush hour, and traffic was a nightmare. Cars were bumper to bumper, and we barely moved at times. Construction barrels were everywhere, and the lane markers were hard to see, but Abe handled it all like a pro, getting us safely to the southwest side of town. That was where the RV park was and where we'd be living while Grandad was at the rehab center. The park was only about fifteen minutes from the rehab center, so we'd easily be able to drive Grandad to and from the center whenever he needed treatment.

Once we checked in and found our spot, Abe parked the RV and unhooked the Jeep. He and Louis got to work setting up the electricity, water, and sewer connections. When the RV was ready, we climbed into the Jeep and headed toward the rehab center.

Abe found a parking spot, and we all filed inside. We checked in at the front desk, and they directed us to Grandad's room. When I walked in and saw Grandad, I rushed over and gave him a huge hug. It felt like it'd been forever since I'd last seen him over winter break. It was amazing to see him again. He looked so strong although one side of his face still drooped a little.

After a few moments, the nurse came in. "You're just in time. He's ready to be discharged to outpatient care," she said with a smile.

"Does that mean he gets to go home with us?" I asked, practically bursting with excitement.

"That's right," the nurse confirmed. "He'll need to come in a couple of times a week for a few hours, but he's strong enough to go home now."

"That's awesome!" Abe said, grinning from ear to ear. He gave his dad a big hug.

"I'll go get the discharge paperwork and the wheelchair," the nurse said. "He'll be ready to go home in about thirty minutes." She left us alone in the room.

"Great news, Terry," the patient in the bed next to him said, his voice slow and slurred. "I'm happy for you." He didn't seem as strong as Grandad. He looked older and was bald but for a ring of white hair around his head. His face was covered in deep wrinkles, and one side of his body drooped. He was bigger than Grandad, with a large belly sticking up under the hospital blanket.

"Tell me about your progress, Dad," Abe asked.

"My arm and leg are still weak, but I can walk with a cane now," Grandad replied. "I can eat by myself, but cooking might still be a challenge."

"I'll help with that, Grandad," I said, smiling.

He looked at me with a crooked smile. "I knew you would, Princess," he said, his voice full of gratitude. "I'm so glad you're here, honey."

"I can mostly get dressed on my own," Grandad went on. "And I can go to the washroom by myself now."

"That's a relief," Louis said, laughing at his own joke.

The nurse came back with the paperwork and a wheelchair. She went over the instructions for caring for Grandad at home, including his prescriptions and his next rehab appointment. Once she finished, we helped him into the wheelchair. Abe left us to pull the Jeep around to the front while Louis and I stayed with Grandad as the nurse pushed him toward the exit.

Abe was already waiting at the curb when we got there. He came around to help Grandad into the car. Grandad stood from the wheelchair, using his cane to help steady himself. He backed up to the passenger side of the Jeep, and with a push from his good leg, he used the cane to help lift himself up.

Abe gave him a steadying hand, and between the cane and his strong leg, Grandad managed to get into the Jeep's high seat. It was a struggle, but he made it.

"Are you hungry, Dad?" Abe asked as he drove out of the parking lot.

"I haven't had anything but hospital food for two weeks. I'd kill for some home-cooked food," Grandad said, glancing back at me in the back seat.

"We're running low on supplies in the RV, but I think we have enough for tonight. I'll need to go shopping tomorrow," I replied.

When we got back to the RV, I went inside to start dinner while Abe helped Grandad out of the Jeep and Louis grabbed the chairs from the storage compartment. We still had some corn, wild rice, and dried meat left, so I decided to make a stew.

Once I had dinner in the stockpot, I stepped outside. The guys had set up the awning and pulled out the chairs beneath it. They'd also started a big fire in the firepit next to the RV. I placed the stew pot over the flames and sat in the last empty chair next to Abe.

As the stew simmered, Grandad led us in a ceremony to bless the RV site, which would be our home for the next few months. He put prairie sage into the fire and used a feather to waft the smoke toward the RV to smudge and purify the site. Louis sprinkled tobacco around the RV, showing gratitude to nature for its protection and for providing what we needed. Grandad blessed the RV and the site asking for peace and protection. We thanked the spirits and the tobacco for its role in the blessing.

After the ceremony was over, I dished out the stew into bowls for all of us. Grandad began telling us stories about his time in the hospital, the long transport from Minneapolis to Houston, and his rehab. We took turns sharing our own stories, like of the crazy snowstorm that had delayed our trip to Houston by a day. It felt good to be together, talking and laughing around the fire. Things were starting to feel normal again.

The Wolf Moon hung above us, its light bright and full. It lit up the night, casting a soft glow over our new home. I realized I'd be spending at least the next six months here in Houston, at this RV park, with Abe, Grandad, and Louis while Grandad worked through his rehab. It was a strange feeling, but also peaceful. I loved these people, my family.

We cleaned up after dinner—I carried the leftovers and dishes into the RV while Abe and Louis folded up the chairs. They helped Grandad inside, one walking in front of him and the other behind. Once he was in, Grandad was able to move around the small space pretty easily. Abe grabbed his travel bag from the Jeep and tucked it into the storage area under the bottom bunk.

We each took turns showering and getting ready for bed. Louis was there to help Grandad when he needed it, but mostly, Grandad managed well. I wasn't worried at all. Between the three of us, we could take care of whatever he needed.

ELEVEN

The next day was Louis's birthday. He was officially an "adult" by American standards, though in our tribe, birthdays weren't a big deal. Instead, we had a coming-of-age ceremony when boys and girls first hit puberty. Other ceremonies were held for milestones in our lives—like the day we got our name, our first steps, the first time we killed an animal, and the annual harvest celebrations—but birthdays weren't one of them. So, for us, Louis's birthday felt like any other day.

While Abe left to check out some commercial office buildings where he could set up his company's office, Louis and I started the day doing schoolwork. This was the first day we were stationary while doing our work, and it was nice to be able to sit at the dinette without the bumps of the road. We still wore our headphones so we could hear our teachers and the instruction videos without bothering each other. I was finishing up my classes from last semester—algebra I, world history, environmental science, and English. I'd been taking

Chaldean at our school, but they didn't offer that at Texas Online School, so I had to switch to Spanish as my language class.

The classes were very different from what I had learned back on the reservation. The teachers there were Chaldean, so the lessons were taught from the perspective of our culture and history. But at the Texas Online School, the lessons were taught from a white person's point of view. I noticed the difference right away when we started learning about the "discovery" of America in world history.

"Can you believe this, Louis?" I asked when I was reading my online world history book. "The way they talk about Natives make us sound violent and primitive while the whites are painted as heroes!"

"Wow, seriously?" he asked, looking over my shoulder to read it. "That's absurd! They kicked us out of our land like we were trash. We were here first and had every right to fight for our land!"

The way they positioned it was hard to take, and I quickly realized most American students were taught this version of history and not the correct version about how poorly Natives were treated.

Abe came back around noon to take Grandad to his therapy session. We stayed behind to continue our schoolwork. Once I was finished with my classwork and needed a break from studying, I decided to explore the RV park.

The RV park was shaped like a rectangle, stretching far back from the main road. Our RV was parked near the back right of the park. Behind it was our firepit, which faced a tall brick wall. In front of our site, there was a small parking lot with a few shade trees.

I started walking down North Avenue toward the front of the park. Most of the park was made up of RV spots, but some buildings on Avenue C grabbed my attention, so I turned right to check them out. The first building was a washroom with showers. The second had a sign that said *Laundry*. I walked inside. The room was full of large, stainless-steel washing machines with circular doors. In the center, there was a long table where an older woman sat, watching a television mounted on the wall. One of the machines was whirring.

"Howdy," she said in a thick southern accent as I walked in. "My, ain't you a purdy lil thang."

"Hello," I replied, blushing. "How do you use these machines?"

"Well, you put your laundry pods in first, then your clothes, and after that, you feed it some quarters to start it," she explained.

She stood and walked over to me. I was standing next to the first machine near the door.

"Phew!" she said, backing away slightly, her nose crinkled up. "You're purdy, but smelly! Ya might need ta do a load a laundry."

I hadn't realized I smelled, but you don't often notice your own scent. We'd been on the road for several days, and I was definitely in need of some clean clothes. She pointed out which buttons to press on the washers and where to put the coins. She took me to the dryer, where her clothes were tumbling around, and explained how that worked, too.

"It was nice to meet you, Isabelle," the woman, Jennifer, said as I walked out the door into the sunlight.

"Nice meeting you, too. Thanks for showing me how to use the machines," I replied, smiling at her as I continued my walk.

The next building I found was the office. I went inside and said "Hello" to the guy behind the desk. He was reading a magazine and barely looked up when I walked in. There was a small convenience store next to the desk, with a fridge full of pop, water, and juice. I made a mental note to buy some laundry pods they were selling. Past the store, open double doors led to a large room with long tables and chairs. It looked like a dining room, and there was a kitchen behind a wall with a pass-through window. On the far side of the room, there was a ping-pong table and a pool table.

After I finished exploring the office and dining hall, I stepped back outside. There was a bus parked at the curb, so I walked up to the driver.

"Where does the bus go?" I asked.

The man tipped his cowboy hat at me. "Hello, pretty little lady. The bus goes to the medical facilities nearby. Do you need a ride?" he asked.

"Oh, no. But my grandad does go to physical therapy at the stroke center nearby. Does the bus go there?"

"It sure does. We leave every hour on the hour to go to the various medical buildings. Tell your grandad we're here for him," the driver said.

"I'll definitely do that," I said. "We got here last night, so I'm exploring the RV park," I explained.

"Have you seen the picnic area yet? It's in the far-left corner by the dog park," he said.

"No, I haven't. I'll check it out. Thanks for the tip!" I smiled at him and turned to head in the direction he'd pointed out.

At the end of Avenue C, I turned right onto South Avenue and headed toward the back of the RV park. The road ended at the dog park and a picnic area. There was a big grove of trees providing shade, and under them, a fenced-in area with a small pavilion. The pavilion had two picnic tables, perfect for sitting while your dog ran around.

On the far side of the dog park, another fence led to a large soccer field behind the RV park. Curious, I walked through the gate to see what else was in the park. Beyond the soccer field, I found a school with an even bigger park area. It had more picnic tables, soccer fields, a recreation center, and even baseball fields. It was peaceful, with lots of green space and trees.

Not wanting to get lost or wander too far, I turned around and headed back through the dog park to the RV park. When

I reached South Avenue, I could see our RV site across the parking lot.

When I got back, Louis was still working on schoolwork. I told him all about my walk, including the laundry room and the park I'd found. I decided to try my luck with the laundry machines, so I grabbed all our dirty clothes from the past few days and stuffed them into a large trash bag. I took some cash Louis had and headed to the office.

Once I got there, I asked the man for some laundry pods and change for the machines. He barely looked up from his magazine as he took my money and gave me the change. I grabbed the pods and coins and walked next door to the laundry room.

Jennifer wasn't there anymore, so I did my best to remember her instructions. When I fed the quarters into the machine, it started, so I must have done it right. I sat at the table to wait. The television was showing a cartoon with puppies dressed as superheroes. I pulled out my phone and texted Mickie while I waited.

hey mick whatcha doin, I texted.

math class, was her response.

ugh my least favorite lol

its not so bad. tell Louis I said happy birthday

will do

Since Mickie was in class, I didn't want to bother her, so I put my phone away. I turned my attention to the television and watched as the puppies saved the day. I spotted a remote on a shelf below the television, so I grabbed it and started flipping through channels. Before long, I heard the machine beep, telling me it was time to switch the clothes to the dryer. I made several trips back and forth between the washing machine and the dryer. After feeding the dryer a few more quarters, I pressed the buttons to start it. The machine roared to life, and the clothes tumbled in circles through the clear plastic window.

My phone buzzed.

where r u? Louis texted.

at the laundry, I texted back.

k, i was worried

im fine, im the only one here. should be done in an hour

k

A guy about my age walked into the laundry room, carrying a full laundry bag. When he saw me sitting at the table, he flashed a huge smile. "Hello," he said, setting his clothes down next to me.

"Hi," I replied, smiling back. It was nice to see someone my age.

"I'm Noah," he said, holding out his hand.

"I'm Isabelle," I told him, shaking his hand.

"Did you just get here?" he asked. "I haven't seen you around."

"Yeah, we got in last night," I said. "Are you staying here, too?"

"Yeah, we've been here for two weeks now," he said. "We drove down from Ohio. I go to the Montessori school next door. Just got out of school, actually."

"My grandad's getting rehab at the hospital nearby."

"Nice," Noah said. He picked up his laundry bag, added some pods to the washing machine, and loaded the clothes inside. He hit the start button, and the sound of the water filling the machine echoed around the room. He looked up and smiled at me. "Mind if I join you?"

"Sure," I said, and he sat across from me. We continued talking as we waited for our laundry.

My dryer buzzed. The time had flown by. Noah offered to help me load my clothes into the trash bag I had brought them in.

"Can I see you again?" Noah asked anxiously as I headed for the door.

"I'm sure I'll see you around. We'll be here at least a couple of months," I told him. I flung the bag over my shoulder and waved as I left the laundry room.

I headed back to the RV, and when I got there, Abe and Grandad were already back from Grandad's therapy. I told them all about my walk around the RV park, the laundry room, and the shuttle to the hospital. It seemed like this RV park had everything we needed to get by for the next few months.

***

We settled into a routine over the next few weeks. Abe found a co-working space he could rent short-term for his company.

Since five of his employees lived in the Houston area, he got a private office that would work for the six of them in case they all wanted to go into the office together.

Grandad was making progress and able to do more each week. He still needed a lot of help, but he was almost at the point where he wouldn't need any assistance in the shower. His mind was sharp, and he even helped me with my math homework, which I was struggling with on my own.

Abe's twenty-sixth birthday came at the beginning of February. I teased him about being over a quarter of a century old, and he teased me about being "a youngin'."

I was getting the hang of grocery shopping and cooking more American meals since we didn't have our usual grocery options available. Things were definitely different down in Texas. No one had ever heard of chokecherries, and the store didn't carry much venison or walleye. I started picking up the recipe cards they passed out on Fridays and trying new dishes.

Grandad was the most hesitant about how we were living and eating. He worried the changes would make us, especially Louis and me, forget our heritage—like they had tried to do to him in boarding school. It had been over a month since we had been to a powwow, and while we still held small ceremonies here and there, life was different in Texas.

***

One night in late March, my phone buzzed. It was Mickie. I was so excited to hear from her. It had been a few days since we'd last talked, and I needed our estrogen chats. I was stuck in a house full of guys, and my only friend in the neighborhood was a guy, too. I missed the late-night girl talks Mickie and I used to have when we shared a room on the reservation. She was my best friend, one who could never be replaced, but lately, it felt like we'd been drifting apart.

guess what, Mickie texted.

chicken butt lmao, I responded. I chuckled at my joke. *jk what?*

i missed my moon

Mickie was very regular. To my knowledge, she had never missed a moon or been late.

it was supposed to start Monday but it never did, she said.

whoa! does that mean your pg?

idk maybe

omg that'd be crazy! so soon!

I know.

have you told nate?

not yet cuz im not sure about it, she said. *I figured id wait until im sure.*

keep me posted, sis

I will

It seemed impossible that Mickie was pregnant so soon. We'd gotten married two and a half months ago. My heart sank. I was happy for her, but at the same time, I couldn't shake the feeling of loss. She might already be pregnant, and here I was, married the same amount of time, but I hadn't even had sex yet. We'd been living in a tiny, unstable place with no bedroom door and my brother and grandfather sleeping ten feet away. I wasn't even sure I could have kids, but I definitely wasn't going to have them when I hadn't even done the one thing that could lead to a pregnancy.

TWELVE

Louis's last day of high school had been yesterday. He could've walked across the stage at a nearby school to get his diploma, but he decided not to. Now that he'd finished high school, he could go to college. He was looking for a job right now, though, so he could help contribute to the family.

As for me, I was scraping by in my classes—barely. Seniors got out earlier than the rest of us, so I still had two weeks left before my school year was over. I was barely passing algebra I and pretty much failing Spanish. My grades were as low as they could get without failing.

Abe had been going into the office almost every day. He hired three more people locally and had to rent more space to fit everyone. His company was still doing well and even growing. Last month, he went to New York for a few days to meet with some investors, leaving the three of us to manage things in the RV. It wasn't too tough, but I couldn't shake this strange, lonely feeling when I had to sleep in our bed alone.

Mickie was definitely pregnant and had made it safely through her first trimester. I had no idea how she was going to juggle being a senior and having a baby at home. Most of the girls in our tribe who got married and pregnant in high school ended up dropping out. It wasn't a huge surprise, either. Girls weren't expected to finish high school. Our value came from bringing new life into the world. But Mickie was different. She was a superstar, and I couldn't picture her dropping out. Maybe she'd find a way to handle both—taking care of a baby and staying in school. But I figured she'd have to give up her extracurriculars if she was going to balance it all.

Grandad had made a lot of progress in the five months since we'd moved to Houston. He could do most things on his own now though he still used his cane when he went for walks. He didn't go to therapy as much, and when he did, he took the shuttle bus. He could get there and back by himself, which made him feel more like his old self—the independent man he'd always been.

I had gotten used to life in the RV in Texas, but I still missed the reservation. It felt like a part of me was missing. My parents were gone, and now my home was, too. My culture and heritage seemed to be slipping away from my memory, and I'd even started picking up a Southern accent in the few months we'd been here. I still wore my braid down my back, but the braid was the only thing left of my Native heritage. I couldn't believe how much had changed in such a short time.

***

Come June, school was over for me, and I had managed to pass all my classes. I was so relieved summer was here. I could put my laptop away and not worry about algebraic formulas or World War II. The weather was blistering hot, and the humidity made it even worse. Louis spent most of the time with his shirt off, showing off his toned, tanned body. A girl about his age had arrived at the RV park, and he was trying to make a good impression.

One day shortly after my school year had ended, Louis was at work—he had found a job at a local mechanic's shop—Abe was at his office, and Grandad was busy editing an article for the medical journal. That left me with free time, so I decided to visit Noah and the new girl, Olivia, who had just arrived at the RV park earlier in the week. Olivia's family's RV was on the same side of the RV park as Noah's family's. They were both free and up for some fun, so we headed to the soccer field behind the dog park to kick the ball around.

We didn't play much soccer on the Rez, so I wasn't sure how well I'd do. But I turned out to be pretty good. We played in the heat until we were sweating like crazy, and finally, we had to take a break and grab some water. Olivia's RV was right next to the dog park, and it was on the way back to mine, so we stopped there. She handed Noah and me each a cold bottle of water from her fridge.

"Do you want to have a picnic at the dog park for lunch?" Olivia asked. "We can make some sandwiches here. It's super close to the picnic table."

"Yeah, sure," Noah and I both said. We helped her make sandwiches, and she grabbed a bag of chips for each of us. We took fresh bottles of water and headed over to the picnic tables under the shady trees behind her RV.

It felt good to hang out with people my age. That was one of the things I missed about going to school on the Rez. My class was small, but at least I had been around other kids my age. The online school this semester had been tough, what with only seeing people over Zoom, though most of them kept their cameras off. Besides Louis, Abe, Grandad, and the few people I'd talked to at the RV park or the grocery store, I hadn't interacted with anyone. It was one of the biggest reasons I still felt heartbroken over losing our home on the reservation.

After lunch, I said goodbye to Olivia and Noah and headed back to the RV. When I opened the door, I heard a strange noise from inside. My stomach twisted as I stepped into the RV and immediately saw something was horribly wrong. Grandad's laptop was tossed carelessly onto the dinette bench where he had been sitting earlier. And then I saw him.

Grandad was on the floor, his body jerking and flailing uncontrollably. I froze. My heart dropped. I rushed forward, my breath catching in my throat. "Grandad!" I shouted, but he didn't respond.

His mouth was foaming, a mix of saliva and blood, and he was gasping for air. His limbs were stiff, his back arched, and his whole body was twitching wildly.

"What's happening to him?" I screamed, my voice shaking. I looked around frantically, like maybe someone would appear out of nowhere to help. But no one did. I fumbled for my phone, tears starting to blur my vision.

"Nine-one-one, what's your emergency?" a calm voice answered.

"My grandad! I don't know what's happening! He's shaking, he's foaming at the mouth, and—" I couldn't finish. I could barely breathe.

"What's your address?" the operator asked.

"We're in the RV park. South Main. Site eighty...I don't know the address!" I said, my words rushing out in a panic. "He won't stop! What's happening to him? What do I do?" My tears mixed with the sweat on my face as I knelt beside Grandad, feeling completely helpless. In the distance, I could hear a siren getting closer, but it didn't feel fast enough.

It felt like hours passed before the ambulance finally arrived. Grandad was still shaking when the EMTs jumped out of the truck and rushed to him.

"How long has he been like this?" one of them asked.

"I don't know," I choked out, my voice barely above a whisper. "I was gone most of the morning."

"Are you a relative?" the EMT asked.

"His granddaughter," I managed, my tears flowing freely now.

They worked quickly, loading Grandad into the ambulance. One of them looked at me. "Do you want to come with him?"

I nodded, my heart pounding hard in my chest. I climbed into the front of the ambulance, and we sped off toward the hospital. It was only about ten minutes away, but it felt like an eternity.

When we arrived at the hospital, the EMTs rushed Grandad into the back to take care of him. They told me I had to wait in the waiting room. I walked into the waiting room and immediately called Abe. He answered right away and said he'd be there as soon as he could.

While I waited, I grabbed Grandad's paperwork and tried to fill out as much as I could. I didn't know all the details, but I did my best to answer the questions while I waited for Abe to show up. When I had filled out all I could, I set the clipboard down on the seat next to me.

The wait felt like it was never going to end, and I had no idea what was going on in the back. This was the second time in six months we were stuck in a hospital because of Grandad. He was getting old—he was one of the oldest in our tribe—but he had always been so healthy before the stroke. And now, this.

Every time I stepped into a hospital, it brought back memories of last September. I remembered sitting beside Mom's hospital bed, talking to her as she took her last breaths. I was the last person who'd been with her before she'd died. I was the last one with Grandad, too, bringing him his dinner right before he had the stroke. And now, I was the last one with him again, this time as he had been seizing on the floor in the RV.

I felt tears well up in my eyes. Why did I always have to be the one closest to death? I was the youngest in the family. I should have been the farthest from it.

"Daddy, I miss you," I whispered to myself, hugging my arms tightly around me, trying to keep my tears in. One tear fell onto my arm, and more followed. I couldn't stop them. I missed the old days, my daddy, late-night talks with Mickie, the sound of school bells ringing, and my friends. I missed the easy, familiar life on the reservation.

Why did this have to happen to me? Why did life have to change? It didn't seem fair, and it felt like I was the one who was losing the most. I sat in the crowded emergency room, surrounded by people, but I felt like I was all alone as I hugged myself and cried, trying to make myself feel better and failing.

Abe walked through the door, and as soon as he saw me crying, he hurried over. He slid into the seat next to me, carefully moving the papers aside, and pulled me into a hug. I turned toward him and cried into his shoulder. In that moment, I felt like a scared little kid, not the grown, married woman I was supposed to be.

"Do we know how he is?" Abe whispered, gently rubbing my back in slow circles.

I shook my head, sniffing. "They haven't told me yet." I fell apart. "It was so awful, Abe!" I sobbed. "He was lying there, shaking so bad. There was blood coming out of his mouth. I couldn't do anything! I felt so useless!" My cries echoed through the busy waiting room. I buried my face back in Abe's chest, not wanting to see everyone staring at me.

It felt like forever before a doctor came to the door and called my name. Abe and I stood together, holding hands, and followed the doctor down the hall to a smaller, private room.

"Your grandfather experienced a status epilepticus," the doctor began. "That means he had a seizure that lasted much longer than normal. We weren't able to stop the seizure with the usual anti-seizure medication, so we had to sedate him completely." He paused before continuing, "He's in a medically induced coma right now, but the good news is, he's no longer seizing."

"Can we see him?" Abe asked, his voice quiet.

"We're still running tests on his brain activity to figure out what needs to happen next," the doctor replied. "But it's not looking good."

"What do you mean, 'not looking good'?" I asked, my voice trembling.

The doctor sighed and explained, "It seems like he'd been seizing for a long time before you found him. During status epilepticus, the brain's electrical activity gets out of control, causing severe disruptions in brain function. From the initial tests, we can see some swelling in his brain. His lack of response to the anti-seizure medication combined with what we've found so far suggests he's suffered brain damage. It may be irreversible." He paused again. "We'll need to do more tests to see if we can restore normal brain function."

I stood in a rage. "No!" I shouted, my voice breaking. "My grandad is fine! He's a doctor! He would've known what to do for this! He's fine! Tell me he's fine!"

More tears came pouring out, and I started sobbing uncontrollably. This couldn't be happening. We came all the way to Houston for Grandad to get better after his stroke, and now things were worse. Now they were telling me he had "irreversible brain damage." How could this be happening?

Abe stood and wrapped his arms around me, trying to calm me down. His scent and the warmth of his embrace helped pull me back to reality. I cried into his chest, letting all my sorrow and fear pour out. I couldn't be strong on my own anymore. It felt like there was too much loss in my world.

The doctor led us back to the waiting room and said he would let us know when we could see Grandad. I turned to Abe, feeling desperate. "Is there anything we can do, Abe? A sacrifice? A smudging ceremony? Something...anything?"

Abe sighed and shook his head. "Let's make sure the others know what's going on," he said, pulling out his phone. He called Louis to fill him in. Louis had gotten home from work and was confused about where everyone was, so he was relieved to hear from Abe. But when he heard what had happened, he was shocked.

I called Mickie next, telling her all about Grandad. There was nothing she could do from Minnesota, but she deserved to know. We were in this together, even if she was far away. Uncle Nate was at work, but Mickie promised to tell him as soon as she saw him.

The doctor gave us the okay to see Grandad. As I walked into the hospital room and saw him lying still in the bed, hooked up to machines, I froze. The scene hit me hard—it was too familiar. Flashbacks of Mom flooded my mind, and I couldn't take another step forward. I had been the last one with her when she died, and I couldn't let the same thing happen to Grandad.

I stood there, paralyzed, before slowly backing out of the room. Abe glanced at me, confused, then looked at Grandad and back at the panic on my face. He seemed to understand without me saying a word. He followed me out.

"I can't do it," I whispered, my voice barely audible. "I'm sorry."

"Don't be," he said quietly. "I understand." He pulled me into a long, comforting hug.

Eventually, I pulled away. "Go," I said, my voice weak and shaky. "You need to be with him. I'll wait out here."

"Are you sure, Princess?" he asked, searching my eyes.

I nodded, forcing a weak smile. I sat in a chair outside the room. Abe studied me for a moment, his expression filled with compassion. He nodded back and disappeared into the room with Grandad.

I was only sitting for a few minutes when Louis ran up to me, a worried look on his face. "Where is he?" he asked. I pointed to the room, and he dashed in.

The boys finally came out of the room, and a doctor followed behind them. He told us they would be monitoring Grandad and running more tests over the next few hours. He promised to keep us updated on his condition. He also mentioned Grandad would likely be in the hospital for a while.

At that point, there wasn't much more we could do. Grandad was still unconscious, and his doctors would be busy with tests, so we decided to head back to the RV. After five months of Grandad going to rehab, it felt like we were back at square one.

That night, I barely slept. Nightmares haunted me, mixing flashbacks of Mom and Grandad in the hospital.

***

Ten days later, Grandad was still in the hospital with no progress. Abe's phone rang early in the morning. It was way too early for a Saturday. The sun hadn't even risen yet, and we were still in bed.

Abe rolled over, picking up his phone. "Hello.... Yes, this is he.... Mmhmm.... Okay. Thank you for letting me know. We'll be there as soon as we can." He hung up and let out a long sigh.

"Who was it?" I mumbled, rubbing my eyes.

"It's over. Dad just died."

THIRTEEN

It was time to pack up and head back home to the reservation. Our only reason for coming to Houston had been Grandad, and now that he was gone, there was no point in staying. I was ready to leave this place behind. I had been homesick our entire stay here, and now, Houston only reminded me of sadness and loss.

Grandad's body had been taken to a local funeral home yesterday and would be transported back to a funeral home in the closest town to our reservation. From there, we would take him home to the reservation for the funeral ceremony at the powwow, like we had done for Mom and Daddy. He would be buried in our burial ground next to them. Abe had made all the arrangements, paid for the coffin, and handled the transport.

Louis and I said our goodbyes to Olivia and Noah before climbing into the Jeep to make the long drive back to Minnesota. I was looking forward to getting home, but the reason we were heading back made the return feel sadder. Memories of Mom and Daddy's funeral kept creeping in, and they'd stick with me until we buried Grandad. No sixteen-year-old should have to deal with this much loss in such a short time.

The drive back home felt long and heavy, like the weight of the world was pressing down on me. It was summer, so the trip was a lot easier and faster than the winter drive to Houston. We made it in three days, like we'd planned, instead of the four days it had taken when we'd driven down. There was no snowstorm to get stuck in, no icy roads, no cold nights spent huddling together by the firepits. Most of the drive was sunny and hot.

After we pulled up to our old house on the reservation, which was Louis's house now, we unloaded his things from the RV and helped him get settled in. Once finished, Abe and I headed to Abe's house, which was now mine, too.

Mickie came over when she heard we were back, bringing some groceries to make dinner. She looked radiant, glowing with her pregnancy, her belly round with the baby. She was so excited to see me and couldn't wait to fill me in on what had happened on the reservation while I'd been away. She helped us unpack the RV, chatting nonstop as we went. Afterward, we spent the rest of the afternoon cleaning out the RV.

That evening, I made dinner for Mickie, Nate, Abe, and myself. It felt good to cook again, to have my familiar foods and a big kitchen to work in. We invited Louis to join us, and for a moment, it felt like old times. The family was all together around the table—but this also made me miss Mom, Daddy, and Grandad. Our family was shrinking.

Mickie, Nate, and Louis went home after dinner. As the day turned to night, I was putting some things away in the dresser when Abe came up behind me, wrapping his arms around me and kissing my neck. "We're alone tonight, Princess," he whispered. "First time since we got married."

I turned around to face him, his arms still around me. I wrapped my arms around him and kissed him back, the familiar spark rushing through me. As I pulled away from the kiss, I smiled up at him. "Yes, finally alone," I whispered.

Over the past five months, I had gotten comfortable with Abe. We'd shared hugs and kisses while we'd slept beside each other in the RV, but we hadn't gone any further, mostly because Louis and Grandad were always close by, sharing the cramped space with us. We had been through so much together in such a short time, and now, I was ready to take our relationship to the next level.

He pulled me into another kiss, this time deepening it by parting his lips and letting his tongue slip into my mouth. I pressed my body closer against his, feeling his desire pressing into me. My body ignited, desire shooting through me.

He backed away slightly and looked into my eyes. "Are you okay?" he asked, his eyes searching mine.

"Yes," I managed to say, catching my breath. I knew he was remembering our conversation from before we'd gotten married, but so much had happened since then. I felt like I had grown up a lot even though I was still only sixteen.

"How are you feeling?" he asked me.

"I want you," I responded. It was true. I wanted him. I wanted all of him.

His hand ran up my back and grabbed the hair at the base of my neck under my braid, tipping my head back as his lips met mine again. He deepened the kiss, pressing our mouths together, exploring my mouth with his tongue.

He slowly backed us up to the bed, our lips still locked in a kiss. He began to undress me, piece by piece. I matched him by helping him out of his clothes until we were skin to skin at the foot of the bed. He lifted me up onto the bed and pressed into me. I felt us joining together, the two becoming one for the very first time. I felt so connected to him, as if our souls had finally become one after months of hovering close by. I was his, and he was mine.

When it was over, we lay next to each other, exhausted. It had been a long day of driving, unpacking, and…"married-people things." I felt so wanted, so connected, so loved. Abe's arm was wrapped around me, his eyes closed, a smile on his handsome face. I hugged him, laying my head on his strong chest. Smelling his earthy smell, I drifted off to sleep.

***

Friday night was the powwow, the night we would lay Grandad to rest and send his spirit off to wherever it went after this life. For the second time in my life, I had to cut my hair as a symbol of mourning. Everyone in our family did it, signifying how deeply we felt Grandad's loss.

When I walked into the dance arena, a wave of nostalgia hit me. I hadn't been to a powwow in five months, and I hadn't realized how much I'd missed the sense of community and belonging it gave me. Our culture and traditions were a part of who we were, and the powwows always reminded me of that in a way nothing else could.

Since it was summer, the regalia was different than it'd been in the winter when we'd left. The men wore less, with their chests exposed, and the women's dresses were lighter and shorter, more suited for the warm weather. My short hair whipped around in the summer breeze, tickling my neck. I wasn't used to it yet, and I wasn't sure I ever would be. I hoped there wouldn't be any more deaths in our family for a long time.

Grandad had always been an important figure in our tribe—and in my life. He'd been a steady presence, especially after Daddy passed. The Serug family was already tightknit, and losing our patriarch was a huge blow. In our tribe, Grandad was an elder who had helped shape our government and played a key role in getting the school built on our reservation. He'd fought to keep our children from being taken away by the US government and placed in boarding schools, where they'd have been forced to assimilate. To our community, he was a hero. The thought of never seeing him again was heartbreaking.

Abe could sense my sorrow. I was sure he felt the same, but men tended to handle grief differently. We sat next to each other on the bleachers holding hands as we waited for the funeral portion of the powwow.

As the smudging ceremony began, a thought hit me. They had done the same thing for our family after Mom and Daddy passed, and it hadn't helped at all. Grandad had still had his stroke and eventually died. I'd still received the diagnosis of endometriosis. I started to wonder if the whole smudging thing didn't work. Negative thoughts and bad spirits still seemed to attack us, even though we'd been smudged every month for as long as I could remember. Maybe it was because I'd been away from the reservation for too long, experiencing the world outside, but the way I saw things had changed.

I went through the motions of the funeral, doing my best to hold back my tears. I didn't want to cry anymore. I wanted to feel happy. I blocked out the funeral happening around me and thought of happy memories. The first snow of the season. Playing soccer in the field behind the RV park. The way I felt when I was with Abe at night. Mickie's big pregnant belly. I focused on these thoughts, and somehow, I managed to get through the ceremony without crying.

But when we moved to the burial ground and the men lowered the coffin into the hole next to Daddy's, it all became too much. All the tears I had kept inside came rushing out. Thinking about Daddy and now Grandad being buried in the earth shattered me. I began to sob as I shoveled a scoop of dirt onto the coffin.

***

In the middle of the night, Abe shot up in bed, his body stiff and unmoving, like he was in a trance. I rolled over, glancing at the clock. It was two in the morning. Confusion filled my mind. Abe was sitting upright, staring at the wall with wide, unblinking eyes.

"What is it, honey?" I asked, my voice soft, but he didn't respond.

He sat there, frozen, staring into the dark.

"Abe?" I asked again, my voice shaking a little. I reached out to touch his arm. His skin was burning hot. "Are you okay?"

He seemed to snap out of it, his body relaxing slightly. He shook his head back and forth. "Did you hear that voice?" he asked, his voice distant.

"No, I didn't hear anything. What did you hear?" I asked. With his hot skin, the strange trance, and now this talk about hearing voices, I was starting to get worried.

"It was the voice of Jehovah. He was speaking directly to me like we're talking right now," Abe said, his eyes still wide.

"What did He say?" I asked, my curiosity piqued despite the strange situation.

Abe took a deep breath as if still in awe of the experience. "He said, 'Go from your country, your people, and your father's household to the land I will show you. I will make you into a great nation, and I will bless you; I will make your name great, and you will be a blessing. I will bless those who bless you, and whoever curses you I will curse; and all peoples on earth will be blessed through you.'"

I blinked, trying to process what he'd said. "What? That's...very strange. What does it mean?"

Abe stared at me, his eyes still wide with the intensity of what had just happened. "I'm not sure exactly," he said slowly. "But it felt so real. It couldn't have been just a dream. I think we need to listen to it."

I sat up, his words sinking in. "So, you want us to leave the reservation again? With no idea of where we're going?" My voice wavered with a mix of disbelief and worry.

"Maybe the trip for Grandad was a way of preparing us for a bigger journey Jehovah wants us to take. I don't know where He's leading us, but I feel like we should go and see."

I shook my head, trying to make sense of it all. "Abe, that's crazy. We just got back. We've barely settled back in. Mickie's going to have a baby soon—our niece or nephew. And now you want us to leave again? Just because you had a dream? I don't know about this."

"He said He was going to 'make me into a great nation,' Princess. That means you're going to have children after all,"

Abe said, his voice hopeful. "The only way I could become a great nation is with children."

I wasn't sure if his words were meant to reassure me or if he believed them. I still felt uncertain. "Abe, I'm barren. The doctor pretty much told me that. I don't think you'll become a great nation through me."

He thought for a moment and suggested, "Maybe we should bring Louis with us. Maybe he'll have children who will be part of the great nation Jehovah is talking about. He's kin to me, after all."

I raised an eyebrow. "I doubt Louis would go for that. It was one thing when he was coming to help with Grandad. Now, there's no reason except for some crazy dream you had. Do you think he'd come just because you had a dream?" I was teasing him a little, trying to lighten the situation. I couldn't take him seriously. This whole thing felt way too out there to be real. "Why don't you try going back to sleep and see if any more dreams help clarify what you heard?" I suggested.

He sighed, frustrated that I wasn't taking him seriously. After a moment, he lay back down, pulling the light blanket over his bare chest. I turned over and tried to fall back asleep.

The next morning, I had mostly forgotten about the weird things that had happened the night before. But Abe hadn't. He was busy, running around the house like a man on a mission, packing for a trip.

"Tell me again what Jehovah said you should do," I said as he threw clothes into a suitcase.

"He said we need to leave the reservation and go to a place He'll show us," Abe replied without looking up.

"So, we're just…going? We don't even know where we're headed?" I raised an eyebrow.

"He'll show us," he said, his voice steady.

"Okay, but what direction are we supposed to go in? Has He at least told you that?" I pressed, trying to make sense of it.

Abe stopped for a moment, clearly thinking. "Not exactly."

"So, you're just going to get in the car and drive, hoping you get another vision on the way?" I asked, half-doubtful, half-amused.

Abe shrugged. "Pretty much."

"And this sounds like a forever thing. Like you're starting a whole new tribe, far away from ours," I said, my heart sinking a little.

"That's what He said," Abe replied, his face unreadable.

"You're okay with just leaving the reservation for good? No coming back?" I couldn't help asking.

Abe stopped what he was doing and looked at me. His gaze softened. "Princess, I feel like this is something I have to do. If Jehovah is telling me to go, I have to listen. I don't know what it means for us or what our future holds, but whatever it is, it's going to be good. He said He's going to bless us."

I let out a long sigh. I didn't get it. But when I'd married Abe, I'd promised I would follow his lead, even if I didn't always understand it.

"I don't want to leave the reservation," I said quietly. "I felt like I lost a part of myself the last time we left. The world outside the reservation is so different."

"I get that," Abe said. "It was tough for me when I went off to college. People made fun of me for being Native. They mocked my hair, called me 'redskin.' It was really hard. But luckily, we didn't run into too many people like that on our trip to Houston. Still, there's a lot of ugliness in the world. We'll probably face some of that when we follow Jehovah's plan. But He promised to bless those who bless us and curse those who curse us. We'll be under His care the whole time."

I felt a lump in my throat. "But we're never coming back? We're leaving for good? I won't see Mickie or her baby or Uncle Nate again? I...I don't know if I can do that," I admitted. I was so tied to my family, the reservation, and the life we'd built here. I loved the powwows, the way the whole tribe came together, and how we connected with the other tribes near the reservation. It was hard to imagine walking away from all of that.

Abe stepped closer, his eyes softening. "We get to write our own story, Princess. We'll start our own tribe, make our own traditions. We'll have our own powwows, wherever Jehovah leads us. It'll be ours, a tribe new and special."

I stared down at my feet, feeling like my life as I knew it was slipping away. After a long silence, I looked up at Abe. He was watching me closely, like he was trying to figure out what I was thinking.

"Okay," I said quietly. "I'll go where you go. Your home will be my home, and your God will be my God."

FOURTEEN

Now that we had made the decision to leave...for good...we had to tell the rest of the family and make preparations. We invited everyone over for dinner on Saturday night to break the news. I cooked walleye, wild rice, and berries, trying to make dinner feel normal. We sat around the table, eating and talking, but the usual comfort of the scene was gone. Knowing we were about to tell them we were leaving for good, I only felt sad.

Mickie smiled as she rubbed her belly. "I can feel the baby kicking now," she said. She was about four months along, and her baby bump was getting bigger every day.

I felt a pang of sadness in my chest, thinking about not being there when her baby was born, not watching it grow up. Mickie would be an amazing mom, and I couldn't help but feel a little jealous of this new chapter in her life, one I wouldn't be a part of.

Nate talked about how well the casino was doing. More people were coming in from all over the state, and he was hoping to turn it into a major vacation spot over the next few years to bring in more money for the tribe. I felt a deep ache, knowing I wouldn't get to see him reach that dream. I could almost picture little Serugs running around, the casino packed with visitors.

Abe cleared his throat. This was it. The big reveal. "We have an announcement to make," he said.

Everyone at the table looked at him with curiosity. I was sure they were expecting good news, like me being pregnant or a big update on his company.

"Princess and I are leaving the reservation...for good," Abe said.

I looked around the table to gage their responses. All of their jaws had dropped, and their eyes had gone wide.

"What? Why?" Mickie was the first to speak, her voice cracking. Tears started to fill her eyes.

"Jehovah, my God, has told us to leave," Abe explained. "He's taking us to another place to make us into a new nation. He came to me in a dream last night and told us to go, that He would direct us where to go, and that He would bless us."

There was complete silence. I looked around the table at everyone's faces. Mickie was crying quietly. Nate's mouth was still hanging open. Louis was staring at us, his eyebrows raised, eyes wide with shock. It was clear they were as heartbroken as

I was. My own tears that had been threatening all night finally spilled over.

Louis broke the silence. "I'm going with you."

I smiled through my tears, but Abe was the first to speak. "Louis, are you sure about this? We're not coming back. This isn't like the trip to Houston."

Louis didn't hesitate. "Yes, I know. But if you're starting a new tribe, you might need more than the two of you to get it off the ground. What if Princess can't have kids?" His words hung in the air, and my unspoken fear was now out in the open. Everyone at the table knew about my endometriosis diagnosis, but I'd never thought it would affect anyone outside of Abe and myself. Now, Louis was thinking about leaving behind his life on the reservation because of it.

"Besides," Louis added, his voice softer now, "Princess is my baby sister. I want to be there for her through a change as big as this. I can't imagine how hard it must be for her to leave her home...for good."

I felt a surge of love and gratitude for him. He always knew what I needed, what I was feeling, even without me saying a word. Louis had always been a good big brother, and I loved him more than I could say. He understood how difficult this was, and his support meant the world to me.

"We leave on Monday morning," Abe said, breaking the silence. "We'll take the RV like we did last time. Louis, if you're coming with us, how long will it take you to get ready?"

Louis didn't hesitate. "I can be ready by Monday. I've barely unpacked anyway."

After dinner, we said our goodbyes. But this time, the goodbyes felt much more final than before. I didn't know if I'd ever see Mickie or Nate again once we left. Mickie and I hugged, both of us wiping away tears. I said goodbye to my unborn niece or nephew, resting my hand on her belly. I felt a tiny kick, and it only made the sadness deeper. I touched my own belly, wondering if I'd ever experience that same feeling.

As Mickie and Nate walked down the front porch steps to leave, Mickie looked back at me, tears still in her eyes. She waved a slow, sad goodbye, and I waved back, my heart heavy.

***

Sunday was our prep day for the long trip ahead. I spent the day making food while Abe went to the elders to get the proper travel documentation. Luckily, the elders were available on weekends, so Abe was able to get all the paperwork in order for a trip to who-knows-where.

Since I had no idea how long we'd be on the road or where we were headed, I figured it was best to be as prepared as possible. Sure, we could stop at grocery stores or buy food from gas stations along the way, but I wasn't comfortable with that. I was still having a hard time leaving my heritage behind, and I much preferred the foods I knew and loved over the processed food we could pick up on the road.

I headed to the general store to buy supplies and ingredients for the trip. We couldn't carry too much because of the limited space in the RV, so I had to be picky about what I bought. I also wanted to use up as much of the food at home as possible since we wouldn't be coming back.

I started making food that would last a while and packed the RV with supplies we might need—pemmican, wojapi, nuts, berries, wild rice, cornbread, frybread, corn, beans, squash, and maple syrup. The freezer was stocked with ground meat for soups and stews, and the fridge was packed full. The cabinets by the microwave were stuffed, too.

By the time I finished preparing and packing the RV, Abe had returned. He had a written statement from one of the elders, who was an elected official, confirming our status as Natives. He also had our equivalent of birth certificates, stamped on the tribe's letterhead. Louis already had a driver's license for his ID, but I still needed a photo ID card, so Abe and I headed to the elder's place to get mine.

Abe also signed over his house and land rights to Nate, and Louis signed his over to Mickie. This way, the property would stay in the family, and Mickie and Nate could use it for their kids in the future.

It wasn't until four o'clock in the afternoon that we felt like we had everything in order to leave the next day—the paperwork, the food preparations, and the packing. We turned our attention to getting the house ready for being shut down for a long time. Even though it was the middle of summer, we winterized the houses so they would be ready for the months ahead. Once we got to wherever we were going and settled in, we'd have movers bring our belongings, what little we had, to us.

The long day came to an end, and it was time for our last night in our own bed. It hadn't been my bed for long, but it was still a lot more comfortable than the cramped space in the RV. And it was definitely better than sleeping with my brother ten feet away. We made the most of our privacy while we still had it.

***

The next day, we woke up with the sun at 5:25 a.m. It was one of the longest days of the year, which meant we'd have a lot of driving ahead of us before we had to stop for the night...wherever that would be.

Louis showed up at six o'clock with his suitcase in hand. He loaded his things into the RV, claiming the storage space under the bunk for himself now that Grandad was no longer with us. Once he was settled in, we all piled into the Jeep, ready for what was sure to be a long drive.

We headed south, the road stretching out in front of us. The sun was bright, and the air conditioning in the Jeep was blasting. It felt like this whole year had been nothing but déjà vu. First, my parents had died, then Grandad had died—two funerals. Then we'd gone on the RV trip to Houston, and now we were on this trip to who-knows-where. It was like my life had hit repeat, and I wasn't thrilled about it.

I was still trying to figure out who I was. My identity had always been tied to the reservation, to being Native, to being a Chaldean Indian. Now, we were leaving that behind for good, and it felt like a piece of me was being left there. Who was I really? Now I was a nomad. A wanderer.

We drove south all day, making it to Kansas City as the sun was setting. We stopped twice for gas and once to eat. By the time we got there, we were all wiped out. It was crazy how tiring sitting in a car all day could be. I couldn't imagine how much harder it was for Abe, who'd been driving the whole time.

We set up the RV at a park right off the interstate. By now, Abe and Louis were pros at hooking up the RV utilities, so they got to work right away. As soon as they got the electricity running, I started making dinner while they took care of the rest of the RV utilities.

The park was well-shaded, with trees surrounding the RV. Each campsite had its own firepit. After the sun set, the temperature dropped to a cool sixty-five degrees, so the guys made a fire and pulled out the camp chairs. We sat around the fire, eating and chatting.

Once we finished eating, Abe asked if I wanted to go for a walk around the park. It was clear he was a little stiff from the long drive, and exercise would do us both good. We held hands as we walked, Abe carrying a flashlight to guide us through the darkness. The moon was only a few days into a new cycle, so it was dark outside without the light.

"How are you holding up, Princess?" Abe asked.

I sighed. "I'm not going to lie. It's not easy leaving the reservation when I know I'm not coming back."

"I get that. It's hard for me, too," he said.

"Then why are we doing this?" I asked.

"When Jehovah calls, you answer. He created this world. He makes the sun rise and set. He controls the rain, the storms—everything. Look at the stars up there," he said, gesturing to the sky. "He made all of those. I don't want to mess with that kind of power. I'm only a human. Nothing compared to Him."

"Yeah, I get it," I said. "He could probably call down a lightning bolt if you didn't listen."

Abe chuckled. "I suppose He could if He wanted to, but I don't think He works that way. He wants our obedience, but He's not going to force it. We have free will. We can choose to follow Him and receive the blessings He wants to give us, or we can go our own way, which might lead to destruction."

I nodded. "Sometimes it's hard to do the things you don't want to do, even when you know they're the right thing."

"It certainly is," Abe said.

We walked in silence until the path ended, and we turned around to head back.

"Have you figured out where we're going yet?" I asked.

"Not a clue. Hopefully, Jehovah will give us some direction soon. Otherwise, I guess we'll drive into Mexico and keep heading south."

"You think He wants us to go to South America?" I asked, surprised.

"No, but I haven't gotten any clear direction from Him yet," Abe said. "So, I'm going to keep going in the same direction. He told me to 'go to the land I will show you.' Eventually, He has to show up and show us where we're supposed to go."

We reached the RV, where Louis was still sitting by the fire, headphones in, lost in his music. He looked completely at ease, like he was okay with whatever came next. I suspected he was bored with life on the reservation. There weren't many options for him, especially when it came to meeting girls, so he was eager to find someone outside of the reservation to make him happy. He definitely saw things differently than I did, but he was the oldest child, more adventurous and rebellious than me.

We packed the chairs back into the RV and covered the hot coals with dirt. It had been a long day, and I was drained. By the time I crawled into bed, it was after ten o'clock, and I didn't waste any time before falling fast asleep.

***

Day two of our journey started off rainy. I had no idea where all this rain was coming from. The sky had been clear the night before when we had been looking up at the stars. Now, the boys were rushing around, trying to stay dry while they unhooked the utilities and got the RV ready to hit the road. The rain poured down, soaking them completely. I looked like a drowned rat after running between the RV and the Jeep. We hadn't brought any umbrellas or raincoats, and I felt unprepared.

It was summer, but the rain on my clothes made me feel cold as I sat in the Jeep. I wrapped my arms around myself, hoping the sun would break through the storm. The windshield wipers were going full speed, but the road was still hard to see through all the rain. We weren't in a hurry, so Abe drove slowly to avoid hydroplaning.

The rain stopped when we got to Jasper, Missouri. We had made it through the storm. The sky cleared up, and the sun peeked through, with blue skies all around us. But there was one strange thing—straight ahead, there was a tall, thin cloud, like a pillar standing in the sky, leading the way.

Abe noticed it, too. We both stared out the windshield, our heads tilted as we looked at the strange cloud ahead of us. It wasn't blowing in the wind or changing shape like the rest of the clouds were doing. Instead, it stayed perfectly still, like giant white legs standing in front of us.

"Louis, look!" I called out, breaking his focus on the book he was reading in the back seat. I tapped him on the shoulder and pointed toward the cloud.

He looked up and stared at it. As soon as he realized it wasn't moving like a normal cloud, he focused on it even more.

"This has to be Jehovah's way of guiding us," Abe said, his voice steady. "It's too strange to be a regular cloud."

"I think you're right," I said. "It's not normal."

Abe kept his eyes on the cloud and drove toward it. As we got closer to Kendricktown, the cloud moved to the west, following the curve of the interstate. When we passed the town, it shifted south again. As we approached the 249 interchange, the cloud turned west once more, so we followed it, taking the loop toward Duenweg. A cloud didn't move like that under normal circumstances, so we were sure it was Jehovah guiding us, leading us to the "land He would show us."

We kept following the cloud as it directed us onto I-44, through Cherokee Nation and Muscogee Nation, and into Choctaw Nation in Oklahoma. By the time we reached the Choctaw Casino and RV resort, the sun was setting, and night had fallen. The cloud disappeared into the darkness of the night, so we decided to stop.

Being in Indian country, I was curious to check out the casino and see how it compared to Uncle Nate's. The RV park we were staying at was nice, and I started thinking it could be a good idea for Uncle Nate's "destination vacation" plan. Overnight accommodations were a big part of making a place a true vacation spot, and right now, Uncle Nate's casino didn't have many hotel rooms. An RV park could be a first step. I took some pictures of what could be seen in the dark to send to Mickie while we were driving the next day.

The casino was only a five-minute walk from the RV park. After we leveled and chocked the RV and hooked up the electricity, we made our way toward it. The casino was in a huge tower, and we were impressed by how modern and massive it was. Uncle Nate had a long way to go. His casino was decent-sized, but it was nothing like this resort.

We had dinner at one of the restaurants inside. A place like this on our reservation could bring the unemployment rate down to zero. But we didn't have enough people among all three tribes near us to run a casino this big. It was definitely more than Uncle Nate could manage right now. Still, he was just starting, and his business was growing. Who knew what it could turn into someday? I snapped more pictures to send to Mickie.

We didn't stay long at the casino. It was getting late, and we had already put in a long day on the road. This whole road-trip thing was exhausting. As soon as we got back to the RV, I collapsed into bed and fell fast asleep.

FIFTEEN

Now that we had the cloud to guide us, I felt a little more at ease. It was clear Jehovah was watching over us. But when Abe woke up the next morning, his mood seemed off, like something was bothering him.

"Abe, you okay?" I asked. "You seem kind of down."

He hesitated then said, "I had this dream last night about going back to Houston and bringing my team from work with us. It felt so real, like I was supposed to ask them to come with us, but...I don't think they'd want to leave."

"That does sound pretty unlikely, especially with how unsure everything is about the trip," I said, trying to make sense of it.

"I guess all we can do is ask," he sighed.

"Well, let's see if the cloud leads us to Houston first," I suggested.

Abe nodded, but his mind was clearly elsewhere.

We packed up the RV and got it ready for the long drive ahead. It would take about five and a half hours to get to Abe's office in Houston. If he was going to talk to his employees, it'd have to wait until tomorrow morning.

We hit the road at around eight in the morning, and the same strange cloud was still there, guiding us as we headed south on US-75 toward Dallas. The sun was already up, casting a warm glow over the road. The city felt alive with its usual energy, but Abe seemed distant, lost in thought about what was coming next. How were we going to ask his employees to join us on this crazy journey?

The cloud led us through Dallas and onto I-45 south, right through the heart of the city. When we got out of Dallas, the landscape started to change again. We stopped at a truck stop for gas and a quick break. It was nearly noon, and the sun was beating down hard. I was starving, so I grabbed some berries from the RV's fridge and passed them around.

The heat made the air feel thick, and we all worked up a sweat walking from the Jeep to the gas station. There, Louis grabbed a pop, his new addiction, and when we returned to the Jeep, he held it to his forehead to cool off a little before popping it open.

The drive between Dallas and Houston was long, with miles of open road that felt endless, especially since we'd driven this same stretch of highway in the opposite direction ten days ago. Once we left Dallas, the city skyline faded behind us, and the highway stretched out in front of us, lined with fields on either side. Some of the fields were planted with crops, others were dry, flat land. Here and there, a gas station or fast-food stop broke up the monotony. As we headed farther south, the air started to thicken with humidity. The trees grew denser, and the smell of the warm, sticky air told us we were getting closer to Houston.

As we neared Houston, the skyline appeared in the distance. The traffic picked up, and the mood shifted. The calm, quiet ride we'd had for the past few hours turned into the chaos of city driving, with more cars, more signs, and the hum of urban life. It was the beginning of rush hour, and the drive through the city was busy and slow.

We were getting close to the RV park where we'd stayed for the past six months. Louis was especially excited to see Olivia again. He'd been texting her while we were away.

It was nearly dinnertime when we pulled up into the familiar RV park on the southwest side of Houston. Abe checked in and paid for a week in case it took that long to convince his team to come. We pulled into our spot. It wasn't the same spot we'd had before, but it was on the same side of the park. As soon as we got the RV leveled and the utilities hooked up, Louis disappeared to find Olivia.

I started making dinner, happy to be walking around the RV rather than sitting in the front seat of the Jeep. The RV wasn't big, but it was a big upgrade from the confines of the seat I'd been sitting in for the past three days. I needed some exercise.

My joints felt stiff, and my back hurt. I stretched and paced the small space as I waited for the food to cook.

I pulled out my phone and texted Louis.

is Olivia coming to dinner?

let me check... Louis texted back a few minutes later. *yep she can come.*

Awesome!

We had more than enough food for one extra person, and I knew how much Louis liked Olivia. It would be good for Abe to meet her, too, even though we weren't planning to stay long. The dinette table in the RV wasn't big enough for four people, so we'd end up eating outside under the awning, in the sweltering heat. It was a far cry from the winter months when the weather had been much cooler and more comfortable. Now, Houston was scorching hot, both during the day and at night. No need for a fire to keep warm, that was for sure.

dinner will be ready in about five minutes, I texted Louis.

Abe was lying on the bed while I cooked, looking exhausted. He had the toughest job of all of us with all the driving. I could tell he was stressing about the conversation he'd have with his team tomorrow. I hated having to wake him up for dinner; he looked so peaceful when he was asleep.

"Abe, honey," I said, gently touching his shoulder. "Dinner will be ready soon."

He opened his eyes and, without warning, pulled me down onto the bed with him. His lips met mine in a kiss. "I miss being alone with you, Princess," he murmured, wrapping his arms around me and kissing me again.

I giggled. "Louis and Olivia will be here any minute, Abe."

"That's too bad," he said. He let me go, and I climbed out of bed to finish cooking. Before I left, I leaned down and gave him one last kiss.

As soon as I stepped back, Louis and Olivia walked through the door, laughing and talking. I rushed over to Olivia and gave her a big hug. Abe sat up in bed, watching us.

"You cut your hair, too!" she said, surprised.

"Yeah, I'm sure Louis told you it's because we're sad about Grandad," I said, running a hand through my short hair. It would be another week or so before it would be long enough to braid again.

"I'm really sorry," she said, pulling me into another hug. "I can't believe it. He was getting so much better."

Louis was busy introducing Abe to Olivia. When we'd been here before, Abe had been working whenever Olivia had been around, so they hadn't had a chance to meet properly.

The evening was relaxed as we ate and talked. Olivia and Louis were clearly into each other. I bet Louis hoped it would take a while to convince Abe's coworkers to join us so he could spend more time with her. We chatted about Olivia's plans for next year now that she'd graduated high school. She didn't have any college plans and was looking for a job instead. Louis joked about her coming with us, but I didn't know how serious he was. We spent the rest of the evening hanging out, laughing, and enjoying each other's company, sitting in camp chairs by the RV. Eventually, Louis walked Olivia home, and Abe and I headed to bed for the night.

***

The next morning, Abe was up early, getting ready to head to his office for the first time in two weeks. He'd kept up with work by doing video calls while we were gone, but today he was going in to see the team in person. He dressed in jeans and a sport coat and tried to make his hair look as close to his old braid as possible by slicking it back.

He grabbed his computer bag and climbed into the Jeep, ready to face the day. Today, he would talk to his team about relocating to God-only-knew-where—literally. I wanted to go with Abe to support him, but I'd only be in the way. Instead, I decided to make the most of my time in Houston and hang out with Louis, Olivia, and Noah.

We played soccer and ate lunch with a few other kids around our age that were new to the RV park. Once Olivia's parents got back home from work, I decided it was time to head back to our RV to see if Abe had returned yet. Olivia's parents invited Louis to stay for dinner, so I said goodbye and walked across the parking lot toward our RV. The Jeep was back, so Abe was already home.

I opened the door and found Abe sitting at the dinette with a glass of water, reading a book. "Hey," I said, smiling. "How'd it go?"

He jumped up and practically ran (as much as you could run in an RV) to give me a hug. His excitement caught me off guard. "It was amazing! Each of them had the exact same dream last night, about me asking them to come with us. They said it felt so real that when I asked, it was like déjà vu! Jehovah works in mysterious ways!"

"So, they're coming?" I asked, surprised at how well his day had gone.

"Yes, every one of them! They all know Jehovah. But they call him 'God.' It seems they all have been to church before where they worship God. They're all going back to talk to their families about the trip," Abe said, grinning.

"It's going to be like a giant caravan following a weird cloud pillar. We're going to look like a crazy bunch!" I laughed, giving him a hug.

"I'm so relieved," Abe said, his smile fading into a look of relief. "I've been stressing about this ever since I had that dream telling me I was supposed to ask them. I guess I shouldn't have worried so much. Jehovah knows what He's doing." He paused, then asked, "Where's Louis?"

"Louis is staying for dinner at Olivia's," I told him.

"Oh, really?" Abe raised an eyebrow and gave me a mischievous grin. "So, we're alone for a while?"

I smiled back at him. "I guess so," I said.

He picked me up and placed me gently on the bed, running his hand through my hair and pulling me close to him, our lips pressing together in a kiss. A feeling of excitement coursed through my veins as he planted little kisses from my earlobe down to the base of my neck.

"You are so beautiful, Princess," he said softly into my ear, letting his breath linger, tickling my neck. Goosebumps ran down my entire body despite the warmth of the summer day. His passion was evident through our clothes as he rolled on top of me, pressing himself against me between my legs.

I kissed him passionately and pressed my body up against his, showing him my desire was as strong as his, that I wanted him. It wasn't long before we were skin-to-skin together, sharing our desires for each other in a tangled mess of RV sheets.

***

Abe's eight Houston-based coworkers had spent the last couple of weeks talking things over with their families and getting their affairs in order and ready for the big move. They would take about two weeks to finish wrapping up their lives in Houston before we could leave for good. All eight employees were coming with us; five of them were married, and three had kids. A total of eighteen people had agreed to this crazy plan to leave Houston and follow a cloud to some unknown land, and Abe's company had inherited five new employees, their spouses, along the way.

In the two weeks before we left, Louis spent as much time as he could with Olivia. They had gotten close, and Olivia didn't want him to leave. She begged her parents to pack up and come with us, but they weren't interested in leaving their jobs or their life in Houston. They both had stable careers and weren't ready to give that up to travel around without a clear destination.

Louis had a conversation with Abe about the possibility of Olivia joining us. We did have an extra bunk below Louis's that she could use. But Abe wasn't thrilled about the idea of them living together before marriage even though they'd be sleeping in separate beds.

***

One day, Abe was at work, and Louis and I were alone in the RV.

"What's Olivia doing today?" I asked, curious why he wasn't with her.

"She's got a dentist appointment. She'll be back in an hour," he said. "I'll be over at her place for dinner, so you don't have to worry about making food for me."

I smiled. I didn't have to make dinner for him much anymore. He was almost always at Olivia's. "You're going to miss her when we leave, aren't you?"

"Yeah," he said quietly, staring down at his hands. "I was thinking about asking her to marry me."

"What?" I gasped. "Are you serious?"

He looked up at me. "Yeah. I can't imagine my life without her. And Abe won't let her come with us unless we're married," he said.

"Louis, don't rush into things. You don't even have a way to support her. You're living off Abe right now. How are you going to take care of her? You're the man in the relationship. You need a job, a way to make money, to live."

"We could make it work," he said, his voice steady. "Maybe it wouldn't be easy, but we'd figure it out."

"Just think about it, okay? Don't rush into it."

He nodded but didn't respond, his gaze dropping again.

"Hey," I said, trying to change the subject and lighten the mood. "Do you want to go play ping-pong in the lodge? Just because Olivia's not here right now doesn't mean we can't have fun."

"Sure, sis," he said, standing up from the couch. "Let's go."

***

We had one more week before we left for our trip to nowhere. It was the fourth of July, and red, white, and blue was everywhere. Olivia's family invited us over for their big holiday celebration followed by fireworks at Hermann Park after dark.

We never celebrated Independence Day on the reservation. As a sovereign nation, our "independence day" was different. Besides, the fourth of July also marked the beginning of terrible things for our ancestors, like the loss of our land and being forced onto the reservation.

But life was different now. We were more connected to Americans than ever before. Still, Grandad would roll over in his grave if he knew we were going to an American Independence Day celebration.

Before the celebration, Louis practically bounced into the RV, grinning from ear to ear. "I did it! I asked Olivia to marry me, and she said, 'Yes!'"

I put my book down and stood from the couch. "Wait, really? Uh, congratulations, Louis." Despite my hesitations about his decision, I pulled him into a big hug.

He stepped back, pacing around the small space. "Yeah, but we can't get married before we leave. It's way too soon. But once we get where we're going, I'll prepare a place for us then come back to get her."

I raised an eyebrow. "What do her parents think about all this?"

He stopped pacing, his eyes lighting up. "Asher gave me his permission. I've been studying every article I can about American engagements and weddings. I don't want to mess it up. I asked her dad on Sunday, and he said yes." He started pacing again and continued, "Well, he was a little unsure at first since we're so young. But I told him Abe said I could work as a customer support associate at his company. So, I'll have a job and can take care of us."

"That's awesome!" I pulled him into another hug. I was happy for him. Olivia was amazing, and I was excited for her to be part of the family.

He practically bounced again. "I used all my savings to buy the ring, and it's not huge, but it's perfect. And she said 'Yes!'"

I couldn't help but smile. His excitement was contagious.

"Her parents are taking us out to dinner tomorrow to celebrate. Somewhere fancy," he said.

"Wow, that sounds nice." I hugged him again. "I'm so excited for you, Louis. Olivia is a great girl, and I know you'll be perfect together."

Louis left to go back to Olivia's, and I got our food ready. Abe would be home any minute, and we would head over to Olivia's house for dinner before the fireworks.

***

We had three days before we left Houston and followed the cloud toward some unknown place. I hadn't seen the cloud since we'd gotten back to Houston two weeks ago, and I couldn't help but wonder if it would show up again to lead us once we started moving. How embarrassing would it be if we had all these plans to leave, and the cloud didn't come? Everyone would think Abe was crazy, and if the leader of the company was crazy, how much longer could the company survive?

What if Jehovah had given up on us because it'd taken us so long to get moving? Maybe He'd moved on to someone else, someone who didn't need so much time to get ready. What if we'd missed our chance completely? I'd had my doubts about all of this from the start, but things did seem to be falling into place. Abe's coworkers had all had similar dreams, dreams clear enough that they'd agreed to follow him when he'd asked. Surely that wouldn't have happened if Jehovah had given up on us.

SIXTEEN

The day came when we were leaving Houston for good. We had a whole caravan with us: four RVs, a Honda Accord, a van, and an SUV. We all met in the back of the Kroger parking lot at nine in the morning.[1]

Everyone was buzzing with excitement. It was a new day, a new life, a new journey for all of us. We couldn't wait to see what Jehovah would do through us and through Abe. I never imagined I'd see so much excitement for an uncertain trip like this.

Once the last person showed up, the cloud pillar appeared out of nowhere, like it knew we were all here. Of course, it knew. Jehovah Himself was creating and guiding it. We made

---

1. See page in the back of the book for a list of co-workers and their families (Caravan Characters) that joined Abe and Isabelle on their trip.

sure all of the vehicles in the caravan had a full tank of gas since no one knew how far we would be traveling.

I climbed into the front seat of the Jeep. With Abe in the lead, we pulled out of the parking lot one-by-one following the cloud down the highway and toward the entrance to I-69 south. We found ourselves moving away from the bustling city and into the quieter, more rural parts of Texas. Past the last bits of urban sprawl, we began to see more open fields, with tall grasses swaying in the wind and the occasional farmhouse scattered along the road. The farther we went, the more the landscape flattened out, with the occasional clump of trees and distant oil rigs dotting the horizon. There was a sense of wide openness, with flat land stretching for miles in every direction.

We followed I-69 until it merged with US-59 in Rosenberg, where the cloud continued southwest. When we got about an hour and a half into our journey, the cloud stopped over a Love's Travel truck stop near Edna, Texas. Abe pulled over into the parking lot, the caravan following behind. When everyone was parked, little Levi burst out of the truck pulling Elijah's RV, doing what appeared to be the pee-pee dance. Sophia grabbed his hand before he ran into traffic in the parking lot, and the two of them ran together into the store to the washroom.

Elijah was the manager of the sales team. He and his wife Sophia had a five-year-old son, Levi. Elijah owned an RV like Abe's, so his family was using that to travel with us. Sophia had worked as a floor associate at a hardware store before this trip, but with the move, she had joined Abe's company as a customer service representative.

Elijah walked up to Abe's window. "That was a close one!" Elijah said. "Levi was complaining about having to go potty since we passed through El Campo. I didn't know if I should call you to stop or what."

Abe laughed. "Jehovah knew. He stopped the cloud right over the truck stop. I guess maybe we all should take a washroom break. I have no idea when or where the cloud will stop next."

Everyone piled out and made their way to the washrooms. With so many people, even in a truck stop with a large washroom, the lines were long. Luckily, we were about evenly split male and female, so the wait wasn't too terrible. After about thirty minutes, we were back on the road again with the cloud moving ahead of us.

At Victoria, the cloud turned farther south along I-69E, continuing southwest along the coast of Texas and merging with US-77. Once we got closer to Kingsville, the landscape changed into the rugged, more arid territory of South Texas. The trees became sparser, and the brush grew thick and wild, stretching across the land in tangled masses. The land started to feel even more untamed, and the heat kicked in as the noon sun relentlessly beat down on us.

On the outskirts of Kingsville, the cloud stopped at the second Love's Travel truck stop of the day so we could take a break and gas up. Some of the folks went into the store or went to the Arby's attached to the store to eat lunch. The kids were getting restless. It had been three and a half hours in the car, plus a thirty-minute stop at the first gas station. Four hours is a long time to be stuck in a car when you're a little kid, so everyone, kids and parents alike, was relieved for the break.

I jumped into the RV to make lunch while the others went to the gas station restaurant. I packed up some nuts and berries to bring into the restaurant as a snack, so we could still eat with everyone. The small seating area was packed with our group. Most of the adults already knew each other, but some had never met the spouses and kids. They were all chatting and getting to know the families they'd be living around for the next few months, or maybe longer.

I handed Abe and Louis their food and sat next to Mia, who was helping little Levi open his ketchup packet for his fries. Sophia had gone to refill their drinks and left Levi with Mia.

Mia was a young single Hispanic girl who worked in customer service. She had been living with her parents before the trip and was planning on staying with Sophia in their RV, helping out with Levi. She wore a blue crop top that matched her eyes, showing off her tanned, toned arms and flat stomach. A small navel ring with colorful gems dangled from her belly button. Her short jean shorts revealed muscular quads and perfectly tanned legs. Her jet-black hair, highlighted with streaks of blonde, fell in soft waves down her back. I wasn't sure if her bright blue eyes were contacts or her real eye color—they looked so different against her tan skin and dark hair.

I caught Henry and Theo both sneaking glances at her while she helped Levi. Henry and Theo were both single Hispanic guys who worked in the product development department.

"He's a cutie, huh?" I said, watching Levi shove a fry covered in ketchup into his mouth, getting it all over his face and hands. His mini sandwich sat untouched beside the quickly diminishing pile of fries. In addition to the ketchup on his face, he had a chocolate milk mustache on his upper lip.

Mia laughed. "Seems like the fries are just a way to get the ketchup into his mouth," she said, trying to wipe his hands with a napkin before he got ketchup all over his clothes.

"He is messy, but what kid isn't?" I said, laughing, too. I loved interacting with kids. That was one of the things I was looking forward to about this trip. Five kiddos were with us, with another on the way, and I was hoping I would get to help out with all of them. If I couldn't be a mother myself, I would take advantage of as much interaction as possible with these kids.

Mia looked around to see if anyone was listening and then bent in closer to me. "You're Abe's wife?" she whispered. "You look younger than me. I mean, you're gorgeous, like a model, so I get why he would want to marry you, but you seem so young."

I could feel the heat in my face at her observation. "Yeah, we marry young on the reservation. To keep the tribe growing," I explained.

"You're trying to have kids already?"

Sophia returned in time for me to avoid the question. She set the three drinks she was carrying next to her tray. Sophia was also Hispanic, about the same height as Mia but with more of a curvy build. Her skin was warm and olive-toned, and her dark almond-shaped eyes were framed by long lashes. Her thick hair was pulled back in a big ponytail to keep it out of the way while she chased after Levi, who seemed to have endless energy. Her low-cut shirt barely stayed in place over her chest as she leaned across the table to hand Mia her drink.

"Where's Elijah?" Sophia asked.

Mia shrugged. "I think he went to the store. Or he's in the washroom." Almost as soon as she finished speaking, Elijah appeared with a full bag of snacks in his hand.

"I got snacks for the road," he said, lifting the bag to show Sophia and setting it down next to his food. He grabbed a fry from the tray in front of him and shoved it in his mouth. Elijah was a big guy, and the bag of snacks explained where his extra weight came from. His pale stomach rolled over the waistband of his pants, and his face was round and red and constantly seemed to glisten with sweat. But he had a friendly, approachable vibe, and everyone liked him right away.

William Junior zoomed past our table with Harper hot on his heels. They were chasing each other around the seating area, laughing and shouting.

Liam, who was the manager of the product development team, and his wife, Amelia, had two kids: Luna, who was nine, and William Junior, who was seven. Amelia was a teacher, and since it was summer break, she wasn't working at the moment. She would tell the school she was not returning the following school year because of the move.

Liam's voice cut through the noise. "Junior! Get back here and finish your food!"

The moment William heard his dad's angry tone, he froze. Harper, who wasn't expecting him to stop so suddenly, ran right into him. They both went tumbling to the ground with a loud thud.

William started crying, not because he was hurt but from the shock of the fall. Amelia was quick to rush over, untangling the two kids and pulling William into a tight hug to calm him down. Harper immediately started smoothing his short, curly black hair from behind him, looking guilty. "I'm sorry, William. I couldn't stop in time," she said, her big brown eyes wide and full of concern.

William sniffled, wiping his wide nose with the back of his hand. "It's okay," he said, his voice shaky. "I'll be fine. I guess I better eat my food."

Amelia smiled, relieved that he was okay, and gently guided him back to his seat. She was strong and curvy, with medium brown skin and thick, wavy dark brown hair. She got her strength from carrying her kids when they were little and chasing after third graders at the school where she taught. Her large, almond-shaped eyes were a warm brown with little flecks of green, perfectly framed by her high cheekbones. Her nose was wide with a high bridge that curved downward, and her lips were full and expressive.

William Junior looked like a mix of both Amelia and Liam. He had Amelia's Mexican eye shape and color along with her medium brown skin, but his hair was Liam's—tight, black, and curly. His sister Luna looked more like Liam, with his same curly black hair, dark brown skin, round face, and thick lips. At nine years old, Luna had already started to grow taller and was almost Amelia's height. Liam was tall, so it looked like Luna was going to take after him.

"Harper, baby, that's why we don't run around in restaurants," Emma said, waving Harper over to the table. "Come sit down and eat."

Emma was the manager of the customer service and support team. She and her husband James also had two kids: Ellie, age eight, and Harper, age seven. James had worked as a nurse at the hospital near where Grandad had his physical therapy. He ended up joining Abe's company on the sales team.

Harper looked like her mom, Emma—blond hair and blue eyes—while Ellie looked more like her dad, James. Ellie had chestnut-brown hair and brown-green eyes, with little freckles on her cheeks and a narrow, turned-up nose. Her long, elegant eyelashes made her look older than she was, like a teenager trapped in an eight-year-old's body.

It took about an hour and a half at the truck stop before everyone finished eating and used the washroom. By the time we stepped back outside, the heat was almost unbearable.

Elijah's shirt was soaked through from walking between the gas station and his truck, and my forehead was dripping with sweat, too. I was definitely not used to the hot, humid summers down here in Texas. It got hot in Minnesota, but nothing like Kingsville.

I opened the door to the Jeep and was hit with a blast of even hotter air. The leather seat felt like it had been baking in the sun, and I didn't want to burn my legs by sitting on it. Abe turned on the air conditioning and rolled down the windows to let the heat escape while the car cooled down. He went into the RV and grabbed towels so we could sit on them and avoid burning ourselves. It worked, and I climbed into my seat, settling in.

The cloud was waiting for us once everyone got settled into their cars and topped off their gas tanks. We followed it out of the gas station, heading back toward the on-ramp for US-77 south. Once we drove past Kingsville, the road opened up, flat and empty, with the occasional farm here and there. There wasn't much to look at, only wide open land with fields of grass and cattle grazing far off in the distance.

As we got closer to Riviera, the landscape started to change. The air felt different, more coastal. The cloud shifted to the east, and Abe turned on his blinker, pulling left onto a flat, two-lane road. We passed more open fields—no trees, no hills. It was like no one lived out here at all.

Eventually, we came upon the first sign of civilization—a few farmhouses, a big metal building, and a windmill, all tucked behind a small group of trees. Trees were rare around here, and I'd never seen so much land with so few of them.

We crossed an intersection, and the trees disappeared again, leaving behind more flat, open fields stretching out with nothing but grass and low bushes as far as I could see. Sometimes, we passed fields with rows of crops, but mostly, it was flat land.

I spotted some trees up ahead. We were getting closer to more civilization. I could make out a few tiny houses, more young trees, and even some palm trees in the distance. We reached an intersection with a small old-fashioned gas station. Beyond the station, I could see water straight ahead, but the road curved to the right, and the cloud followed. I couldn't imagine what we must have looked like—seven vehicles driving through this tiny ghost-like town, if you could call it a town at all. It had to have been the most traffic they'd seen in ages.

As we drove on, we passed more crops on the right and scattered houses on the left. A small inn sat by the water, next door to a sign for an RV park. The cloud drifted ahead of us, and we followed, turning right and passing a big hunting lodge. Eventually, the fields gave way to the beach, with water on both sides of the road and a bridge over a lake. It was a beautiful sight, and for a moment, it reminded me of the lake back on the reservation.

We crossed over the bridge, and the cloud turned off the road to the left. We passed a huge sign shaped like a sailboat that read "SeaWind RV Resort, Memorial Park." The road was so narrow, it barely seemed wide enough for one car. We followed the signs toward the RV park, and soon, we saw RVs parked behind a fence. The water was visible on the driver's side while the RVs were parked on the passenger side. The view was nice, including picnic tables and even an observation tower near the beach. We kept going, heading toward the RV park's office. The cloud stayed right above us, like it was guiding us there. It seemed like a good place to stop for the night.

It was still only mid-afternoon in July, so we could've kept going for hours, but with the kids, we had to take more breaks. They got restless quickly and needed more stops than Abe, Louis, and I did. It was a lot different traveling with kids, but Jehovah was definitely looking out for them.

The RV park was huge and had tons of cool activities. It sat right on Baffin Bay, a part of the Gulf of Mexico, so the views were breathtaking. The park had a big, round lake, a shuffleboard court, a horseshoe pit, a fire ring, a nature trail, a skeet shooting field, and even a game room. The park next door had playgrounds, walking paths, and a pier that lit up at night. There was also a recreation hall with a full kitchen, perfect for our large group.

Abe and I walked into the office to check in. The man behind the counter was friendly and, to our surprise, greeted us like old friends. After hugging both of us, he said, "We've been expecting you! I'm so excited to host your group tonight, here on the southern edge of King Ranch."

That welcome caught us off guard. "Did you tell him we were coming?" I whispered to Abe.

He shook his head, as surprised as I was.

The others started filing into the small office, and it was clear there wasn't enough room for all of us. The man welcomed each one with the same warm hug, and everyone else looked as shocked as we did.

"Your group is big, and I want to make sure you get the best spot," he said. He pulled out a paper. "Now, who is Abe Serug?"

SEVENTEEN

Our faces must've been a picture of confusion. Abe hadn't called ahead, and none of us had known where we were going, so there was no way we could have made a reservation. Plus, it was the middle of the afternoon. If it were up to Abe, we'd still be driving. We pushed ourselves to go as far as possible before stopping. This was the earliest we'd ever pulled over—except for that blizzard, when we'd had no choice but to stop.

Jehovah must have somehow told the man we were coming. The man checked in Abe and gave him directions to site number 206. He then called for James Williams, who was as surprised as the rest of us to hear his name. James wasn't even using his own RV, and this was his first time at an RV park.

The man checked in Elijah Brown and Mateo Martinez and looked at the others who hadn't been called yet. By now, we all had a strange feeling about this. Maybe this man was an angel.

Mateo had joined Abe's company as their CFO right when this trip had been suggested. He had been a controller at another company, but with Abe's business growing so fast, Abe needed someone to take care of the company's finances. His wife, Charlotte, had already worked for Abe in the customer service department.

Charlotte and Mateo didn't have kids, but they had two dogs and a cat. They had a motor coach and a smaller towable RV they had lent to Emma and James for the trip. They had invited the two single guys to join him and Charlotte in their motor coach.

"Liam Johnson and Lucas Flores?" the man behind the counter called out. They both stepped up. "I know you're not traveling in RVs, so we have cabins available for you at Baffin Bay Inn, down the street. It's only about five minutes away. You passed it on the way here."

"I remember passing it," Lucas said. "Thanks so much for helping us all get settled." Lucas worked in the sales department on East Coast deals. He had some of the biggest accounts like Bank of America and Truist. His wife, Ava, was pregnant with their first child, due in four months. Ava was the most hesitant about the move because she wasn't sure if there would be proper prenatal care wherever we were headed. But when she found out James was a maternity nurse, it made her feel a little better. Ava had joined the company as a customer service representative until the baby arrived.

"You're welcome to stay here as long as you want and enjoy the amenities the park has to offer. There's an overflow parking lot next to Abe's site. The Inn will let you check in as late as you need," the man said. "If you need anything, my name is Kleberg."

"Out of curiosity, how did you know we were coming?" Abe asked Kleberg.

"God Almighty came to me in a dream and told me to welcome his prophet," he said. "He told me what to expect."

Abe stepped forward and shook the man's hand. "Amazing. Thank you for your hospitality and for making us feel so welcome."

The man smiled. "Abe, I know you'd do the same for me. I hope you enjoy your stay."

We all scattered to explore the RV park and the county park next door. Mia went with Theo and Henry to try their hand at horseshoes. Charlotte took her dogs to the dog park to let them run around. Lucas and Ava headed to the nature trail; she said she needed to walk and get the baby some exercise. The kids were set loose on the playground at the county park next door while the guys stayed behind to hook up the RVs. I went with Amelia, Emma, and Sophia to keep an eye on the kids and get to know them better.

"So, you're Abe's wife," Amelia said. "Aren't you a little young to be married?"

"We marry young on the reservation," I said, my face turning red. *How many times will I have to answer this question?*

"Is that even allowed?" Sophia asked.

"In our tribe it is. It's actually quite common."

Amelia made a 'hmm' sound, but didn't ask any more questions about it.

"Once school starts again, I'd love to help teach the little ones with you, Amelia," I offered, hoping to show her I was responsible enough to be married.

"That's a great idea!" Emma said excitedly. She clearly didn't care that I was young. "I've been thinking about what to do for the kids' education. But with a teacher here and you helping, too, we could easily homeschool them."

The guys walked past us with fishing poles. Louis was leading the group, pulling a wagon loaded with supplies. Daddy had taught him how to fish, so he was the expert around here. He wasn't into hunting, but he loved fishing. The lake calmed him, and now it looked like he and Abe were going to teach James, Elijah, and Mateo how to fish.

"Hi, sweetie," Elijah called out, breathing heavily as he walked past Sophia. She looked shocked when she saw the fishing pole in his hand. "Louis is going to teach us how to fish. We're going to catch dinner!" Elijah said proudly, wiping sweat from his red face.

"Wow, hon!" Sophia said in amazement. "Stay hydrated. It's so hot out. Did you bring some water?"

"Yeah, Louis made sure we're all prepared," Elijah said, wiping his forehead with a towel. He gave her a quick kiss before huffing off with the others down the pier.

Sophia and Amelia giggled as he walked away. "I never thought I'd see the day when Elijah did anything other than sit on the couch after work," Sophia said, laughing. "He's definitely not the outdoorsy type."

"Fishing's mostly just sitting, honestly," I said. "It's sitting in the heat...or the cold, depending on the season. Maybe he'll find it's his new hobby." I laughed along with the others.

It turned out Elijah was great at fishing. With Louis's help, he caught the biggest speckled trout of anyone in the group. After hours of fishing, they had enough to feed everyone for dinner. Maybe it was a miracle from Jehovah, or maybe the fish were biting like crazy in the afternoon sun.

We all gathered in the rec hall, where I showed Sophia and Ava how to cut the fins off the fish, scale them, and remove the heads and blood. I sent Louis to grab the wild rice from the RV, and we cooked up fish and rice for the whole group. There was plenty to go around, and some even went back for seconds.

Abe and I sat with the Johnson family. I was excited to get to know Luna and William Junior better. Junior wasn't too into the fish and barely picked at it, but Luna dug in and even had seconds. She was definitely a tween—head down, scrolling through her phone when she wasn't eating. She showed me the selfies she'd taken on the playground, with all her cute filters.

Before long, everyone had eaten their fill, and Amelia, Emma, and Charlotte took care of the dishes. The Johnson family, along with Lucas and Ava, left to check in at the inn down the street. The rest of us headed back to the RVs to settle in for the night. Ellie, Harper, and Levi were put to bed, and the adults gathered around in camp chairs outside the RVs, chatting and getting to know each other better.

The full moon lit up the night, its glow reflecting on the surface of the lake. Kleberg hadn't been kidding about giving us the best spot—our site was an end spot, with a perfect view of the lake on one side and the bay on the other, across the road. I sat in my camp chair under the awning of our RV, watching the moonlight dance on the water and thinking about all that had happened. It was clear Jehovah had been with us all day. The cloud had been an obvious sign, but there were others, too. The stop in time for Levi to use the washroom. The way Kleberg had already known all our names. The catch of fish big enough to feed everyone. All these things felt like signs that we were being watched over by a force bigger than us.

The first day had been a success, full of surprises. I could only imagine what tomorrow would bring.

***

The next morning, I woke up around 6:30 a.m. to an empty bed. Abe was gone. After fifteen minutes of waiting, I knew he wasn't in the RV. I slipped on my moccasins and stepped outside. The spot in front of our RV was empty, and I didn't see him near the other RVs in our group either. I squinted toward the beach, just in case. What I saw wasn't what I expected.

I left the RV park through the main gate and walked down the dusty, potholed road. The road forked past the exit. To the left, it led to the highway. To the right, it curved toward the bay and the beach. I took the right fork. On my right, a wooden sign listed the park hours. Beyond it was a field dotted with picnic tables shaded under a cluster of mesquite trees. Grills, trash cans, and even a few exercise stations with pull-up bars filled the area. There was a horseshoe pit here, too.

To my left was a huge open field. Way in the distance sat a giant aluminum building with a long covered front area. It looked like a place they'd hold festivals or big gatherings. The parking lot in front of it was empty. A little farther down, near the beach, was a small pavilion with picnic tables and, across from that, an observation tower overlooking the water.

But none of that was what grabbed my attention.

In the middle of the open field on the left, all by itself, stood a single oak tree. The tree's trunk split low at the base, forming two main sections that curved outward and then up, like giant arms in a perfect V shape, spreading into leafy green canopies. The leaves were soft and feathery, making the tree look full and alive. At the base of the split, a small cluster of grass pushed up from the dirt.

The sun had started to rise over the bay, spilling golden light across the land. The tree cast a long shadow that reached toward me. If I were up in the observation tower, the view of the sunrise would've been stunning. But I wasn't here for the scenery. I was here because of Abe.

And there he was.

He stood on the far side of the oak tree next to a pile of rocks. Three rocks were in the pile—two big ones at the bottom and a third flatter rock on top. Together, they looked like a little stone pyramid. Abe had his arms raised high, and in his hands, he held a bottle of olive oil.

I stopped and watched, stunned, as he poured the oil over the top rock. It ran down in shimmering trails, catching the light as it spilled onto the base rocks. The whole pile glistened like tiny little diamonds catching the morning light.

What in the world was Abe doing?

At first, I didn't move. Abe clearly wanted to be alone, doing...whatever this was. It looked like a ritual, but not one I'd ever seen back on the reservation. I stood back and stared as he poured the entire bottle of olive oil over the rocks. When it was empty, he set it down by his feet, raised both hands to the sky, and started swaying gently. I stood there, frozen, my mouth hanging open.

After a minute or two, he turned, like he could feel me staring, and smiled. With a small wave, he invited me over. I hesitated but slowly started walking toward him. My feet felt heavy, like they weren't sure they wanted to move.

"Today is going to be a good day, Princess," Abe said as I reached him. He pulled me close and draped his arm around my shoulder. Together, we stood in front of the shimmering rock pile, the morning sun bouncing off the oil like it was alive.

I had to stand on tiptoe to peek over the top rock and see the bay water beyond.

"What are you doing, Abe?" I whispered, my voice low, like I didn't want to disturb whatever this was.

He looked down at me, eyes bright with excitement. "Last night, I had a dream. Jehovah appeared to me, like before, and said, 'To your offspring, I will give this land.'"

My eyes went wide as I stared up at him, waiting for more.

"I built this altar to thank Jehovah," Abe continued. "I gave Him our best oil, to honor all He's done for us and all He's going to do." I couldn't tell if he was excited or in awe. Maybe both. His voice dropped, like he was sharing a secret. "Princess, the dream felt real. We didn't even have to go far, did we? Only four hours from Houston, and here we are. This land—it's going to be ours." He stopped, then added, "Well, not ours. Jehovah said He'd give it to our offspring."

I frowned, confused. "What does that even mean? What are we supposed to do now?"

Abe shrugged, thoughtful. "I'm not sure yet. But I know we're following Him. We're doing exactly what He wants."

"So...we're staying here? At this RV park?" I asked, glancing back toward our site.

He shook his head. "I don't think so. Jehovah said He's giving us this land. I think we're supposed to see it first. All of it."

"When are we leaving?" I asked. "It's not so bad here. We've got everything we need—the big kitchen, the bay with all those fish, the playground, and the beach for the kids."

Abe chuckled. "Maybe we'll stay for a little while. I'll talk to Kleberg and see how long we can keep our spot. But then...." He stared at the horizon, like he could already see the future. "Then we'll go. We'll see the land Jehovah promised us."

I glanced at him sideways. "And what about the whole 'offspring' thing?" I teased.

He gave me a sly grin and pulled me closer in a one-armed hug. "I guess we'll have to work on that," he said with a wink.

***

We spent a week at SeaBreeze RV Park, soaking in the scenery and making the most of the place. The eighteen others in our group started getting used to life without the comforts of the city. It was a change, but we were managing. On Sunday, the boys decided to go hunting. They grouped together and set off to see what animals were in the area. Again, Louis was the expert, but Abe also knew how to hunt with a bow. They taught the men what they needed to know, and they ended up coming back with armadillos, jackrabbits, and prairie dogs—enough to keep us fed for the week.

Adjusting to the food wasn't easy. Jackrabbit meat was tough, and we quickly realized we needed to get creative with it. The fish were plentiful, but Ava was careful not to eat too many since she was pregnant and didn't want to risk mercury poisoning. I'd never tried armadillo before, and I had to figure out how to cook it right.

During the week, Abe and most of the adults set up shop in the rec hall every morning. They worked from their laptops, using the park's Wi-Fi until quitting time. Amelia and I were left to watch over the five kids. Since school was out, we took them swimming, taught them how to fish, showed them how to trap jackrabbits and squirrels, and let them climb trees and play on the playground.

I was having the time of my life. I felt like I had been born to take care of the kids, each one with their different needs. I loved it. Yet as much as I adored the little ones, I couldn't stop thinking about the future. I longed for the day when our own child would join us. My body ached to have a baby of my own.

***

After a week of getting settled, it was time to pack up and hit the road again to explore more of the land Jehovah was giving us. Abe wanted to start in the northern part of the territory he'd dreamed about and work his way south. He'd bought a map of Texas at the RV park's little store and marked the area he remembered from his dream. It stretched from the Rio Grande River in the south to the Nueces River in the north.

We left SeaBreeze in Riviera, Texas, and set our sights on Alice, Texas—only about an hour away. There was no need to hurry. We took our time saying goodbye to Kleberg. He had shared a couple of meals with us, showing real kindness and hospitality during our stay. We thanked him for all he had done for us and wished him well, and he sent us off with good wishes for the journey ahead.

Back on the road, our caravan rolled through small towns and endless fields that stretched on forever. We turned northwest on US-77, heading back toward Kingsville. This stretch of road felt familiar since it was the same route we had taken the week before. We passed Ricardo, a tiny place with a gas station and a few scattered houses along the highway. There was some road construction as we navigated through Kingsville, turning off onto Sixth Street and winding northwest until we hit TX-141.

Once we left town, it was back to the wide, open fields, miles of nothing but sky and brush with hardly a soul in sight. We passed a little regional airport and turned right onto US-281, which took us all the way to Alice. We stopped to fill up the gas tanks. We could see the familiar white-and-orange-striped roof of a Whataburger, and the kids cheered. They could get what they called "normal food."

With everyone fed and the RVs fueled up, we turned left onto TX-44 and headed for Progeny Ranch RV Park. The road stretched out ahead, and it felt like another adventure was beginning.

Eighteen

Progeny Ranch RV Park wasn't much of a park. It was more like a parking lot in an open field in the middle of nowhere, right next to the railroad tracks. There was plenty of space for all our RVs, but it didn't have the same amenities as SeaBreeze or South Main. Not much was around here, so fewer people came to visit. It wasn't like the bay area, where tourists would come to enjoy the water. Here, it was fields, trees, and oil rigs for miles.

We were greeted like we had been at SeaBreeze, with the owner welcoming us like old friends and giving us all hugs. He also listed out our names, and he told the Floreses and Johnsons to head over to a bed and breakfast in San Berry, down the road. We weren't as shocked this time since we'd seen it before, but it felt different since we weren't following the cloud anymore; we were driving on our own, passing through the land that had been promised to us.

Once we parked our RVs, hooked up the utilities, and settled in, Abe told me he was going for a walk in the field by the woods. He was hoping to hear more from Jehovah.

After he left, we took the kids to the field next to the parking lot to burn off some energy. We played games like tag and red light, green light until they were all tired. It wasn't long before Levi was ready for a nap, so we went to his RV to tuck him in. The other kids followed us to Ellie and Harper's RV to play card games and watch television. Emma had made lemonade for everyone, so we relaxed and waited for Levi to finish his nap.

When it was almost dinnertime, Abe still hadn't come back. I started to get worried.

"Louis, should we go after him?" I asked.

"It has been a while since he left, huh?" Louis said, glancing at the sky. "Let's go find him, Princess." He grabbed his bow and slipped his knife into the waistband of his pants.

We set off to look for Abe. He had said he was going to the edge of the woods, which was across the field beyond the fenced-in area. I couldn't see him from where we were, so I scanned the entire edge of the field. No sign of him.

"He could be anywhere along the tree line," I said. "How are we going to find him?"

"Abe!" Louis called out, his voice carrying toward the trees. There was no answer.

When we reached the tree line, we looked both ways. The thick forest of oak trees curved around the giant field, stretching about a half mile from the railroad tracks to the back of the RV office area. The field was cut in two by a wire fence, as if made to hold in cattle. We didn't see Abe in either direction along the tree line, so he must've gone into the woods.

Louis used his bow to push aside some of the lower branches so we could peer into the trees. The ground was covered in brush, and we couldn't see a clear path from where we were standing. We decided to walk along the edge of the tree line, hoping to find a trail or a break in the trees. We kept walking, moving farther away from the RV park, until we found a narrow trail leading into the woods.

We trudged down the trail, scanning every corner of the woods, hoping to catch a glimpse of Abe. The thick canopy above us made the air cool and the light dim, and our eyes struggled to adjust. The trees were short but dense, and the ground was covered in brush except for the trail we were walking on. I didn't think Abe would have wandered off into the thick brush, so we stuck to the trail.

I heard a rustling sound coming from the bushes off to the side. I jumped, my heart racing. A squirrel darted out and climbed up a tree. I let out a breath I hadn't realized I was holding.

Louis chuckled beside me. "You're jumpy," he teased.

"It's scary in here!" I shot back, giving him a playful punch on the arm.

"You never would've made it as a hunter," he laughed.

I rolled my eyes and kept going, ignoring him. "Abe!" I called, the sound of my voice swallowed up by the trees around us.

We walked deeper into the woods, growing more anxious as we searched for any sign of him. A creeping sense of panic began to rise in my chest. Surely, Abe couldn't have gone this far into the woods.

I took a deep breath, and a mouthwatering smell drifted through the air, like someone was grilling dinner. I checked my watch. It was about four o'clock. Maybe the people at the RV park were starting to cook. But the scent was coming from ahead of us.

"Do you smell that?" I asked Louis.

He paused and sniffed the air. "Yeah, smells like dinner," he said and started walking toward the source of the smell.

Soon, the trees parted, and we stepped into a clearing. The sky was filled with gray clouds, like it was about to rain. In the middle of the clearing was a single oak tree, standing alone. And right next to it, we found Abe. For a second, I felt another wave of déjà vu. Abe had gathered some rocks and built an altar, like he had before. But this time, instead of olive oil, there was a dead animal, lying on a pile of wood, burning on the top of the rock pile. Smoke from the fire on the altar was rising in a thin pillar up to the clouds. The smell of burning meat was stronger here.

I felt like we were interrupting a private ceremony. I stepped back under the trees, not wanting to get too close. I glanced at Louis, who was frozen in place. His eyes were wide and his mouth slightly open, as he stared back and forth between Abe and the fire. Abe had his arms raised to the sky, humming and swaying.

Louis snapped out of it and moved closer to me, whispering, "What on earth is he doing?"

"He's worshiping Jehovah."

"That's...a weird way to do it."

"It's not the first time," I whispered back. "He made an altar like this at SeaBreeze, but that time it was olive oil, not an animal cooking."

Louis watched Abe for a few more seconds before asking, "What do we do now?"

"We can either wait or go back. At least we know he's okay."

Louis looked back at Abe and frowned. "Safe for now. But what about the way back? Anything could happen in these woods. There's a reason you hunt in a pack."

"So, you want to wait?" I asked.

Louis glanced over at Abe, still lost in his ritual. "How long do you think he'll be at it?"

"I have no idea," I replied. "Last time I went looking for him, he stopped when he realized I was behind him. But he wasn't cooking an animal then. I don't know what he's doing now or how long it'll take."

"It's nothing I've ever seen before," Louis said, shaking his head.

"Yeah, nothing like we did on the reservation. I'm not sure what to expect anymore."

"Maybe he's making up a new ritual for our new tribe? Trying different things?" Louis suggested.

"Maybe," I muttered. "I really don't know."

We sat on a fallen log near the edge of the woods, still hidden in the shade of the oak trees. From where we sat, I could see Abe clearly, so I figured if he looked in our direction, he'd see us, too.

The smoke from the fire kept rising, thick and heavy, while the animal slowly burned. Abe shifted between kneeling in front of the altar, his face pressed to the ground and arms stretched out in front of him on the ground, to standing with his hands raised toward the sky, mimicking the smoke. I counted at least seven times he did this while we sat there, watching him. By the seventh time, the animal was charred and black.

The clouds broke apart, and a beam of sunlight sliced through the sky, landing almost directly on the altar. The sunlight glittered through the smoke, lighting up Abe's body, the tree, and the altar. He dropped to the ground, kneeling in front of the altar again, face pressed to the earth, arms stretched out. He stayed like that until the sun disappeared behind the clouds once more.

Abe slowly stood, his movements calm. The fire was nearly gone now, the wood and the animal almost completely consumed. For the first time, he turned toward us. His face glowed, peaceful, like he had finished a special moment. His eyes were closed, and he seemed to be soaking in the moment. When he opened his eyes, his smile widened, reaching his eyes, and he looked right at me.

Abe walked toward us, his steps steady and confident. When he reached us, he pulled me into a tight hug, his hand resting gently on the back of my head as he smoothed my hair down. His voice was calm but strong as he spoke.

"We're doing everything right," he said. "Just as Jehovah wants." He pulled back slightly, enough to meet my eyes. "Our children will inherit this land, Princess. We have to keep moving, keep exploring. We need to see all of the land He's giving them. We'll travel on the weekends, explore new places, and stay near different parts of the land during the week."

***

That week, we stayed at Progeny Ranch RV Park. The adults who worked for Abe's company set up their workspaces in different RVs, organized by department. Surprisingly, the Wi-Fi was fast and reliable, so Abe's employees could still do their work. The small town of San Berry had a little market where we could buy food, but it didn't have a big rec hall like SeaBreeze. Instead, we all cooked in our RVs and ate outside, sitting in camp chairs under the awnings, trying to stay cool. It was the middle of summer, and the Texas heat was relentless.

With the adults busy with work, Amelia and I had to keep the kids entertained. There wasn't a playground or a beach here, only a big field to run around in and some woods to explore. Even though we could buy food at the market, the kids were more interested in trapping rabbits. So, we set up some traps around the outskirts of the woods and waited to see what we could catch.

A couple of nights during the week after work, we drove to nearby towns to explore. We let the kids have some familiar fast food and stopped at the market on the way back to pick up groceries.

As the week drew to a close, I was glad we would be heading away from this area. There was a lot less to do here than at the last place we had stopped, and the kids were getting restless. They had all exhausted tag and other lawn games and were tired of playing cards and watching television. Abe and Mateo seemed to be tired of us invading their workspace in our RV with the kids when they got too overheated outside, too.

***

On Saturday morning, we packed up the RVs and got ready to head to the next stop. By the time we hit the road, it was already mid-morning. We passed through Alice and kept driving south. Terrain RV Park was off the highway near Falfurrias, Texas, about forty minutes away. We rolled in around eleven o'clock and got the usual warm welcome—a hug, a reservation for each RV, and a recommendation for the hotel for anyone who needed it.

We followed the same routine that week: the adults worked from their assigned RVs while Amelia and I kept the kids busy. We didn't have laundry facilities at Progeny Ranch, so we had a mountain of laundry to do when we got to Terrain. We made sure to get it all done before we left at the end of the week.

Alongside laundry facilities, Terrain had a pool and a spa that the kids could enjoy. They also had horseshoe pits, and the kids were getting better at it each day. The horseshoes were a little too heavy for Levi, but the older kids could manage as long as they stood a little closer than you're normally supposed to. There was also a shuffleboard court, and Amelia taught all of us how to play.

***

The following week, we drove to Hebbronville, Texas. Lucas's and Liam's families stayed at a Garden Inn while the rest of us got our usual welcome at Philanthropy RV Park on the northern side of town. By this point, we had the routine down pretty well. The kids were getting used to RV life and looked forward to the new experiences each week. By the time Friday rolled around, they were eager to help with the prep work—laundry, grocery shopping, whatever needed doing for the next stop.

Over the next month, we made stops in Encino, Raymondville, Edinburg, and Harlingen, staying a week in each place. When school started again in mid-August, we had to work out a new schedule. Once we got to Raymondville, the kids spent a good portion of the day doing schoolwork in the RV. We took breaks for recess and PE, and Amelia and I split up to work with them on math, reading, science, and history. We had a range of ages: Levi was in kindergarten, William Junior and Harper were in second grade, Ellie was in third grade, and Luna was in fourth grade.

Labor Day weekend took us to Brownsville. The city sits on the southern tip of Texas, right on the border where the Rio Grande River divides the United States from Mexico. Brownsville is a mix of American and Mexican cultures. Everywhere we looked, we saw colorful street art, heard people speaking Spanish, and noticed a slower, laid-back vibe that felt different from most other places we had been to so far.

Since it was near the coast, we decided to take a break from school and work. We left the RVs at the park and piled into the cars for a trip to South Padre Island. Abe even set everyone up with a hotel room on the beach, and we got a little taste of life outside the RVs, enjoying the sand and surf for the holiday weekend.

After a relaxing long weekend, we packed up to head back to the RV park and return to our routines. We had loaded up the cars to leave the island and were standing in line to check out of the hotel when all our phones buzzed at the same time with an emergency alert. Hurricane warning. We all crowded around the television in the hotel lobby, watching the latest news report. The biggest hurricane on record was spinning in the Gulf of Mexico, rapidly gaining strength, and heading straight for South Texas.

Nineteen

I had never worried about hurricanes in northern Minnesota. It would take a true catastrophe for a hurricane to hit us, like the end of the world. Our biggest concerns were below-zero temperatures and white-out blizzards. Hurricanes? Never even crossed my mind. But now, here we were, facing this new challenge.

"Hurricane Gert is rapidly gaining size and strength," the weatherman said on the television. "It's now a Category Five hurricane with wind speeds reaching two hundred fifteen miles per hour." The screen showed a radar image of a massive storm, with rain bands covering all of the Gulf of Mexico.

"This slow-moving monster is on track to break several records," the weatherman continued. "Gert's outer bands extend from the bottom of the Yucatán Peninsula to the top of the state of Mississippi. It's almost as big as Typhoon Tip of 1979, the largest tropical cyclone ever recorded. Gert is also tied with Hurricane Patricia in 2015 for the most powerful hurricane in terms of maximum sustained winds.

"This storm came out of nowhere," the weatherman continued. "Two days ago, it was barely a minor disturbance. But the warm waters of the Gulf have fueled it, and it has rapidly organized into a major threat to the Gulf Coast."

The screen switched to a map with colorful lines pointing straight at South Texas, passing through Corpus Christi and across the southern tip of Texas before turning north then east again over Dallas. The red hurricane graphic showed the storm as a Category Five at landfall on Thursday over Corpus Christi.

"Gert looks like it will cover most of Texas as a hurricane before it weakens and heads east across the United States, bringing much-needed rain to the Southeast," the weatherman said. "We'll keep you updated with the latest, so stay tuned to Channel Two."

We all looked at each other, shocked and scared. Now what? Jehovah had called us down to South Texas, and one of biggest storms on record was headed straight for us. Had Abe misheard what Jehovah had told him? Of course, if we had stayed in Houston, we would have been on the northern side of the storm and still have been feeling the effects of Gert as badly.

"Okay, everyone," Abe said, breaking the silence. "Let's regroup when we get back to the RVs and figure out what to do."

We piled into the cars and headed back to the RV park in Brownsville. At every gas station we passed, cars were lined up onto the street, waiting to fill up. I was glad we'd topped off the tanks when we'd first gotten to Brownsville on Saturday. I hoped there'd still be gas left when we got back to fill up again. The storm was causing a lot of panic, and it seemed like gas might run out soon.

When we got back to the RV park, the adults all gathered in Mateo's motor coach to watch the news and figure out what to do next. I decided to take the kids to the pool to keep them occupied while Abe and the others talked. They'd gotten so good at swimming this month; it was their favorite thing to do, and the heat was unbearable without it. The "feels like" temperature was over a hundred degrees.

The pool was at the front of the RV park while our RV sites were way in the back by the pond, putting green, playground, bocce ball court, and corn hole area. I gathered up all the kids' swimming gear and towels and told them to get dressed in their swimsuits while I changed into mine. I loaded the swim gear into Louis's wagon, and we walked down the main road toward the entrance. At the front were most of the park's amenities like the pool, hot tub, shuffleboard courts, pickle ball courts, fitness center, laundry, showers, and welcome center. The pool was kidney-shaped, well-maintained, and looked like it belonged in a resort. There was already a group of people swimming when we arrived.

Brownsville seemed like a retirement town, or "snowbird" town as Amelia called it, because most RV parks around here were for people fifty-five and older. It had taken us a while to find one that worked for younger families. We had stopped at one place and didn't get the friendly welcome we were used to, but they were kind enough to point us toward Prevailing Winds RV Park. Like SeaBreeze, Prevailing Winds had all of the amenities we could possibly need to stick around long-term...if it weren't for the hurricane coming our way.

As I floated in the pool on an inner tube, watching the kids swim, I couldn't stop thinking about our situation. The last few months had been incredible—driving around South Texas, exploring the land we hoped to build a future on. Now that same land was in danger of being destroyed by a hurricane. Any normal person would pack up and go home, but I doubted that thought had even crossed Abe's mind.

We were supposed to be building our own nation, our own tribe. But it felt like we were taking bits and pieces from different places and trying to blend them all together. We still had our fishing and trapping traditions, but we also bought most of our food from grocery stores and fast-food joints like everyone else. It felt like we were living more like the white people of America than our ancestors ever had. Our group was a mix that included three Natives—Abe, Louis, and me—five white people, four Black people, and nine Hispanics. The Chaldean tribe had always been proud of its Native roots, but now we were becoming a melting pot, much like the United States, the founders of whom we'd always resented for kicking us off our land.

I couldn't help but wonder if, in some ways, we were doing the same thing to others. Would we be pushing people off their land, or would we find a way to fit in? Were we any better than the people who had taken our land? I didn't know anymore. I kept wondering if this was the plan Jehovah had for us or if we were making it all up as we went along.

I shook my head, trying to clear my thoughts, and checked on the kids to make sure they were safe and having fun. Levi was splashing around in his life jacket, laughing like he was having the time of his life. Luna was tossing diving toys into the pool for William Junior, Harper, and Ellie to find. I decided it was a good time to help Levi with his swimming, so I took off his life preserver and helped him float on his back before helping him swim to the side of the pool. He was getting better every day.

We stayed at the pool for a couple of hours, enjoying the last relaxing hours at this RV park before it was time to head back and see what the adults had decided. When we got back to the RVs, I helped the kids change into dry clothes and did the same myself. I set them up with lunch either in front of the television or at the dinette to keep them busy while I went to see what the plan was.

I walked into Mateo's RV, and everyone turned to look at me. The place was crowded, with the whole crew sitting in or leaning against any space they could.

"Well?" I asked, glancing around. "What's the plan?"

"We're heading south, away from the storm, until it passes," Abe said. "Then we'll come back and check the damage."

"South?" I said, surprised. "We're already as far south as we can get unless we cross into Mexico."

"Exactly. We're going to Mexico," Mateo said, grinning. "Some of us have family there, so we're heading in their direction until the storm passes. Once it's safe, we'll meet up and continue with the original plan."

"So, we're splitting up?" I asked. "How many of you are staying with family?"

Abe walked over and put his arm around me, giving me a reassuring squeeze. "Mateo, Ava, Sophia, and Mia all have family in Mexico. They'll head there to stay with them. Mateo's letting Liam's family use his RV, and they'll take Liam's van. Theo and Henry will stay with us until the storm passes, and we'll all meet up again later."

I nodded, trying to wrap my mind around it all. "That's a lot of moving around. Is that what Jehovah wants us to do?"

Abe's smile disappeared. "I haven't heard from Him about what to do. No dreams, no visions, nothing," he said, shaking his head. "But He controls the storm, so there must be a reason it's coming this way. We can't sit here and let it destroy us. I'm sure they'll issue evacuation orders soon, anyway."

The image of the swirling storm filled the television screen, hanging in the Gulf like a giant, angry cloud. "What's the storm doing now?" I asked.

Emma glanced up at the screen, her face tense. "It's getting closer. But it's slowing down, which makes it worse," she said, her voice tight. "The warm water in the Gulf is feeding it, making it stronger. If it doesn't speed up, it could hit harder."

I swallowed, feeling a knot form in my stomach. It was like the storm was building up, waiting for the right moment to strike. The air felt thick, like the world was holding its breath.

Abe squeezed my shoulder again, pulling me out of my thoughts. "We'll be fine," he said, though his voice carried an edge of uncertainty. "We need to stay ahead of it."

Even as he spoke these words, I could see the worry in his eyes. None of us were sure what to expect, but one thing was for sure. This storm wasn't going to leave us alone.

"It looks like we don't have much time left before we need to head out," Liam said, glancing at the television, too.

As soon as Liam finished speaking, the voice of the weatherman blared through the RV's speakers. "Hurricane Gert is now the strongest hurricane on record. Wind speeds have reached two hundred and twenty miles per hour, and the barometric pressure has dropped to eight hundred eighty mbar. This makes Gert stronger than Hurricane Wilma, the previous strongest Atlantic hurricane, which hit a pressure of eight hundred eighty-two mbar back in 2005."

The weatherman paused for a moment then kept going. "We now have a hurricane nearly the size of the largest in history, with the highest sustained winds ever recorded and the lowest barometric pressure ever measured. Gert is breaking records left and right. This is going to be one massive storm. It's time to make your preparations. The storm appears to be set to make landfall in under three days."

We all stared at each other in shock. It was time to move, and fast.

"Louis, have you talked to Olivia?" I asked.

Louis nodded. "Yeah, I talked to her about an hour ago. Her family is already on the road north. They're heading to Oklahoma City to ride out the storm," he said.

"Phew," I exhaled, not realizing I'd been holding my breath. "I'm glad they're getting out of there."

"She said traffic was a nightmare," he continued. "I hope we don't run into the same problem heading south. I doubt as many people will go to Mexico as will try to find somewhere else in the States to escape to."

"Probably not," I agreed.

"Alright, let's get these preparations started," Abe said. He started handing out tasks, and we all split up to get things done.

I had never been outside the country before. Every new place we stopped felt like a whole new world to me. I had no idea what to expect when we crossed into Mexico.

We decided to get the RVs ready in case we had to boondock once we were in Mexico. After all, Mexico was a third-world country, and we had no clue what we might run into. We weren't sure if we'd find any decent RV parks like we had in South Texas. Heck, we didn't even know if we'd have to park in public lots or random spots. The motor coach had a generator, but the other RVs ran on battery or solar power. If we had to boondock, it would be a whole new experience for us, and Mateo and Elijah wouldn't be around to show us what to do. We were doing our best to learn from them before we all went our separate ways.

We filled up the freshwater tanks in all three RVs, making sure we had enough water for the trip. Amelia and Emma went into town to grab groceries and try to get extra propane tanks while I took the kids to the laundry room to wash and fold all our dirty clothes.

Everyone in town was rushing to get ready for the hurricane. The RV park was nearly empty, just us left, and the owners were boarding up the windows of the buildings and moving items that could get blown away, like the pool chairs. The grocery store was nearly wiped out, and Amelia and Emma were lucky to find whatever they could. They split the propane they'd bought between us so we'd have enough for the road when we left the next day. They also made sure to get things the kids could snack on in case the ride was long without options of places to stop to eat.

While we worked, Abe and Mateo adjusted work schedules so the remote employees could cover the others' work while we were away. Abe had about thirty employees who worked outside of Texas, so he was busy making sure their clients would still be taken care of while we were on the road.

We were leaving first thing in the morning. The plan for the RV crew who wasn't staying with family was to start driving south at sunrise and stop when the sun set. We'd make stops when we needed to, mostly for the kids. The RVs were all gassed up, so we'd keep driving until we couldn't anymore. Hopefully, there'd still be gas stations open along the way. The farther south we went, the fewer people would be freaking out, and we were hoping supplies would still be available down there.

***

Everyone had finished getting ready for the long trip ahead before we settled in for the night. Abe pulled me aside and asked if I wanted to go for a walk.

"Princess," he began as we walked, his voice serious, "depending on who we run into, some of the people in Mexico can be aggressive and dangerous."

I stopped in my tracks, shocked. Half of our group—Theo, Henry, Mia, Sophia—was Mexican. I had never seen any violence or signs of danger from any of them.

I must have looked confused because Abe quickly added, "Not the Mexican Americans. They're fine. I'm talking about the cartels, the drug lords and their people. If you cross them the wrong way, they can be extremely dangerous."

I felt a pang of fear.

"Do you remember Grandad talking about when he was forced to go to those boarding schools when he was little?" Abe asked. I nodded, not seeing the connection between the boarding schools in Minnesota and the cartel. "Well, neither he nor our great-grandparents had the power to stop them. The cartel is even worse. They don't take 'no' for an answer. If you refuse them, they'll kill you and everyone around you."

My stomach dropped. His words sent a cold shiver through me. Was he taking us into a situation like that?

Abe seemed to sense my panic. "Look," he said, his voice quieter now, "I know you're beautiful. If anyone asks, tell them you're my sister. It'll go better for me, and my life will be spared because of you."

I blinked at him, confused. "You want me to lie and say I'm not your wife?" I asked, my voice shaky.

Abe chuckled softly, but I saw no humor in what he was saying. "It's not really a lie, more of a white lie, I guess. Once your father died, you became Grandad's daughter. And I'm Grandad's son, so in a way, you are my sister." He paused, studying my face. "If they think you're my wife, they'll kill me but keep you alive. But if they think you're my sister, they'll want to impress me because they'll want you for themselves. That way, we both stay alive."

My heart sank. I could barely whisper, "You'd let them take me?"

His words hit like a punch to the stomach. *Is he suggesting that if the cartels think I'm not married, they will think I'm available?* My mind spun. *Is this what he's asking me to do? Am I supposed to go along with this?* I didn't want to be some pawn in their game, especially not with the cartel. I was married, and that was the end of it.

"No, of course not," Abe quickly replied. "I don't think they would take you. But they'll treat us well if they like you. Once the storm passes, we're heading back home anyway. We'll tell them we're not sticking around for long, and they'll get over it."

I didn't buy it, but I tried to push the doubt aside. Abe was older and had been through more than I had. If he thought this was the best way to handle things, I would trust him.

TWENTY

We left first thing in the morning, like we always did, rising with the sun. Three of the families didn't have a Mexican family to stay with—James and Emma's family, Liam and Amelia's family, and us. The other two families were using Mateo's RVs. Theo and Henry split up, with Theo going with James and Henry with Liam.

As we pulled out of Brownsville, the road was lined with palm trees and small shops. The drive into Mexico felt like more than just crossing country lines—it felt like crossing between two completely different worlds. From busy American streets to quiet rural highways and winding mountain roads, the landscape shifted as much as the culture. Each mile marked a new change in language, architecture, and lifestyle.

We followed US-77, heading south toward the border. The neighborhoods mixed suburban houses with local markets, with signs in both English and Spanish, a constant reminder of the area's deep Mexican roots.

About fifteen minutes into the drive, we saw the Veterans International Bridge ahead. That was when things started to feel different. The closer we got to the border, the more signs of security appeared. On the American side, the buildings were big and industrial, with fences running along the road. It was chaotic, with cars, trucks, and buses all lined up, waiting to cross, everyone in a hurry but no one able to move quickly due to the long process of getting through customs.

As we approached the bridge, Abe slowed down. This was the first checkpoint, where we had to show our documents, everything Abe had gotten for us before we had left the reservation. We got our papers ready, and Abe made sure to have the car's Indian registration and proof of insurance for Mexico. He handed the paperwork over to the customs officer.

The officer asked a few basic questions: the purpose of our trip, how long we'd be staying, and if we were carrying unusual items. Abe answered calmly, assuming most people in the line were escaping the hurricane, like we were. They walked us through filling out the information on the kiosk for the tourist visa so we could pass through Mexican customs and immigration. Abe filled it out, paid the fees, and after about ten minutes, we got our tourist cards.

Once we were through US Customs, it was time to cross the bridge. From there, we had a perfect view of the Rio Grande River, its muddy water marking the line between the US and Mexico. The crossing didn't take long, but it still provided a moment for us to look around. On the US side, Brownsville looked modern, with wide streets and big shopping centers. But as we reached Matamoros on the Mexican side, the city looked more crowded, more chaotic. The streets were lined with houses, little shops, and street vendors. It had more energy. It was less organized, but definitely busier.

As we drove into Matamoros, the vibe started to feel even more different. Abe got ready to show our paperwork to the Mexican customs official at the next checkpoint stop.

The officer gave me a long look that made my stomach tighten. He started speaking to Abe in Spanish, perhaps assuming we spoke it due to our dark skin and hair. Abe said, "English?" The officer nodded, but his eyes narrowed a little. In English, he asked to inspect the RV, so Abe stepped out to let him in. When the officer came back out, he told Abe to wait while he went to talk to his boss. We exchanged glances, confused.

After what felt like forever, the officer came back with two others. All three of them were about average height, muscular, with short dark hair and almond-shaped brown eyes. One of them had an intense, hostile look in his eyes, like he was looking for a fight. The other guy had a softer expression, like he was the good cop of the pair. The third officer stood back, watching us. They all had semi-automatic guns strapped to their bodies, which made me uneasy.

They peered into the Jeep at Abe, then at Louis, and then their eyes landed on me. I held their gazes, trying to stay calm, but in the pit of my stomach, I felt a sense of danger. They kept glancing between Abe and me, and the mean-looking one asked, "Is this your...?"

"Sister," Abe answered quickly.

The officers exchanged knowing smiles, and my stomach flipped again. They started talking quickly in Spanish, and we couldn't understand a word. We were the only car in our group without anyone who spoke Spanish.

One of the officers, the one standing off to the side, appeared to take a picture of us with his phone. They handed Abe back our paperwork.

"Where are you staying in Mexico?" asked the kinder officer in English.

"We're not sure yet," Abe said. "We're with two other RVs, and we're heading south to stay ahead of the storm. We're hoping to make it to Victoria, if we can."

The sky had darkened, and the first raindrops from the storm began to fall. Time was running out.

"We know a good place north of the city," the kind officer said. "It's far enough south to stay clear of the storm."

"That sounds great, thank you," Abe said, giving him a smile.

"It's off the highway in a town called Güémez, not far from Victoria. Go to the restaurant Taquería Roy. Tell my friend Juan that Sánchez from the border sent you. He'll help you out with a place to stay."

"That's very kind," Abe said, shaking his hand. "We appreciate your help."

The officer nodded and waved us through, but the mean-looking one never stopped staring at me. I was glad when we drove away.

"I don't like the idea of meeting this guy's friend," I said, my voice tight.

"Why?" Abe asked. "He seemed nice. Like he wanted to help."

"Abe, did you see how that one guy was looking at me?" I shifted in my seat. "It made me feel...cheap. Like I'm an object he could take."

"I noticed it, too," Louis said from the back seat. "It was creepy."

"Thanks, Louis. I'm glad it wasn't just me," I said.

The rain started coming down harder as we drove away from the immigration center. Once we crossed the checkpoint, there was a clear change in the surroundings, especially in the architecture.

We started driving through the streets of Matamoros. The roads were straightforward, and we switched onto Mexican Highway 101, which would take us south to Ciudad Victoria. The rain made the road slick, but the conditions were mostly good. Some bumpy patches caused our vehicles to shudder, especially as we left the more developed parts of Matamoros. The traffic was heavy with everyone evacuating due to the storm, and we moved slowly through town and onto the highway.

I called Amelia and Emma to make sure they had made it through customs without any issues. We had gotten separated due to the extra questioning we had experienced, so they were ahead of us, but not by much. We decided to keep up with each other through text and meet at a stop close to the city if we didn't find each other on the road before then.

As we passed through Matamoros and headed toward Ciudad Victoria, the road felt different. When we left the city behind, the landscape changed. We were driving through the flat, scrubby land of northern Tamaulipas. The area looked desert-like at first, with scattered ranches, farms, and small villages. The rain felt out of place in this desert, and the road was congested.

Along the route, several Mexican checkpoints stopped our progress. These were manned by the Federal Police, the Mexican Army, or Immigration Services, all armed with weapons. Unlike the US border, these checkpoints were quick stops. The officers' questions were routine, but we still had to stay alert and follow their instructions. At each checkpoint, they asked to see our documents again. Sometimes they'd take a quick look inside the RV, but nothing too extensive—and we didn't come across anyone like the creepy guy in Matamoros.

The highway from Matamoros to Ciudad Victoria was a narrow two-lane road, much smaller than the big highways back home. As we passed through the small towns, tiny supermarkets and a few restaurants caught my attention, most of them with parking right off the road—nothing like the big parking lots we were used to. We caught up with Emma near El Moquetito when the Williamses had to stop for Harper to use the washroom. They parked in a tiny hospital lot off the side of the road. We pulled in beside them to take a quick break, too.

As I climbed back into the Jeep, I noticed a big black SUV parked about half a mile behind us down the road. I nudged Louis with my elbow and pointed toward it.

"Did we pass that car before we stopped?" I asked him.

Louis glanced at the SUV, then back at me. "I don't remember seeing it, but I wasn't paying attention."

We kept going and eventually caught up with Amelia after a stop for Ellie to use the washroom near San Germán. They had parked at a small restaurant in the city, which didn't have a parking lot—only a dusty patch of road in front of the building. When we saw them, we all tried to park, but the space was tight. We had to squeeze our long vehicles in, using the side of the road to make it work.

Since we'd already stopped thirty minutes ago, we stayed in our cars. James came over to Abe's window when he was done with the washroom, holding an umbrella.

"Good to see you again! Glad you found us," James said. "What took y'all so long at customs?"

"I'm not sure," Abe replied. "They were asking questions, then they had to go get their boss for some reason. Did they search your RV?"

"Yeah, but it didn't take long. Maybe because of your Indian paperwork?" James suggested.

"Could be," Abe said, shrugging. "It's not like the normal passports they see."

"Well, let's get going. How much longer until we get to Victoria?" James asked.

"It's probably still about two and a half hours," Abe said, looking up at the sky. The rain had turned into a light drizzle, and the traffic had eased up. James nodded and went back to his SUV.

The side-view mirror showed the other families climbing back into their cars, but a glint of sunlight caught my eye. It was coming from the same black SUV, parked on the side of the road about a quarter mile behind us.

"Uh, Abe," I said slowly. "I think we're being followed."

He gave me a skeptical look. "Why do you think that?"

"There's a black SUV back there. I don't remember it being there when we stopped, but it's there now. And it was parked at our last stop, too." I glanced at Louis. "You saw it at the last stop, right? It's back again."

Louis tried to look out the window, but the RV was blocking his view. "Can you see it in my mirror?" I asked.

He shook his head. "I saw the one at the last stop, but I can't say for sure if this is the same one. I can't see it from here."

"Well, they haven't threatened or stopped us, so I guess we keep going," Abe said. "Maybe they'll forget about us after a while."

Our group was all back together now, so we continued driving, the roads getting emptier as most of the evacuees turned off. The highway felt more open and lonelier now with only us on the narrow road.

As we got closer to Ciudad Victoria, the landscape started to change. The flat plains began to rise as we reached the foothills of the Sierra Madre Oriental mountains. The air grew cooler, and the dry scrubland gave way to thick green trees. The road started to wind, but it was still an easy drive.

The rain had stopped. We must have driven out of the storm. We passed by the town of Güémez, the one the customs officer had mentioned. I even spotted the small restaurant he'd talked about. To my relief, Abe kept driving.

***

After about four total hours of driving and another two hours or so stopped at immigration and other checkpoints, we reached the outskirts of Ciudad Victoria, the capital of Tamaulipas. It was almost two in the afternoon, and the hunger was starting to hit. We had been driving for hours, and everyone was ready for a break. As we cruised down the road on the outskirts of the city, we spotted a small run-down restaurant on the side of the highway. It had a dusty parking lot big enough to fit our RVs, which was a relief.

I hopped out of the Jeep and glanced around. I couldn't shake the feeling that someone was watching us, and I couldn't help but look for the black SUV. But as I scanned the area, I didn't see it. Maybe it was my nerves getting the best of me.

The restaurant looked old—paint peeling off the walls and a faded "TACOS" sign hanging crookedly above the door. But it was better than nothing, and everyone was starving. We walked in, the little bell above the door jingling as we entered. There was a wooden line, like a cue for a ride at an amusement park, leading up to the counter. Behind the counter stood an older Mexican woman, smiling at us warmly.

"Hola!" she greeted us. "¿En qué puedo ayudarte? ¿Qué te gustaría pedir?"

Theo, always the translator, stepped up and began talking to her. He smiled, his Spanish flowing easily, and I couldn't help but feel relieved to have him and Henry with us. They made communicating so much easier.

The menu was simple—mostly tacos, which wasn't a problem, but it wasn't what I was used to. No fancy combos or sides were offered like at the restaurants in Texas. The place was small, and we quickly realized our huge group was enough to nearly double the restaurant's usual capacity.

Once we'd all ordered, we moved to the tables on the right side of the room. They were old, long wooden tables that looked like picnic tables, except the benches weren't attached. They creaked under the weight of us all as we sat. The restaurant had a rustic vibe, with exposed rafters above us and bare wood walls that felt unfinished yet gave it a homey feel.

The tacos arrived, and even though I wasn't a taco expert, I could tell these were special—fresh, warm, and bursting with flavor. These were hands down the best tacos I'd ever tasted. I could tell everyone else was enjoying them, too. Liam and Abe were practically inhaling theirs, and even the kids were quiet for a change, focused on their food.

As we ate, the conversation shifted to what we'd do for the night. We needed a place to park the RVs, somewhere safe and preferably free. Liam suggested we find a Walmart Supercenter. He'd heard a lot of RVs parked in Walmart lots overnight; the lights and the fact that people were around made it feel safer.

Safety was the big thing on my mind, too. The customs officials earlier had given me the chills, especially the way they'd looked at me, like they knew something I didn't. And that black SUV...I kept glancing over my shoulder, half-expecting to spot it. It had been a tense day in Mexico, and I was starting to wish we were back in Texas, where things felt a little more familiar, even if it did mean we would have storm damage to deal with.

Abe pulled out his iPad and opened Google Maps. "Two Walmarts in Victoria," he said, tapping the screen. "This one's got a bigger parking lot than the other."

The lot with the bigger space was on the western side of the city, farther than the other one, but it seemed like the best option. I hoped the area was safe enough.

We finished our tacos and left the little restaurant feeling satisfied and full—so full that I wanted to stretch out and take a nap. As I climbed into the Jeep, the sun was low in the sky, casting long shadows across the dusty parking lot. I absentmindedly scanned the road behind us.

My stomach tightened. There it was. The black SUV. It was parked on the side of the road about half a mile back, tucked behind a row of trees, enough to blend in but still noticeable if you were looking.

I didn't want to make a big deal out of it, but I couldn't shake the uneasy feeling crawling up my spine. I nudged Louis, trying to be as discreet as possible, and nodded toward the SUV.

Louis followed my gaze and froze as his eyes locked onto the SUV. He quickly turned back around, and I could tell by the way his face went pale and his eyebrows shot up he was as freaked out as I was.

"That's got to be the same one," he muttered under his breath, his voice tense.

Abe started the Jeep and pulled out of the parking lot, but my eyes kept darting to the side-view mirror. The black SUV stayed far enough back to look like any other car, but I couldn't shake the feeling that it was always there, lurking behind us.

Louis was silent, his jaw clenched tight. We both knew this wasn't normal. The odds of running into the same car in the middle of nowhere, twice in one day, possibly three times? Slim to none. We were being followed. But why?

I tried to stay calm, but the longer we drove, the less I could ignore my gut feeling, the one that said we weren't just being followed...we were being hunted.

TWENTY-ONE

Ciudad Victoria had more of an urban feel than Matamoros, with a mix of old colonial-style buildings and modern ones. The streets were wide, lined with government buildings, parks, and busy markets. Street food vendors were everywhere, and the city had a slow but lively pace to it. It was smaller than the big cities in the States I had been in but full of culture and life.

We pulled into the Walmart parking lot, steering the RV toward the back corner near the Sam's Club. It was away from the main traffic, so we wouldn't be taking up any spaces that could be used by customers. A large field with trees and grass stretched out right across from where we parked, and a line of trees separated us from the next row of parking spaces. It felt like a perfect spot to settle in, far enough from traffic and customers but still close enough if we needed to go into the store for something.

Once we were parked, we all piled into Liam's RV, which had the generator running, so we could watch the news and keep track of the storm. The television flickered on, and we saw the latest updates. The storm had shrunk in size but was still enormous, now covering almost the entire Gulf of Mexico south of Louisiana. The outer bands weren't reaching as far as they had the day before, but it was still a massive storm, and the rain bands would likely hit us in the middle of the night.

The eye of the storm was well-formed and menacing, the winds still howling at two hundred twenty miles per hour. It was now officially the strongest storm on record. The eye was predicted to hit Corpus Christi tomorrow night. We all stared at the screen, knowing things were going to get a lot worse before they got better. After a few minutes, we turned off the television to save power.

We checked in with Elijah's, Mateo's, and Lucas's families. They'd all made it to their relatives without any problems. They'd be working from home this week. We had satellite internet, too, but we didn't want to use up any more electricity than we had to since we didn't have proper hookups. So, we kept things quiet for now, waiting for the storm to do its worst.

There was a sharp knock on the door. I froze, my heart racing, and quickly looked around to make sure everyone was accounted for. Thirteen. That was how many we were supposed to have. My mind raced. Was it someone from Walmart or Sam's Club telling us we couldn't park here overnight?

Liam was closest to the door, so he stood to answer it. I couldn't see outside from where I was sitting deep inside the motorhome, but whatever he saw clearly shocked him. I could see it in his eyes and the way his expression froze for a moment.

"Can I help you?" Liam asked cautiously, sounding as though he was trying to keep his voice steady.

A man's voice replied, but the words were muffled. "Estamos buscando a Abe Serug."

Liam gave him a confused look, clearly not understanding what the man was saying. But before he could ask, Theo pushed past him to talk to the visitor in Spanish.

"Hola, amigo," Theo greeted. He then backed up, his arms raised slightly, a clear sign of surprise, or maybe fear.

A cold chill ran down my spine. Without thinking, I pulled the kids closer to me, guiding them into the back of the RV and out of sight. Could it be someone from the black SUV? The one that had been tailing us? Why else would Theo look so startled, even a little scared?

I heard the man's voice again, but it was too soft for me to catch the words from the back of the RV. It didn't matter. I was trying to distract myself and the kids by starting a card game. I needed to take my mind off the uneasy feeling that'd been growing inside me ever since we'd crossed the border into Mexico.

I glanced out the window of the RV bedroom where I had taken the kids. My heart skipped a beat. Two men were standing outside, both holding guns that looked like the ones the

Mexican customs officers had carried. They were talking with Theo and Abe. Why were they interested in Abe? How did they even know his name? Could they have memorized our paperwork at the border? Was this all somehow connected to the way they'd questioned us or the strange looks they'd given us?

It was hard to focus on the card game, and the kids easily beat me. My heart was racing and my forehead slick with sweat. I peeked out the window again. Theo, Abe, and the two Mexicans were still talking, their voices low and urgent. One of the men looked in my direction, and I quickly ducked out of sight.

After about twenty minutes, Amelia came into the room. Her expression was tense, her lips pressed together like she didn't want to tell me what was going on.

"We're hitting the road again, Izzy," she said.

I blinked, surprised. "What? Where are we going now?"

"A town farther south. You'll have to ask Abe for the details on the way," she replied, but there was hesitation in her voice. "Okay, kids," she said, turning to the others. "Time to get back in the car."

Groans echoed around the room. They were all tired of being cooped up in the RV and the endless driving. Slowly, they got up and left the room, dragging their feet as they headed for the door.

Once they were gone, Amelia leaned in close, her voice barely a whisper. "I don't know what's going on, Izzy, but I don't like it."

I shook my head, the worry pressing down on me like a heavy weight. "Me neither," I muttered. "I hope Abe knows what he's doing."

***

We were back in the Jeep, the rain falling in steady sheets as we drove southeast. Another outer band of the storm had rolled in, the dark clouds swallowing up the sky, even though it was still two hours before sunset. The road stretched out in front of us, wet and slick, but the storm didn't seem to care. It was almost like the weather mirrored the tension inside the car—heavy, oppressive, and worsening by the minute.

Abe hadn't said much since we'd left the Walmart parking lot, and he still hadn't given me any explanation about where we were going. But I hadn't asked either. I could feel his stress radiating from him, like for the first time in his life, he wasn't sure if he was making the right choices. His hands were gripping the steering wheel so tightly his knuckles were white, and his jaw kept clenching and unclenching. Louis sat quietly in the back, staring out the window, lost in his own thoughts.

I couldn't take the silence anymore. The questions swirling in my head were getting louder and louder, and I needed answers. "Where are we going, Abe?" I asked, my voice breaking through the heavy quiet.

He glanced at me briefly, his expression tight. "To an estate about an hour away."

So, he was going to play this game, the one where he gave as little information as possible. I wasn't having it. "Whose estate is it?" I pushed.

"It belongs to el jefe," he said, as if that meant something to me.

"And who is el jefe?" I asked, already knowing I wasn't going to like the answer.

Abe let out a long, slow breath but didn't look at me. "The head of one of the Mexican cartels."

The words hit me like a slap to the face. I felt my pulse spike. "We're going to the home of a drug lord?" I squeaked, my voice barely above a whisper.

"We've been summoned," he said, his tone flat, like it was no big deal. But the way his fingers gripped the wheel told a different story.

"Summoned?" My voice shot up an octave. "What does that even mean?"

Abe exhaled sharply, the sound almost like a growl. "Jefe Hernández requested our presence at his estate."

"But why?" I asked, trying to keep my voice steady. The fear I'd been trying to push down ever since we'd crossed the border was bubbling to the surface, rising up like a tidal wave. The customs officials, their eyes lingering on me with a dark and hungry look...it was all making sense now. They'd been watching me. Watching us. And now Abe was leading us right into the lion's den.

I shook my head, my heart pounding. "This can't be what Jehovah wants. Associating with the cartel, being anywhere near them, is dangerous, probably illegal. Now we're going to the house of the head of the cartel? What are you thinking, Abe?"

He let out a long, frustrated breath, his gaze locked straight ahead as he spoke. "The border patrol saw how beautiful you are, Princess," he said, his voice low and strained. "They told Jefe Hernández about you. El jefe gets what he wants, no matter what, or who, is in his way. He sent his people to follow us. When we didn't stop at the bar where Sanchez told us to go, they followed us here and confronted me. Hernández invited us to his estate so he could meet you...personally."

My stomach dropped. I could hardly believe what I was hearing. The thought of this dangerous man, the leader of a cartel, knowing about me...wanting to meet me? It was too much.

Abe continued, his voice more distant now. "He has houses all over the country, but he is at this one. It's only an hour away, and it's far enough from the hurricane. He had his people bring us to him there."

I stared at him in disbelief. "Is this all because you lied about me being your sister?" I asked, my voice shaking. The tears were already welling up, but I didn't want to let them fall. "If you had told them the truth, that I'm your wife, none of this would have happened."

Abe's grip on the wheel tightened even more, his knuckles paling further. "No, Princess. If I'd said you were my wife, I'd probably be dead by now," he said, his voice flat but fierce. "Hernández gets what he wants. No one says no to him. Not even the law."

I felt a lump in my throat, the reality of it all crashing down on me. "What are we going to do now?" My voice trembled with rage and fear. "What if he wants me and won't give me back to you?"

Abe didn't even blink. "Let's hope that doesn't happen," he said, his tone grim.

I wanted to scream, to demand answers, but nothing would change. We were in this mess, and we had no choice but to face it head-on. The storm outside was nothing compared to the storm about to hit us.

***

The rest of the drive was quiet except for a few sniffles that escaped from me as I tried to hold back my fear. I felt like I was heading straight into a nightmare I couldn't wake up from. Abe, who was supposed to protect us, seemed to be driving us right into the danger he knew was ahead.

We turned off the highway onto a narrow path, a long driveway that seemed to stretch on forever. After a while, the mansion came into view, standing imposingly behind a guardhouse and tall iron gates. The estate looked like a fortress, built from pale limestone that had faded from the sun, its walls warm and golden in color and rising from the thick green hills that surrounded it. It was a strange mix of old Spanish colonial charm and modern luxury. The windows were framed in sleek black ironwork, with grand arches above them, giving the mansion a majestic, eerie look.

Our caravan of RVs rolled up to the guardhouse, and I immediately noticed the two armed guards standing near the entrance. Their guns were not slung casually over their shoulders like the customs officers. These men held them firmly in their hands, ready to act at a moment's notice. Abe rolled down his window and gave them his name. They nodded, their faces hard and unreadable.

"Can I see your documents?" one of the guards asked with a thick accent.

Abe reached into the glove compartment, pulling out the paperwork. As he did, the guards subtly raised their weapons, their eyes trained on him. I held my breath. Abe handed the documents to the guards and kept his hands visible. They shuffled through the papers then handed them back, keeping some cards for themselves.

"You'll get your tourist cards back when you leave," the guard said.

"The two RVs behind me are with me also," Abe added.

The guards glanced at each other and nodded. One of them turned and went into the guard shack, making the massive iron gates creak open.

The entrance to the estate was through a grand courtyard. The cobblestone driveway stretched out in front of the gates, winding between lush hedges of bougainvillea. Their bright purple and red flowers spilled over the vines, casting splashes of color along the path. Stone statues of mythical creatures stood along the way, their faces weathered by time but still standing tall and proud.

The gardens surrounding the mansion were carefully manicured, with tall palm trees swaying in the soft breeze. At the center of the courtyard was a wide fountain; its water glistened in the sun as it bubbled gently. Beyond the gardens, the land stretched out into wide fields with tall, bushy plants whose bright green, serrated leaves rippled in the wind.

The mansion's roof was covered with terracotta tiles, weathered by years of sunlight. Several tall towers rose above the roof, each crowned with a decorative dome. The tallest tower had a sharp spire that seemed to reach toward the sky.

We drove up to the circular drive, a wide space that easily fit all of our RVs. The black SUV that had been following us earlier was parked in front of the house, and we took our places behind it, feeling out of place in front of such a grand estate.

Once parked, we walked up the front steps to a set of huge wooden doors. The doors were polished to a shine, with detailed carvings of swirling flowers and vines. They were flanked by towering stone columns, and above them was a wide balcony that curved around the second floor, held up by intricate iron railings.

Before Abe could knock, the door slowly creaked open. A small elderly woman stood behind it, dressed in a servant's uniform. She gave us a quick nod, opened the door wider, and motioned us inside.

The foyer was nothing short of breathtaking. As soon as we stepped inside, I was hit by the sheer grandeur of the space. The walls were made of polished marble, a creamy beige color with veins of gold and gray running through it, reflecting the light from every angle. The ceiling stretched at least twenty feet above us, painted with scenes of grand battles, mythical creatures, and peaceful landscapes.

In the center of the foyer hung a massive chandelier, its crystals sparkling in the light like a thousand tiny diamonds. The walls were lined with large, framed paintings—some by famous European artists, others depicting Mexican landscapes and historical figures. Each frame was gilded in gold, adding to the room's luxurious feel.

The floor was made of black-and-white checkered marble tiles that seemed to shimmer as we walked over them. At the far end of the foyer, two grand staircases with wrought-iron railings decorated with vines and flowers spiraled upward in perfect symmetry, their marble steps gleaming. At the base of the staircase stood a large mahogany table, its surface glistening with polish. On it rested crystal vases filled with bright flowers—roses, lilies, and orchids. Above the table, a massive mirror framed in gold leaf reflected the entire foyer, making the room feel twice as large as it was.

Tall windows lined the walls on either side of the doors, draped with heavy red velvet curtains that were pulled back enough to let in the dim light from the setting sun. The soft shadows they cast added to the room's mysterious air. The air smelled faintly of fresh flowers and polished wood, mixed with the old leather scent of the antique chairs sitting against the walls.

We were led by the woman through an arched doorway to the left into a sitting room. The room was equally impressive—vast, with high, vaulted ceilings, ornate wooden beams, and deep crimson velvet sofas lining the walls and framing a massive stone fireplace. The soft, golden light of sconces flickered around the room, casting long shadows across the rich fabrics and dark-wood furniture. The space was filled with a quiet luxury, one that made me feel small and insignificant.

Sitting in one of the velvet chairs was an imposing man that could only be Hernández, holding a short glass with amber liquid. He stood as we entered, his presence filling the room. Tall and broad-shouldered, he had muscles that came from years of maintaining both physical and mental strength. His black hair was neatly trimmed, streaked with gray at the temples. His face was hard, with sharp cheekbones and a jawline that seemed to be chiseled from stone and covered in a short but thick beard of dark hair. His eyes, dark brown and cold, fixed on us as if he could read every thought we had.

His clothes were expensive, designed to be casual but unmistakably high-end—a leather jacket, tailored shirt, and designer jeans. His platinum watch gleamed under the soft light, and he wore a gold chain around his neck. His very presence screamed power, and there was a dangerous calm in the way he held himself.

"Welcome to my home," he said, his voice low and deliberate. Each word seemed carefully chosen, calculated to intimidate.

Abe stepped forward, offering a firm handshake.

Hernández nodded and gestured to the many couches in the room. "Please, have a seat," he said, his expression unreadable.

TWENTY-TWO

Everyone shuffled in and took a seat on the plush couches. Harper tugged on Emma's shirt and asked, "Mommy, what are we doing in this castle?" Her voice echoed off the high ceilings.

I gasped, my heart jumping in my chest. I had no idea what Hernández would think of such a question.

His gaze snapped to Harper, and the room seemed to freeze. He snapped his fingers, and we all jumped in our seats. The servant who had led us into the room rushed back in and stood stiffly in front of Hernández, waiting for his next command.

"Lleven a los niños a la sala de juegos. Sus madres pueden ir con ellos." Hernández's voice was firm and cold, the words sounding like a command rather than a suggestion.

The woman bowed and backed away, turning toward the children, who were fidgeting on the couches. She pointed to them, then to Amelia and Emma, and waved them toward the door. Amelia and Emma exchanged nervous looks.

Theo, who was sitting next to Emma, leaned in and whispered, "She's going to take you and the kids to a place where they can play."

Emma nodded and stood, gently herding Ellie and Harper in front of her. Amelia followed with Luna and William Junior trailing behind her. I felt a rush of relief knowing the kids would be out of the room.

Now, I was the youngest person left in the room. I wished I could join the kids, but I was stuck here, and the silence felt heavier than ever.

Hernández broke the quiet first. "Would you like a drink?" He raised his glass slightly then casually waved his other hand toward the bar at the far wall.

The bar was an impressive sight—dark mahogany and lined with bottles of top-shelf tequila, rum, and whiskey. Behind it, a massive wine rack showcased rare vintage bottles while shining glassware and silver cocktail shakers were neatly arranged within easy reach.

Abe seemed to freeze, unsure of what to do. What was the right thing to do when el jefe offers you a drink? If we turned him down, would Hernández think we were disrespecting him? But if we accepted, would it cloud our judgment when we tried to figure out why he'd brought us here in the first place? Either way, it felt like a trap.

"A very kind offer, but no, thank you," Abe said, trying to sound as polite as possible.

I held my breath as we waited for Hernández's reaction.

Hernández didn't seem offended. Instead, he gave a small, amused smile. It was a smile that didn't reach his eyes—more of a grimace, like whatever he was thinking was not going to be good for us. "It's right down to business, then," he said. He looked directly at Abe. "Abe, I will speak to you, as you are obviously the head of your group."

I tensed, dread creeping up my spine as Hernández's eyes shifted toward me. "I brought you here because one of my halcónes told me about a beautiful woman entering the country," he continued, his voice smooth and casual, like we were discussing the weather. "This woman, more beautiful than any of my other wives, is your sister, Isabelle." His gaze lingered on me, a look of desire flickering across his face.

My stomach twisted, and I struggled to swallow the knot in my throat.

James, sitting next to me, whispered in my ear, "Sister?"

I nudged him hard in the ribs, hoping he'd stay quiet. The rest of the group hadn't been in the car when Abe had told the customs officer I was his sister. We hadn't thought we would have to lie about it, but now, with the situation spiraling out of control, it seemed like a mistake.

Thankfully, it seemed Hernández hadn't heard James's question. "Where are your parents? Her father?" Hernández asked, his tone still casual.

Abe responded carefully, "Our parents are no longer among the living."

"So, as her older brother, you would be the one to decide her future?" Hernández's eyes didn't leave me as he spoke, his words sharp.

"I suppose that is the case," Abe replied, his voice tense.

Hernández nodded then continued as if he were making a casual business proposal. "I have many homes, like this one, scattered around the country, on routes we frequently use in our business. One of my wives lives in each of my homes. They look after the place while I'm away. Now, they don't do any of the work. I wouldn't let my beauties do work. I have servants for that, like Maria, who you met earlier. But they are here for me when I am here."

He paused and looked around the room, letting his words sink in. "As you can see," he continued, "my beauties live in luxury, and their families live in luxury as well. As her brother, you will receive much wealth as a dowry of sorts for your sister."

Dowry? My mind reeled. It was clear now that Hernández had no intention of letting me leave. He was treating me like property. My blood ran cold.

Abe turned to Hernández, speaking about me like I wasn't even there. "There's something you need to know about her," he said, his voice flat. "She can't have kids. She's barren. She won't be able to give you an heir, to carry on your family name."

Maybe he thought that would make Hernández back off, change his mind about taking me. Maybe he thought it would keep me safe. But it hurt, more than I expected. When Abe had talked about marrying me, he'd promised he wouldn't care if I was barren. Now I could see it was always there in the back of his mind, a secret he couldn't shake. Maybe he was hoping if Hernández took me, he could be free of the burden of me, the woman who couldn't give him the family Jehovah had promised.

I'd never felt smaller.

If Abe thought saying it would make Hernández change his mind, he was wrong. Hernández didn't even blink. "I don't need her to have children," he said, his voice cutting through the air. "I've got plenty of other wives who can do that.

"You will all stay with me," Hernández continued. "No need to stay in your RVs. There is plenty of space here. You will be well taken care of."

With a snap of his fingers, Maria appeared again, standing at attention.

"Estas personas se quedarán con nosotros. Consigamos a nueve de las sirvientas para que las cuiden y llévenlas a sus habitaciones," Hernández instructed.

Maria nodded and quickly left the room.

"I will have your RVs parked in our back lot," Hernández added, clapping twice. A man in a servant suit immediately entered the room. "Hand Alejandro your keys," Hernández ordered, looking at Abe, Liam, and James.

Reluctantly, each of them handed over their keys, and I realized there was no way out. We were stuck here, surrounded by security and danger, with no escape in sight.

Maria returned with a young woman in a servant's uniform. She pointed at me and motioned for me to follow her. My heart raced, panic rising in my chest as I glanced at Abe. I didn't want to be separated from him. He met my eyes with a look that said he was sorry, but there was nothing he could do. I took a deep breath, trying to steady myself, then stood and followed Maria and the other girl out of the room. We climbed the staircase, my legs shaking as I ascended. We turned right down a long hall and stopped at a door on the left.

The room I entered was breathtaking. The walls were painted a soft, creamy color with gold trim along the edges, making the space feel quiet and elegant. Huge arched windows, draped with dark velvet curtains, covered one wall. As the sun began to set, the light flooded in, casting a warm glow over the room.

The bed was in the center of the room, massive and impressive, with a dark mahogany frame that gleamed; it was a bed fit for a royalty. The headboard was carved with delicate vines and flowers, so detailed they seemed alive. The bedspread was a thick, soft comforter of white Egyptian cotton embroidered with gold, and pillows in shades of burgundy, cream, and gold were scattered across the bed. It looked too perfect to touch, like it was meant for display, not use.

On either side of the bed, an antique nightstand stood with a tall lamp made of brass and crystal, casting a soft glow. There was also a plush armchair with a matching ottoman by a marble table on which a vase of white orchids rested. The floor was covered in thick Persian rugs in shades of red, gold, and beige.

A large gilded mirror covered one wall, reflecting the room and making it feel even bigger. On the opposite wall, a sleek, dark-wood dresser stood with porcelain figurines and a set of elegant jewelry boxes arranged on top. The air smelled faintly of fresh flowers and old wood.

Maria left me alone with the other girl and disappeared down the hall. We stood in silence, unsure of what to say. The language barrier between us felt thick.

"Do you speak English?" I asked quietly.

She shook her head, her eyes a little sad. She couldn't have been much older than me, maybe Louis's age, but she looked like she'd seen a lot more of life's harshness than someone her age should have.

I put my hand on my chest and said, "Isabelle."

She repeated it then said, "Honey."

Honey pulled a tape measure from her apron and started taking my measurements—chest, waist, hips, length. She wrote them down quickly on a small pad then walked through a door to the right. With nothing else to do, I followed her.

The door led to a washroom.

"Wow," I whispered, my mouth hanging open.

The washroom was as stunning as the bedroom. The marble floor was swirled with veins of gray and white that formed intricate patterns. The walls were also marble, but its tones were softer, whites and creams with gold highlights that shone in the light from a chandelier overhead. The freestanding bathtub sat in the center of the room beneath a tall arched window, its white porcelain surface gleaming. Soft, fluffy towels were neatly stacked nearby, ready for use.

Off to the side was a glass shower stall, its walls frosted for privacy. The shower had a rainfall showerhead, and stone tiles lined its floor. A marble vanity with shiny silver faucets stretched across the opposite wall, and above it hung a large mirror. The sink was a deep basin made of polished marble and surrounded by jars of lotions, perfumes, and a few candles that gave off a soothing lavender scent.

The washroom also had a walk-in closet big enough to hold an entire wardrobe. The walls were lined with shelves and racks for shoes, bags, and coats, all empty currently, and at the far end stood a full-length mirror.

Honey moved around the washroom, checking that everything was in place—fresh toilet paper, shampoo, and other supplies I might need. I wouldn't need to worry about retrieving my toiletries from the RV.

Honey began filling the bathtub with hot water, the steam rising into the air as she crushed a bubble bar under the tap. Thick, frothy bubbles started to form on the water's surface. She pulled a soft, fluffy towel from the stack under the sink and placed it next to the tub along with a washcloth.

I'd never had a bubble bath before. My last few showers had been cramped and uncomfortable, taken in the RV. I was filthy, and maybe I even smelled. Was that why she'd drawn the bath for me?

Once the tub was full, Honey motioned for me to get in. I hesitated. I was nervous about undressing in front of her, so I quickly turned my back, undressed, and climbed under the bubbles, hoping she wouldn't notice how uncomfortable I felt. To my surprise, she pulled up a chair behind the tub and started shampooing my hair. I sat there, unsure of how to react. When she was done, she left the room and came back with fresh underwear, a white lacy thong and matching lacy bra.

Honey stayed with me for the next hour, doing things I didn't want but couldn't refuse. She plucked my eyebrows, waxed my legs and bikini line (which was super awkward), curled my hair, and applied makeup. The process made my stomach turn. Whatever she was getting me ready for couldn't just be bedtime.

She brought in a dress, a long, flowing white gown covered in lace and pearls with delicate floral designs along the bodice. The skirt was full and layered with soft satin. She also brought in a silk rebozo embroidered with bright, colorful patterns and a short lace veil. It was unmistakably a wedding dress.

I shook my head so hard I almost gave myself whiplash. No way. I held out my hands in front of me to object. I couldn't wear that. I couldn't get married. I had to stop this. I had to tell someone what was going on. This wasn't happening.

I couldn't shake the memory of what Hernández had said in the sitting room. He had so many wives. How many, exactly? I had no idea. But the way he'd spoken made it clear every one of his estates deserved a new wife to go with it. I could be already married and wearing a wedding ring for all he cared. It wouldn't stop him. He might kill Abe and take me anyway. The thought made me shiver. There was no escape, not when dealing with el jefe. They took what they wanted, no matter who they had to destroy along the way.

Reluctantly, I let Honey dress me in the wedding gown. She wasn't giving me a choice. She brought out a necklace with a beautiful silver cross covered in diamonds, worth more than the RV we'd been living in. Along with the necklace, she gave me a pair of delicate gold sandals that glittered in the light. She even tucked small white flowers into my hair, making me look like a fairy tale princess.

When she spun me around to face the full-length mirror in the closet, I barely recognized the person staring back at me. The girl in the reflection was not the one who had been in the RV, fighting to stay strong. This girl looked elegant, more beautiful than I could have ever imagined. Could that really be me? I felt like I was looking at a stranger.

Honey smiled at my stunned expression, clearly pleased with the transformation. She had turned me from a simple girl into someone entirely different—someone who could walk into a room and command attention without saying a word.

She guided me out the door, her hands light on my shoulders, steering me down the hall and toward the stairs. My heart pounded in my chest, and my mind raced with questions. Where were we going? What was happening? I didn't dare ask. It wouldn't make a difference, anyway.

We ended up in a part of the house I hadn't seen before. It was a small mudroom, not much more than a hallway. The door at the far end led outside to the back patio.

The enormous backyard was like a different world. The patio was lined with cushioned seating areas surrounded by dense, vibrant greenery. In the middle of it all was a huge swimming pool, the water shimmering under the moonlight. Above me, chandeliers hung from the ceiling of the veranda, their lights casting a soft golden glow.

Beyond the pool, a long cobblestone path stretched toward a large open lawn. Rows of white chairs were neatly arranged, facing an archway covered in ivy and flowers. The chairs were already filled with people, all dressed in clothes similar to what Hernández had been wearing, their eyes turned toward the arch. The air was thick with anticipation. The yard was lit by strings of café lights crisscrossing above, illuminating the pool in a warm, romantic glow. The atmosphere felt like a dream, or a nightmare I had no idea how to wake up from.

And there, under the archway, stood Hernández.

How did they pull this off in two hours? Am I about to be married to this man? Fear bubbled up inside me, but I couldn't move, couldn't speak. It was like the ground had vanished beneath my feet, and all I could do was float forward toward my fate.

Honey pushed me to the start of the long walkway then gave me a gentle shove forward, leaving me standing there by myself. As I slowly walked down the aisle, music began to drift through the air, playing softly from hidden speakers along the lawn. My eyes scanned the crowd, searching for Abe. I spotted him and Louis sitting in the front row. They were dressed in expensive suits and had gold chains hanging around their necks, but their faces were filled with concern. It was obvious they were being treated well, like I had been, but it was also clear there was nothing they could do to stop this. I was alone in this.

The moon hung high in the clear sky, its light bright and full. The corn moon had only been two days ago, so it was still almost at its peak. I glanced upward, hoping the storm would come in full force and ruin the wedding, saving me from this fate. But it seemed distant, its outer bands nowhere near us. The stars twinkled peacefully, as if nothing was wrong. *How can this be happening?*

I thought back to all we had believed a couple of months ago. We had been so sure we were following Jehovah's will. Jehovah Himself had confirmed it in the clearing with the sun shining directly on the altar of charred animal remains. He had promised us land in Texas and a future for our children.

But since then, silence. We hadn't heard from Him at all, not even when the storm had been approaching. Jehovah had done nothing to stop it.

Abe had made the decision to leave, to flee to Mexico without Jehovah's guidance. Had we failed Jehovah's test? Since we had crossed into Mexico, the plan and the promise started falling apart. The storm. The constant fear and uncertainty. And now this. I stood in a foreign country, alone, and forced to marry a dangerous man.

Jehovah's promise about offspring, the future of our family, all of it was slipping away.

TWENTY-THREE

The ceremony felt like a blur, like I was floating above myself, watching a scene I couldn't quite believe. I wasn't the girl standing there in the white dress, listening to the priest's words. That was someone else. A stranger. Just as I hadn't recognized the face in the mirror a few minutes ago, now I didn't recognize the girl in front of me.

My hands trembled slightly in Hernández's as he held them, his grip firm, like he was trying to keep me from disappearing. I wanted to pull away, but my body didn't move. I felt numb, as though my emotions were locked inside a cage. A few tears slipped down my cheeks, and I quickly wiped them away, praying he wouldn't notice. I wanted to break down, to cry so hard I couldn't breathe, but I couldn't. Not here. Not in front of him. Not in front of anyone. I was too scared of what would happen if I let myself fall apart.

Hernández stood there, tall and confident, with a face that could've been carved from stone. He was handsome in a way that didn't feel comforting. He wasn't like Abe. Abe had been kind, protective, a shield. Hernández was a man who didn't ask for permission, a man who got what he wanted no matter the cost. And here I was, standing beside him, about to make promises I didn't want to keep.

When the ceremony ended, Hernández took my arm in a smooth, possessive gesture and led me past the arch, away from the altar. I walked without thinking, my feet moving on autopilot. The path led us into a large open space where a few clusters of guests were already gathering. White tents covered round tables, each draped with a white cloth and a colorful floral centerpiece. Roses, lilies, and orchids brightened up the space, their sweet scent heavy in the air.

A mariachi band was setting up off to one side, tuning their instruments and testing the sound. The lively strum of a guitar and the soft notes of a trumpet filled the air, but they didn't bring me any comfort. The music felt too upbeat for this nightmare. The wooden dance floor in the center of one of the tents was empty for now, but I could imagine it filling with guests, their laughter and chatter blending into the sound of the music.

I forced myself to breathe, to act like I was fine, like I hadn't promised myself away to a man who wasn't Abe. But nothing felt fine. And I didn't know how I was going to get through this night.

I scanned the main tent Hernández had led us to and caught sight of Emma and Amelia, both dressed in stunning gowns with their hair styled in elegant updos. Emma looked out of place in the sea of Mexican strangers. James and Liam walked beside them, each of them in sharp, expensive suits that made them look like they belonged in a world far removed from their normal middle-class Houston life. The children were nowhere to be seen, which I hoped meant they were tucked safely in bed, being watched over by a servant.

Emma and Amelia took their seats at one of the tables, joining Theo and Henry on the far side of the main tent, across from me. I longed to walk over to them, to escape Hernández's firm grip on my arm and sit where I felt I belonged. But Hernández steered me away, pulling me to a table at the head of the tent.

At the center of the table were two seats, one for him and one for me. To my right sat five beautiful women, all of them dressed to perfection, and to his left sat five men who looked like they'd walked straight out of a nightmare, with cold eyes and intimidating stances.

Again, I wondered how this entire wedding, from the decorations to the flowers to the food to the band, had been pulled together in a few hours. Had they planned it all the second they saw us at the border? Hernández always got what he wanted when he wanted it. And it seemed like everyone in Mexico answered to him without question.

Hernández left me alone at the table to mingle with his men, disappearing toward the bar. I had no idea what to do with myself. I didn't belong here, not with these people.

"Hola." A soft voice beside me broke through my thoughts. I turned to find a woman smiling at me, a little more relaxed than everyone else in the room. She must have noticed my terrified expression during the ceremony because she leaned in closer and whispered, "Relax. He's not as scary in private as he seems in public."

Relief flooded through me. Someone who could speak English! Maybe she could help me find a way out of this nightmare.

"I'm Regina," she said with a quiet smile. "His Monterrey wife."

My heart sank. His wife? The hope I'd held onto for a brief moment vanished like smoke in the wind. If she was his wife, how could she possibly help me escape this situation?

She was a stunning brunette with a slender waist and an impressive chest. Her olive skin was a sharp contrast to her striking blue eyes, which matched the color of her low-cut gown. She reminded me of Mia, elegant, confident, and completely at ease in her surroundings.

"Are all of you his wives?" I asked quietly, my gaze drifting down the table at the other women, each of them as beautiful as the last. I felt like a fish out of water, surrounded by women who looked like they belonged.

Regina nodded, her smile flickering. "Yes, we're all his wives." She gestured toward each woman as she spoke. "Valentina from Chihuahua, Romina from Guadalajara, Victoria from Culiacán, and Camila from Hermosillo. He has another one, Renata, in Mexico City, but she's eight months pregnant and can't travel."

I swallowed, feeling small. Hernández had been right when he'd said he surrounded himself with "beauties." Each one of them was breathtaking, but they all had one thing in common. They were Mexican, with rich, dark features and deep connections to the culture. Then there was me, from northern Minnesota, with no Mexican blood running through my veins. I was the outsider here, the one who didn't belong.

Why did he choose me? What is it about me that makes him think I'm the one he needs?

I needed to learn as much as I could from these women. They didn't seem like enemies or rivals; they were other women caught up in this mess, just like me. "Tell me about what to expect," I said, my voice barely more than a whisper.

Regina hesitated then leaned in slightly, her eyes scanning the room to make sure Hernández wasn't nearby. "He treats us with the utmost respect," she began, her voice steady but careful. "We're probably the only ones he treats well. All the other servants, the workers, and the...well, the mulas are treated like dirt. He expects a lot from them. And if they can't deliver, heads roll."

My breath caught in my throat. *Heads roll?* I swallowed hard, trying to control the fear rushing over me. "Have any of his wives' heads...actually rolled?" I asked, my voice shaking slightly.

Regina's expression darkened, and she looked down for a moment before answering. "I've only known of one. The wife who used to manage this home. But it wasn't because she couldn't do her job. She tried to rat Hernández out to the police." She paused, and her lips pressed together in a thin line. "The thing is, the police are all on his side. They're in his pocket. So, when she tried to make a move, they told him. He wasn't happy about that, and she hasn't been seen since." Regina's eyes searched my face. "Now we have a new wedding, a new Tampico wife, and here you are, Isabelle."

My mind was reeling. I tried to push down the lump in my throat but couldn't. "So, the moral of the story is 'don't rat him out to the police.' Got it," I said, trying to keep my voice casual even though my heart raced. "Anything else I should know?"

Regina gave a small, knowing smile, though there was no warmth in it. "Don't try to escape. That would be pointless." She looked me dead in the eyes, like she was warning me rather than merely advising me. "Relax and enjoy the ride. This is the best gig in all of Mexico. You get everything you could possibly want, and then some. But don't ask about the business. Stay out of it. The less you know, the better. If you don't know anything, no one can blame you if things go south."

I sat back in my chair, trying to breathe through the panic rising in my chest. No escaping. No going back to my real husband. No going back to the life I'd known, the one that felt like it was a world away now. I was trapped in a life that wasn't mine, surrounded by women who had learned to survive by playing along.

I closed my eyes for a moment, letting it all sink in. If there was any hope of getting out, it was slipping further away by the second. I was stuck here, at Hernández's mercy.

Hernández came back, holding two drinks, and set one in front of me. It was a margarita on the rocks with a rim of salt glistening in the light. I stared at it, unsure of what to do. I had never had alcohol before, and the sight of the drink made my stomach tighten.

"I don't think I'm old enough to drink this," I said softly, my voice barely above a whisper.

Hernández laughed, a deep, throaty chuckle that sounded like it belonged to someone else. It was the first time I'd heard him laugh, and I wasn't sure how to react. "Isa," he said, shortening my name with his thick Spanish accent. No one had ever called me Isa before. It was always Izzy. "No one will stop you. Drink."

I glanced at Regina. She gave me a small nod, encouraging me with her eyes, and I felt a strange sense of calm wash over me. "It's only one drink," I said to myself. "It's not a big deal."

I hesitated for a moment longer before lifting the glass to my lips. The first sip was more intense than I expected. The cool, tart taste of lime hit my tongue, sharp and refreshing. It made my mouth water, almost too sour at first, but the moment I swallowed, the warmth of the tequila followed, smooth and strong as it slid down my throat. The slight bitterness of the orange liqueur coated my tongue, balancing out the tartness of the lime with an edge that made my taste buds tingle.

The salt rim was the final touch, a little bit of salty crunch that completed the drink and brought out the flavors even more, making it taste fuller, richer. It was all so unexpected, so intense, and before I knew it, I wanted another sip.

I lifted the glass again, this time taking a larger gulp, letting the mixture settle in my chest. The warmth from the tequila spread through me, a little fiery but not unpleasant.

I glanced around, trying to focus, but the world seemed a little fuzzier, a little further away. My head felt lighter, my thoughts slower, like I was in a dream. It wasn't bad, not at all. It was...comforting, in a strange way, and my nerves felt softened, my fear removed. The more I drank, the more I felt like I could forget about everything—about being here, about Hernández, about this entire mess.

Hernández and Regina watched me with curiosity, and I couldn't help but feel a little dizzy. The tent was spinning slightly, the edges of the café lights softening.

Maybe it was the drink, or maybe it was what Regina had told me earlier, but for the first time, I felt like I could let go, let the drink do its work, let the warmth fill me up. I didn't think about how I was here against my will, how I wasn't supposed to be drinking this at all, or what it might mean for me. For a few seconds, I felt light, almost weightless, as if the world had shifted, and I wasn't quite so trapped anymore.

Before I knew it, I had finished the glass.

The mariachi band played loudly, filling the air with lively music. The guitars strummed in perfect harmony while the trumpet blasted a bright, cheerful tune. Guests swirled around the dance floor, laughing and clapping to the rhythm of the song, a colorful blur of swirling dresses and sharp suits under the warm glow of the tent's string lights. The scent of spices and sizzling meat floated through the air, making my stomach growl.

Servants moved through the crowd, holding trays loaded with food—tacos, tamales, and fresh salsas. The flavors of Mexico filled the air, and my mouth watered at the sight of the dishes being passed around. A servant, his white shirt crisply pressed, approached me and silently took my empty margarita glass. He replaced it with another, but I barely noticed, my eyes locked on the food.

I hadn't eaten since that roadside restaurant at two in the afternoon, and now it was well past nine. My stomach was growling in protest, and I realized how hungry I was. It wasn't like me to eat so late. Normally, I would have been in bed by now, wrapped up in a blanket, half asleep with Abe by my side.

If I was going to make it through this reception, I needed some energy. I glanced at the tacos again, noticing the soft tortillas piled high with seasoned beef and shredded chicken, topped with fresh cilantro and onions. The tamales, wrapped in corn husks, steamed gently in the warm air. I picked up a taco and took a bite, the flavors exploding in my mouth—spicy, smoky, with the right amount of salt.

I kept eating, one taco after another, not paying attention to the guests around me or the music that continued to play. My focus was on the food filling the empty space inside me. I didn't want to think about the rest of it, about what I was forced to be a part of.

"Don't eat too much," Regina warned me with a teasing smile. "You've got to keep that beautiful figure of yours. And you don't want to get all bloated."

I nodded, taking a slow sip of my drink.

"Cheers." Regina raised her glass, and we clinked them together before I took another long swallow. I had a feeling we would become good friends if I couldn't figure out a way out of this situation. That was the only thing keeping me sane right now.

I glanced around the room, searching for Abe. There he was, sitting at a table in the corner, his elbow resting on the wood, chin in his hand, watching me closely. My heart rate picked up. I gave him a silent look, hoping my thoughts were clear: *Help*. He didn't smile back, but a flicker of understanding lit his eyes. This wasn't what I wanted. This wasn't what either of us wanted. But we had no choice but to play along.

The reception felt like it was dragging on forever, but I wanted it to last as long as possible to avoid the moment when the guests would leave and I'd be alone with Hernández. As the night stretched into the early morning, the band wrapped up their last song, and the bartender called out "Last call!" Alejandro's team began pulling up cars for the guests. I quickly drained the rest of my margarita, hoping the alcohol would numb whatever feelings I had left.

The moment the last guest left, Hernández appeared at my side. He took my arm gently but firmly, his grip like a chain around my wrist. Without a word, he led me toward the back patio. He didn't ask permission. He swept me into his arms. I froze, but he didn't seem to notice. He carried me across the threshold, his stride steady as he walked me up the stairs and into the room where I was supposed to spend my wedding night.

I couldn't breathe.

The bedroom was quiet, too quiet. The soft light from the lamps on the nightstands flickered, casting shadows on the walls. Hernández set me down on the bed with a soft thud. His hands lingered on my waist before he stepped back, eyes fixed on me. I wanted to say something to stop this from happening, but the words were stuck in my throat.

"Are you ready?" he asked, his voice low. It sent a chill through me.

I swallowed, my heart racing. I wasn't ready. Not at all.

TWENTY-FOUR

When I woke up the next morning, sunlight was pouring through the heavy velvet curtains of the tall windows. The room was quiet, still, and a little too perfect. Hernández was gone, and I was alone in the soft white sheets of the king-sized bed. My head throbbed from dehydration, and I felt a wave of nausea roll through me. I sat up, wrapping the sheets around my bare body, my skin still tingling with the remnants of the night before.

I closed my eyes tightly and shook my head back and forth, trying to shake the memories of last night out of my head. I felt like I had betrayed Abe, the only man I'd ever been with. He was my true husband, and I loved him. But there was nothing I could have done to stop Hernández. And after the wedding ceremony, Hernández had no idea he had done anything wrong.

I balled my hands into fists and pounded the mattress on either side of where I sat. *Why did Abe tell them I'm his sister?* None of this would have happened if he hadn't done that.

Jehovah, where are you now? Where were you last night? How could you let this happen to me? What about your promises? Tears prickled in the corners of my eyes.

Trust Jehovah, my Princess.

My eyes darted around the room at the voice, but no one else was there. *Who said that?* I pulled the sheets closer around my body, more aware of my nakedness than I had been before I heard the voice. I sat, tangled up in the sheets, waiting for the voice to speak again, but nothing happened.

After ten minutes of silence, I glanced down at the floor in search of my underwear. I spotted them folded and placed on the ottoman. "Honey must have done that," I said to myself, trying to push the images of the previous night out of my head.

The room was still, and I felt exposed. I untangled myself from the sheets and got up quickly, pulling on my underwear and walking to the washroom. The large walk-in closet was filled with expensive, elegant clothes, all of which I knew would fit me perfectly. Dresses, skirts, blouses—all new, all made for someone who belonged in this world. Someone who didn't feel like a prisoner. Someone who wasn't me.

On the edge of the bathtub lay a soft white robe. Below it, on the floor, were a pair of fluffy white slippers. I slipped them on, feeling a little more secure now that I was covered. But it wasn't enough to erase the feeling of being used, of being cheap. The previous night haunted me. Hernández had been a perfect gentleman, and under any other circumstances, it would have been a wonderful night. But I felt like I was betraying Abe. I felt like I had been purchased from him like property. I felt dirty.

I wanted to wash everything away—every touch, every scent, every memory. The thoughts of last night made my skin crawl, and I was desperate to find some way to feel clean again. Turning on the hot water at the bathtub, I waited for the steam to rise, but before I could climb in, I heard the bedroom door open and shut.

My heart skipped a beat, and my mouth went dry. *Is he back already? Is Hernández coming for more?* I rushed to close the washroom door, trying to block myself from view.

"Señora?" A soft voice called from the other side of the door. It was only Honey.

I let out a sigh of relief and opened the washroom door. She stepped in, holding a fresh pair of underwear in her hands. I pointed to the bathtub and said, "Bath?" I wasn't sure if she understood the word, but she smiled softly and reached beneath the sink to grab a bubble bar. She crushed it under the running water, and soon, the bathtub filled with soft, frothy bubbles. When the water was high enough, I quickly undressed and slid into the tub, letting the warm water wash over me.

Honey sat behind me, gently working the hairspray and styling products out of my hair with careful strokes. I grabbed a washcloth and began scrubbing my skin, trying to get rid of every trace of Hernández, the night, the guilt, and the feeling that I was nothing more than an object to be used. The warm water soothed my aching body, but it did nothing to soothe the ache inside me.

I mimed drinking from a glass, and Honey understood right away. She stood, dried her hands, and left the room. A few minutes later, she came back with a bottle of water, unscrewed the cap, and handed it to me. I drank it down quickly, hoping it would help with my pounding headache.

I didn't want to leave the bath. I felt so much cleaner in the warm, bubbling water. My skin was tingling, my thoughts a little clearer. But I couldn't stay here forever. *Is this going to be my life now?* I had never imagined being trapped in a world like this.

Hernández wasn't just any man. He was like a god, a man who controlled the largest cartel in Mexico. He'd made a name for himself. Everyone, from the richest to the poorest, answered to him. He had all the power and wealth a man could want, and he had built an empire. In his world, luxury was normal. Any girl would be happy to live in his mansion with servants at her beck and call and endless clothes and jewelry.

But I wasn't made for a life of luxury. I was a girl of the reservation, a girl from poverty. I was supposed to follow Jehovah to the land He promised, where I could raise my children in peace. I wanted a man who had given up the chance to make a name for himself by the very act of choosing me—a barren woman—as his wife. I wanted a peace Hernández's empire could never give me—the peace of Jehovah and the simplicity of a life with Abe, where I could trust Jehovah would provide for us no matter what.

The warm water was starting to prune my skin, so I stood and reached for the towel Honey handed me. She helped wrap it around me as I stepped out of the tub, and I slipped into the fresh underwear she'd brought. I pulled on the robe again, feeling a little more like myself.

Honey helped me with my hair and makeup, but this time, it was simpler. No fancy wedding look, just a look for a regular day. I walked over to the closet, unsure of what to wear. I had no idea what the day would hold, and I was about to ask Honey when I realized I didn't know how to ask in Spanish.

It hit me. My phone! I'd had it in my back pocket yesterday. I turned to Honey and mimicked talking into a phone. She nodded and quickly left the room, returning a moment later with my phone. I turned it on and opened the Google Translate app. Using voice-to-text, I spoke into the phone, asking, "What are we doing today? What's on the agenda?" I hit the speaker button, and the app's robotic voice said, "¿Qué vamos a hacer hoy? ¿Qué hay en la agenda?"

Honey's face lit up with a huge smile, clearly fascinated by the technology. She took the phone from me and replied, "Almuerzo y visita a la finca. Paseo a caballo por los alrededores." I hit the speaker button and heard, "Lunch and visit to the farm. Horseback riding in the surrounding area."

I smiled back at her, relieved we now had a way to communicate.

I picked out a pair of designer jeans and a simple red V-neck blouse and held them up to show Honey. They seemed perfect for a casual day like the one she described. If I needed to change later, I could always do that. She nodded, so I quickly dressed. She added a stunning diamond necklace and tear-drop earrings to my outfit. Normally, I would never wear jewelry like that on a regular day, but she seemed to know what she was doing, so I went along with it.

I followed Honey downstairs and into a huge dining room that immediately took my breath away. The ceilings stretched high above us, painted in soft shades of gold and cream. Hand-painted mythical scenes and swirly patterns covered the walls, giving the room a magical feel. In the center of the ceiling hung an enormous chandelier, its crystals catching the light coming from the tall windows and scattering it across the room like glitter.

At the center of the room was a massive dark-wood dining table. It was so big it could easily fit twenty people, maybe more. The surface was so shiny it almost looked like a mirror, reflecting the grandness of the room around it. A crisp white table runner stretched down the middle of the table, the edges decorated with delicate silver stitching that sparkled under the light. Each place setting was perfectly arranged with fine china, crystal glasses, and polished silverware.

On either side of the dining room, tall windows stretched from floor to ceiling, framed by rich red and gold velvet curtains. Through the glass, I could see the lush gardens outside, with fountains and winding paths leading off into the distance. Sunlight poured in, warming the room.

The floors were made of smooth terracotta tiles, their earthy red tones balancing out the room's fancy decorations. Colorful antique rugs covered parts of the floor, their bright patterns adding warmth to the space. At the far end of the room was a giant black marble fireplace, currently unlit.

The group was already seated when I walked in. The head of the table was empty, waiting for me. Abe and Louis were closest to my seat. Amelia and Emma were trying to keep the kids from knocking over the fine china as they squirmed in their seats, waiting for lunch to start. I was relieved to see Hernández wasn't with them.

As soon as I was in my chair, servants appeared from all sides, moving quickly around the table. One filled our glasses with water while others set down huge platters of food in the middle of the table. The lids were lifted, revealing steaming empanadas, fluffy rice, beans, and fresh salsa. Another servant brought glasses of a milky-looking drink (which I later learned was horchata) and handed one to each adult. They replaced the kids' fine china with plastic plates and gave them plastic cups with the same drink.

Once everyone had food, the servants quietly slipped away, leaving us alone in the dining room. Thankfully, the kids were making enough noise to keep everyone distracted, allowing me to avoid talking about what had happened yesterday.

Louis broke the silence. "Hernández gave me a brand-new motor coach, Princess. Now Olivia and I will have a home when we get back to Texas."

I winced at Hernández's name but forced a smile. "That's cool. I'd love to see it." I was happy for Louis. He and Olivia deserved the very best, and he likely wouldn't have been able to afford a place for them to live on their own. They would have had to stay with us in our RV had we not run into Hernández.

Louis continued, clearly proud of his new gifts. "He gave Abe a brand-new Range Rover P530 and upgraded his RV to the best one on the market." He paused, looking at Abe across the table. It was clear Abe wasn't going to discuss it. I wasn't sure if he was more embarrassed by the gifts he had accepted or worried about what had happened to me last night. "He also invested over a million dollars in Abe's company," Louis continued.

"Wow!" I said, trying to sound impressed. "Abe is a good negotiator with investors!" It was generous of Hernández, but I wasn't sure how I felt about it. These were things I'd never get to enjoy, things I wouldn't even see much now that I was stuck here in Mexico. I guessed this was his version of a "dowry" for me.

"When we get back to Texas, Abe's letting Liam's family use your old RV so it's not so crowded," Henry added excitedly.

They all seemed so thrilled about the new things they were getting. I glanced at Abe. He hadn't said a word. He was poking at his rice with his fork, staring at his plate. He must have been embarrassed. He had lied, essentially sold me to Hernández, and now he was benefiting tremendously from the "deal." I was furious with him, but a lot of what had happened was out of his control, and he looked like he was suffering, too.

When everyone had finished eating, servants came to clear the plates. All but one servant left. The remaining servant was young, maybe in his late teens or early twenties, with short dark hair and brown, almond-shaped eyes that crinkled when he smiled. He was handsome, about average height with a muscular build that showed through his uniform.

He smiled warmly at us and said, "Hola, my name is Eduardo, but you can call me Eddy. I've been looking after Abe during your stay, but since I'm the only servant here who speaks fluent English, I'll be your tour guide today as we explore La Mansión de Tampico." He waved his hand around the room.

"La Mansión de Tampico isn't in Tampico. It's about an hour and forty-five minutes north, tucked away in the rolling hills along the Tampico/Ciudad Victoria route. The house was built in 1979 by Jefe Gallardo, but Jefe Hernández has owned it since the pandemic in 2020."

He continued, "La Mansión de Tampico is one of seven homes, all similar to this one, that Jefe Hernández controls. They're all built along the drug routes in Mexico. Jefe Hernández visits each house when he has business in the area. This home employs about a hundred servants who cook, clean, look after the people, take care of events like the wedding yesterday, drive, maintain the gardens, work security, and take care of the horses and stables. There are also fields of marijuana worked by another two hundred people, mostly forced labor brought here from other countries. Señora Isa," he nodded toward me, bowing slightly, "is now the head of this home and the grounds, which we'll explore today.

"We'll do a quick tour of the house then head out to the stables to take the horses around the grounds. Please follow me," Eddy said as he turned toward the swinging double doors the servants had used when bringing in the food earlier.

Eddy brought us through the massive kitchen, complete with double ovens, industrial refrigerators and freezers tucked into the cabinetry, a massive stove with multiple burners, griddles, a wood-fired pizza oven, and a special area for making Mexican dishes with a grinding stone for masa and a molcajete for salsas. In one corner, a smaller space was set up for baking, complete with a marble countertop, an antique rolling pin, and rows of traditional clay baking dishes.

He pointed out the wooden doors that led to the impressive pantry and a glass door that led to a wine cellar. Along another side of the kitchen, there was a casual dining nook with high stools at a bar. Bright handwoven textiles, draped over the stools and hanging from the windows, added pops of color.

I had never seen a kitchen so amazing and imagined cooking meals here myself. I doubted I'd get the chance to do so, though, since servants made the food and waited on me hand and foot.

Eddy led us to the end of the kitchen near the dining nook and through swinging double doors that led to a playroom. The moment we entered the playroom, the kids jumped up and cheered. This must've been the room they'd been in yesterday when Hernández had talked to us before the wedding. It was a huge square room with high ceilings, and it was filled with an indoor playground. Colorful tubes snaked across the ceiling, with five different slides curving down to soft play mats below. There was a hanging bridge about eight feet off the ground between two of the tubes and a ball pit near one of the slides. A fake rock wall led up one side to more playground tubes, and on the other side, a giant toy bin overflowed with all kinds of toys.

"If you'd like, we can leave the kids here while we continue the tour," Eddy suggested, glancing at Amelia and Emma. "Ruby and Crystal will be happy to watch them." The kids looked up at them, bouncing in excitement and nodding eagerly.

"Please, Mommy?" Harper tugged on Emma's shirt.

Emma smiled and nodded. "Sure, that's fine." She turned to Eddy. "Can you make sure they have our cell phone numbers in case they need us?"

"Absolutely," Eddy assured her. "They'll be well taken care of. Ruby and Crystal are amazing with kids."

We left the kids behind with the two middle-aged servants and continued our tour through the main level of the house. We passed through the mudroom and into the last room on the main floor, the ballroom.

I'd had no idea houses could have ballrooms. The space was massive, with high ceilings covered in beautiful crystal chandeliers that sparkled like diamonds in the sunlight coming through the tall arched windows along the far wall. The floors were covered in hardwood that resembled a zebra's pelt, with dark and light stripes alternating along the wide space. The left wall was covered in mirrors giving the illusion the room went on forever.

Off the ballroom were large washrooms, both men's and women's, designed like conference center washrooms, with multiple stalls and sinks. The floor-to-ceiling doors of the stalls were ivory-painted wood with carvings of vines and flowers. The vanity was thick ivory marble with veins of gray and silver.

After the ballroom, we went through the study where we'd been the day before then back into the grand foyer with its sweeping staircases.

Eddy took us upstairs to show us the bedrooms. Eight bedrooms lined the second-floor hallway, each with its own washroom. None of the guest rooms were as big as mine, but they were as luxurious, decorated with similar styles but different accent colors. The guest rooms for Liam's and James's families had small studies off to the side where bunk beds had been set up for the kids. Hernández's suite was right next to mine. It was the only bedroom bigger than mine, big enough that our entire house from the reservation would have fit inside it. It had a full study separated from the bedroom by double French doors.

This place, with all its rooms and their extravagant décor, felt more like a five-star hotel than a home. I couldn't believe how much my life had changed in one year, from living in poverty to living in a mansion. But this new life, full of luxury, also came with danger.

TWENTY-FIVE

After we finished touring the huge house, Eddy led us outside to show us the grounds. We stepped out through the mudroom and onto the back patio, and immediately, the thick, humid air of the Mexican countryside hit me. Above us, dark clouds swirled and twisted, churning like they were alive, ready to explode and drench the world below. The wind whipped through the bushes and tall palm trees, bending them slightly as they tried to hold their ground. The storm wasn't here yet, but it was coming. The hurricane was still on track to hit Corpus Christi tonight. We were far enough from the eye of the storm that we wouldn't get the worst of it, but we could feel its outer bands. The air was thick with tension, the trees groaned under the pressure of the wind, and the sky seemed to press down on us.

Eddy saw me looking up at the sky. "We better get going before the rain comes. We have ponchos in case it starts before we're done."

The water in the pool in front of us was moving with the wind, almost like a river's current. To the left of the pool stood a large pool house, its white exterior blending nicely with the lush greenery around it, which was also bending with the wind.

Eddy pointed it out. "That's where all the pool equipment and toys are stored—floats, noodles, beach balls, that kind of thing," he said. But there was more to it than that. We walked over to the wide-open doors, which revealed a full-sized gym inside the pool house. We could see rows of cardio machines, like treadmills and stationary bikes, along with racks of Olympic barbells and dumbbells. It was a fitness buff's dream.

I raised an eyebrow, glancing at Eddy's well-toned arms peeking out from under his shirt. "Do you use this gym, Eddy?"

He smiled. "Yes, señora. Every day," he said, a little proudly. "Hernández does, too. He can lift way more than me, though."

I had no doubt about that. Hernández was built like a man who could handle the challenges that came his way. I had been able to see every bit of his muscular arms and legs and perfectly toned abs last night. I couldn't help but be impressed by Eddy, too. His muscles spoke of his hard work.

Beyond the gym, the pool house had a kitchen, smaller than the one in the mansion but still much bigger than the one I'd grown up with on the reservation. It also had a bedroom and washroom, both of which looked like mini versions of the ones inside the house.

Eddy motioned for us to follow him, and we walked past the pool and the pool house down a stone path lined with flowers and tall trees. The path led to a large building I hadn't noticed before. It looked more utilitarian than any of the other buildings on the property.

"This is where the servants' quarters are," Eddy explained as we neared the building. "Many of the staff come and go from their homes in the village, but there are some that stay here permanently. This is where I live."

The building had a more modest feel than the mansion but was still well-kept. It was separate from the main house and was much like a dormitory at a college or boarding school.

We continued down a long cobblestone path to the right of the servants' quarters to a large stable. Several carriages and horse trailers were parked in front of it. Inside the stable was a large riding ring with stalls around the edges. Horses were available for each adult, and several stable boys were getting them ready for the ride.

"All of our horses are specially trained with calm tempera-ments," Eddy said. "Is there anyone here who's never ridden before?"

Most of the Houston group raised their hands. Despite Texas being full of ranches, most of them came from the city, where there weren't as many opportunities to ride. Abe, Louis, and I had ridden horses before on the reservation.

"Hmm...maybe we should take the carriages, then," Eddy said. He turned to the stable boys and spoke quickly in Spanish. They started leading the horses toward the carriages to hook them up.

"I'd like to ride a horse," I said. I hadn't done it in a while, but I would rather ride than sit awkwardly next to Abe in a carriage.

"Of course, señora," Eddy said with a smile. "Anyone else?"

"I will," Louis said, grinning at me.

Eddy spoke more to the stable boys in Spanish, and they got the horses ready for us. Once two of the carriages were prepared, Liam, Amelia, James, Emma, Theo, Henry, and Abe climbed into them. Eddy helped me swing into the saddle of my black stallion while Louis got onto his. Eddy mounted a third horse and led the way, with the carriage drivers following behind us.

Eddy showed us the two large back lawns that had been used for the wedding the day before. Now, they were quiet and empty; the chairs, tents, and tables from yesterday had been removed. Only the meticulously manicured grass and rows of bushes and flowering plants along the edges remained. Beyond the lawns, a tall fence separated the estate from fields of cannabis blowing in the harsh wind and stretching for miles. We could see the wide-brimmed hats of workers harvesting the plants scattered across the fields.

As we rode through the grounds, Eddy kept talking. "I was born in Texas. That's why I'm one of the few English speakers here. Most of the servants are local, born or at least raised in Mexico."

"Were you here when the last wife was still around?" I asked.

"Yeah. That was a disaster. She was too good for her own good, if you know what I mean," Eddy said, glancing over at me from his horse.

I nodded. I remembered what Regina had told me.

"She was a Catholic school girl. Very beautiful. Won the local beauty contest in Tampico—Miss Teen Tampico," Eddy continued, his voice casual, like he was enjoying the conversation. But I couldn't shake the feeling that his loose lips could get him into trouble if he wasn't careful. "She was only sixteen when Hernández took her, right out of her home, against her will. Her parents got a nice amount of money for her. Families always get taken care of, you know? But she couldn't handle it. She was young, naive. She was in love with another man and thought if she turned Hernández in, she could escape and run away with him. Now both of them are missing."

The story made my stomach twist. Sixteen. Like me. She was in love with someone else, like I was with Abe. My heart sank. I'd been so hard on Abe, but was it his fault? He was trying to protect us. He had done the best he could under impossible circumstances. But what if, by following Hernández's plans, we had signed our own fate? What if we ended up like her...missing? I pushed the thought away.

We moved on through the fields, the thick green of the marijuana plants stretching out before us. Eddy kept talking, his voice steady and confident as he gave us a tour of the operation. He explained how the marijuana was grown, how it was processed, and how Hernández also trafficked cocaine from Colombia through this very route. This estate wasn't merely some rich guy's playground. It was part of a farm, a network, one of many in Hernández's sprawling empire.

"Jefe Hernández is a dangerous man," Eddy said, glancing over at me, his eyes serious now. "He's built this from the ground up over the past twenty years. Anyone who lasts long in the cartel is either lucky, smart, or both."

I felt his words settle in my chest. Hernández wasn't just some criminal. He was powerful, ruthless, and smart. He wasn't someone you could walk away from. Every part of this place, from the fields to the mansion, was built on danger, and every second we spent here dragged us deeper into this trap, like we were sinking into quicksand.

When Eddy finished the tour, he led us back to the stables to drop off the horses and carriages with the stable boys.

"Did you like the horse, Louis?" Eddy asked.

Louis grinned, clearly still feeling the excitement from the ride. "Yes, very much. It's such a beautiful creature. So smooth and calm. And so well-trained."

Eddy's eyes brightened with pride. "That's great to hear because it's yours. Hernández is giving you and Abe the horses that you and Señora Isa rode today."

Louis's jaw dropped. "Really?" He blinked, his eyebrows shooting up.

"Yes, if you want them. Hernández says you're starting your own ranch up in South Texas when you get back, and he thought the horses would be the perfect start to your new venture," Eddy explained. "He's even sending two of the stable boys with you to help. They'll drive the horse trailer and can take care of the horses on the way and help you settle them in."

Louis's eyes widened even more, and he gave the horse a gentle pat on its neck. "Wow! That's way too generous!" He shook his head in disbelief. "But you're right. I honestly have no idea how to take care of horses. We had some on the reservation, but they weren't ours, so I never had to look after them."

Eddy nodded knowingly. "Well, now they're yours. And the stable boys can help you with them. They're good at building things, too, so they can help you set up the stables. They're very handy."

"That's pretty amazing," Louis said, his voice quieter now, more thoughtful. "It's...a lot to take in."

"Hernández wants to make sure you are well taken care of," Eddy said with a smile.

After we left the horses with the stable boys, we walked around the side of the house to the overflow parking lot. "This is where Alejandro and his team park the cars when we have events," Eddy explained.

I spotted the RV we'd been using for the past year along with Abe's Jeep. Nearby were Mateo's two RVs and James and Emma's SUV.

Also in the parking lot was a shiny new black Range Rover hooked up to the biggest RV I had ever seen. This must have been the SUV and RV Louis had been talking about earlier, the one Hernández had given Abe in exchange for me. They were both extremely nice and extremely expensive, toys reserved only for the very wealthy.

Next to that one was something even more impressive—a luxury motor coach that gleamed under the sun.

Louis's face lit up the moment he saw it. "Princess, you've got to see this!" he said, practically bouncing with excitement. He grabbed my hand and pulled me toward the motor coach. It was like he had discovered treasure.

I couldn't blame him for being so excited. The RV was unlike any I had ever seen. It was way more luxurious than the trailer we had back on the reservation. This was a mobile mansion. It must have cost a fortune, but it was nothing to Hernández. For him, it was another luxury item purchased to launder his money. Louis was right; it was the perfect home for him and Olivia. I tried to muster a smile, to pretend I was happy for him, but inside, I felt miserable. Was Louis going to accept this, a house bought with money from drug trafficking?

I couldn't help but think about the last Tampico wife, the one who had been "too good for her own good." I was more like her than not. The thought of accepting gifts bought with drug money made me feel sick.

But more than the money, my sick feeling came from the way Hernández thought of me. The way he made it clear that the gifts he gave us, these RVs, the clothes, the horses, came with a price. It made me feel small, like I wasn't a person, but a possession. Something he could buy and own like any other object. I felt like I was losing myself piece by piece.

And by accepting all these gifts, it was like Abe was giving up, admitting I now belonged to Hernández...forever.

TWENTY-SIX

When the tour ended, it was siesta time. Most of the servants took a break, resting before the evening activities began, and the house grew quiet. But the calm didn't last long.

The rain started shortly after we got back. It began with a few light drops but quickly turned into a downpour. It was like someone had turned on a faucet on full blast and forgotten to turn it off. The rain slammed in sheets against the western-facing windows, the sound echoing through the house, constant and deafening. The wind picked up, howling through the vents in the walls, sending chills down my spine. Its eerie whistle seemed to bounce around in the empty spaces, making the house feel even bigger, colder. We were more than four hundred miles south of the hurricane's eye, but the storm was so massive we could still feel its power. The wind and rain stretched out over the land like an angry beast, reminding us how far-reaching it was. We weren't in the worst of it, but its fury was impossible to ignore.

We huddled together in the sitting room playing board games, waiting for the storm to pass, thankful we weren't still in South Texas. I couldn't imagine how terrifying it must have been there if it was even half as bad as it was here. This would be the first Category Five hurricane to hit South Texas since Hurricane Allen in 1980, and I worried about the people who lived there and hoped they had all managed to evacuate. The people we'd met in South Texas had been so kind, welcoming us with hugs and making sure we felt at home. I hated to think about what they were facing right now.

Out of nowhere, the front door flew open, and Hernández stumbled inside, drenched from head to toe, water dripping from his body and clothes onto the marble tiles in steady streams. He looked disoriented, his face pale and his legs unsteady. For a moment, he stood there, swaying, as if trying to make sense of where he was. With a quiet groan, he collapsed to the floor, crumpling like a rag doll.

The rain poured in through the open door, soaking his still form. I was frozen, staring at him in shock, when another man hurried in after him. I recognized him as one of the tenientes who had been sitting with Hernández at the wedding ceremony the day before. After shutting the door behind him, closing out the rain and wind, the teniente dropped to the floor beside Hernández, his hands quickly checking for signs of life. I could see the shallow rise and fall of Hernández's chest, but it was faint, barely noticeable.

The house was eerily quiet, with no servants around due to the siesta. But the teniente spotted us in the sitting room and shouted in panic, "¡Rápido! ¡Necesitamos un médico!" His voice echoed through the house. "¡Ayuda! ¡Ayuda!" he yelled into the air.

In an instant, servants seemed to appear out of nowhere, rushing from every corner of the house. They shouted to each other in fast Spanish, moving quickly and with purpose. I couldn't understand most of it, but I could tell by the frantic energy in the air that something was seriously wrong. My hands went to my mouth, and I stepped closer to the doorway between the sitting room and the foyer. Hernández's body twitched, his face pale, and his breath came in shallow gasps. It reminded me of the day I'd found Grandad seizing on the floor in the RV.

One of the servants checked Hernández's pulse while another felt his forehead with the back of their hand, whispering urgently to each other. Several male servants carefully lifted Hernández's limp body off the floor and began carrying him upstairs. The teniente followed closely behind them, his face full of worry, and they disappeared down the upstairs hallway.

"What's happening?" I asked, turning to Theo and Henry, who both spoke Spanish.

"He's sick. High fever," Theo said quietly. "They're taking him to his room until the doctor arrives."

The servants were now cleaning the water that had flooded in with Hernández. They moved with quiet efficiency. I felt completely useless.

"What can I do?" I asked, the words coming out in a rush. "Theo, ask them. Can I see him?"

Theo turned to one of the servants who was mopping the floor. "¿Puede Señora Isa ver a Hernández?" he asked gently. "Ella quiere estar con él."

By now, everyone in our group had gathered behind me, watching in stunned silence as the scene unfolded. The servant paused, looking up from her work, her eyes flicking toward us. She raised one finger, signaling for us to wait, then disappeared up the stairs, heading toward Hernández's suite.

I felt like an outsider, trapped in a moment I couldn't control. All I could do was hope the doctor would get here soon enough.

As if the universe had heard my desperate thoughts, there was a sharp knock on the door. Maria rushed to answer it, revealing the doctor standing in the doorway, his black medical bag in hand and a stethoscope draped around his neck. It felt surreal. I'd never seen a doctor make a house call before. The doctor nodded to Maria and walked past her up the stairs without a word, rain dripping from his coat onto the tiles. He seemed to know exactly where he was going, as if he had been here many times before.

I stayed put, trying not to let my nerves show. The minutes stretched on, but before I could get too lost in my thoughts, the servant returned and told me I could go up and see Hernández.

I climbed the stairs slowly, my footsteps echoing in the quiet house. The hallway was dimly lit, and I hesitated outside the door for a moment. It was slightly cracked, so I pushed it open. Hernández was lying on the right side of the king-sized bed, his shirt gone, a cold compress pressed to his forehead. His body was covered in a red rash. Bright, angry patches stretched across his chest and stomach.

The doctor was sitting on the edge of the bed, his eyes focused on Hernández's body as he examined the large, discolored marks on the man's chest. The teniente perched on an armchair by the window, his brow furrowed. There was a worried look in his eyes.

I cleared my throat, stepping into the room. The doctor looked up, and so did the teniente, who rose from his chair respectfully.

"Señora," the teniente greeted me, his voice low. He gave a slight nod of acknowledgment, his eyes scanning me briefly before returning to the doctor's examination.

"How is he?" I asked, my voice barely above a whisper as I approached the bed. I was trying not to show how scared I was, but the sight of Hernández in such a condition made my hands tremble.

"He's very weak," the doctor replied, his accent thick but understandable. I was grateful he spoke English. "His fever is high, too high. We must be careful. This could be something serious."

I swallowed hard, trying to process his words. As I moved closer to the bed, I could see the full extent of the rash. It wasn't a simple irritation. It was spreading quickly, red and blotchy. A few of the patches even looked swollen, raised above the skin. It was like the disease was eating away at his skin through the painful boils.

"How did he get that rash?" I asked, my voice cracking slightly. "It wasn't there last night."

The doctor frowned, jotting notes down in his notebook. "That's what I'm trying to figure out. A rash like this doesn't show up so suddenly, especially when there was no sign of it yesterday."

"None at all!" I said. "He was perfectly fine last night. We...we consummated our marriage. He seemed in good health."

"Good to know," the doctor said, his pen scratching against the pad as he continued his notes. He turned toward the teniente. "When did he start feeling unwell?"

The teniente shifted uncomfortably in his chair, his face drained of color. "He said he wasn't feeling well right around noon today. We were in Tampico. He wanted to go home, so we left. But it got worse on the drive back."

The doctor nodded thoughtfully. "Very strange. What did he eat today? Anything unusual?"

The teniente paused, trying to remember. "We had a late lunch, fish. Nothing out of the ordinary."

"Hmm...." The doctor rubbed his chin. He leaned over to inspect Hernández's face more closely. His skin had taken on a yellowish tint, and his lips were dry and cracked. Small, ulcer-like sores were starting to form along the edges of his mouth. "I've seen this before," the doctor said slowly. "This could be a case of syphilis, or possibly leprosy. Both of these conditions can cause sudden fevers and rashes like this."

I felt my blood run cold. Syphilis? Leprosy? I'd heard of their terrible symptoms, how syphilis could start with rashes and sores before turning far worse if left untreated. And leprosy, the slow, creeping disease that ate away at skin and nerves. But both diseases seemed like they belonged in another time, another world.

"Is he contagious?" I asked, my voice tight with fear. We had been close last night, after all.

The doctor's expression remained calm, though his eyes were full of concern. "It's possible. Both diseases can be transmitted through direct contact. But we need to confirm what it is before we can be certain."

As the doctor finished speaking, the teniente turned pale, his hand clutching the armrest of his chair. He let out a soft groan, his eyes fluttering. Before anyone could react, he slumped back against the chair, unconscious.

The doctor and I exchanged a look, both of us surprised. "Maybe you should check him out, too," I suggested, my voice a little too light, trying to cover up my unease.

The doctor stood and walked over to the teniente, checking his pulse. He bent over the teniente, and I couldn't help but notice the look of confusion on his face. This wasn't a coincidence. Something was wrong with both men.

A servant rushed into the room, speaking quickly in Spanish. The doctor listened carefully, and they exchanged words for a few minutes before the servant left.

"The whole Monterrey household has similar symptoms to Hernández and Romero," the doctor explained, his brow furrowed with concern. "I think we need to do check-ups on everyone in the house."

I nodded, feeling a mix of worry and confusion. "Can we start with me? I was in closer contact with Hernández than anyone else here...if you know what I mean."

The doctor glanced at me. "Yes, of course. Let's go into your room so I can do an exam."

I led him next door to my room, my heart beating faster than I wanted to admit. The doctor didn't waste time. He did a thorough examination, checking my whole body, including the most private parts, since syphilis needed to be ruled out. I felt a little uncomfortable, but I reminded myself it was necessary.

When he was finished, he seemed satisfied. "You're fine," he said. "No signs of infection. No fever, no rash, nothing abnormal. You're healthy."

I let out a quiet breath of relief. "What about Honey, my personal servant?" I asked. "She was in and out of this room, too."

The doctor nodded. "We should check her as well."

I wasn't sure how to summon her, but as if on cue, Honey's head appeared in the doorway, her brown eyes wide with curiosity. She must have been standing outside the door, waiting for her name to be called.

The doctor explained what he was doing, and Honey nodded, her face a mask of uncertainty. "I'll step out so you can examine her," I said, stepping back from the door.

Honey's examination didn't take long. When the doctor finished, he called back into the room. "She's healthy as well. No signs of anything concerning."

I was glad to hear it, but I still couldn't shake the unease gnawing at me.

The doctor must have felt it, too, because he didn't stop there. He moved on to examine everyone else in the house. He was methodical in his approach, checking each servant who lived on the grounds, each member of our Houston group, and the other servants and people who worked in the house but lived offsite. One by one, they were all cleared. Everyone, except for Hernández and Teniente Romero, was healthy. It seemed like a small miracle.

By the time he finished his rounds, reports began to trickle in from the other households under Hernández's empire. Mulas who worked along the routes between Tampico and Brownsville and through Monterrey started falling sick, showing symptoms similar to Hernández's. Then came the news from Mexico City. The entire household there had developed a rash like his, bright red, spreading, and concerning.

Whatever was happening, it wasn't contained. It was spreading.

Most of the group had gathered in the dining room after their exams, sitting in tense silence. The doctor was there, too, looking over his notes and trying to figure out what to do next. His brow was furrowed, and I could tell he was worried, maybe even more than he was letting on. The rain, battering against the windows, was the only sound.

I broke the silence, my voice cutting through the quiet. "Do we know Hernández's movements before yesterday? Which homes did he visit and in what order?" I glanced around the room. "We've gotten news from Monterrey and Mexico City. What about the other homes?"

The question hung in the air, unanswered. The best person to answer that was the teniente, but he was getting worse by the minute.

"Is there another teniente we could call to ask?" I pressed, my frustration growing. "Does anyone here know his schedule?"

It was crazy how little anyone knew about Hernández's movements. I supposed it was for security, keeping everyone in the dark in case things went wrong with the operation, but it was a major disadvantage now.

Abe, who had been quiet the whole time, was watching me intently. His gaze was steady, but there was something about it that made me uneasy. I couldn't read what he was thinking. Maybe he was wondering why I cared so much about Hernández, a man I barely knew, who had taken advantage of me, who had ripped me away from my rightful family, and who could end both of our lives without a second thought. I should have been relieved he was incapacitated. That meant he wouldn't be sleeping with me again tonight.

Despite all that, I didn't feel as relieved as I thought I would. Instead, a part of me felt...lost. *Had I already fully accepted my fate here? Had I already given up on whatever hope I'd clung to, the land and children Jehovah had promised us? Had I started to care about Hernández, of all people?*

It had only been about twenty-four hours since we'd arrived, but it had felt like a lifetime. So much had happened, it had gone by in a blur. The wedding, the...er...wedding night, the lavish gifts, the grand tour of the house and grounds, the storm, and now this. It was too much to process in such a short time. No matter how I tried to deny it, feelings deep inside me had changed. Whether or not I'd wanted to be there, I had been pulled into Hernández's world.

TWENTY-SEVEN

The storm outside had grown fiercer, the wind howling like a wild animal and whipping the trees around like they were twigs. Rain continued lashing against the windows in relentless sheets. But the storm inside Hernández's empire was even worse. It wasn't just Monterrey and Mexico City anymore. Now, the Guadalajara and Chihuahua households had also joined the ranks of the sick. Even the mulas working the routes around those cities were being hit with the mysterious illness.

Louis, who had been quiet for a while, spoke up. "Have we heard from anyone outside of Hernández's organization getting this sickness? Is it a disease that's spreading nationally? Like the Covid-19 pandemic?"

The doctor shook his head. "I haven't heard anything about anyone outside the organization being affected," he said, his tone measured but tired. "I don't usually talk to people outside this circle. I'm here to serve Hernández's operation. He likes to keep his people separate from the outside world to prevent any leaks."

Louis frowned, looking unsatisfied but understanding. The secrecy made sense. Hernández ran a tight ship, and any information getting out could be dangerous.

Liam, who had been pacing nervously in the corner, chimed in. "Do you have any former colleagues or classmates you trust? Maybe someone who still works in public health or medicine? You could ask them casually if they've heard of any disease like this happening outside the cartel."

The doctor hesitated for a moment then nodded slowly. "I could try. It's a risk, but it might be worth it."

I could see the wheels turning in his head. The doctor was clearly thinking about his next move, weighing his options carefully. If this illness was contained to Hernández's people, it could remain a mystery for a while. If it was spreading to the general population, though, it could be much more serious.

Meanwhile, Hernández himself had not gotten any worse, but he hadn't improved either. He hadn't left his bed except to use the washroom, his body still wracked with fever. The doctor was doing all he could, but his condition seemed stuck, hovering between life and death.

There was a small part of me that wondered what would happen if Hernández didn't get better. With most of his network down with whatever this sickness was, it could cripple his operations, at least for a little while. For a brief moment, the idea of the cartel's influence being weakened felt like a twisted sort of hope.

I caught myself. *What do I want? Do I want to see Hernández get worse, to see his empire fall apart? Or do I merely want a way out of this nightmare, even if that means losing a few cartel lives? Even if his empire does fall apart, will I be in the clear?* I knew a lot about his operations, more than I should know, more than I ever wanted to know. *Will I have a target on my back to ensure I remain silent...forever?*

The storm outside mirrored the one inside my head, confusing, chaotic, and violent. I wasn't sure if I could weather it.

Eddy walked into the dining room. "We got word from Hermosillo," he said. "They've been hit with the sickness, too."

The room fell silent as everyone processed the news.

Then James spoke up, his voice filled with concern. "So, in a matter of hours, the entire cartel has been affected. The entire cartel except for the people employed in this house." He paused, eyeing the group. "Are we next?"

A chill ran through me. The thought of the sickness spreading to us felt inevitable.

Emma, who had been holding her breath, turned to the doctor. "How do we stop this thing?" she asked, her voice shaky. "We have children in the house. We don't need them to get sick."

The doctor ran a hand through his hair, looking as exhausted as everyone felt. "It's hard to say without knowing exactly what it is," he answered, his tone low. "I need to call the other doctors in the cartel to compare notes. It might even be time to contact the World Health Organization to see if anyone else is being affected." He stood, his face set with purpose, and left the room to make the necessary calls. As soon as the door closed behind him, a heavy silence settled in again.

Out of nowhere, Abe perked up. His eyes narrowed as he motioned for Louis and me to follow him. He led us into the hallway, away from the others. When we were out of earshot, he spoke quietly but urgently. "What if this is Jehovah's way of saving us?" Abe asked, his voice full of hope. "What if we're supposed to make a run for it while everyone in the cartel is sick? While they're all vulnerable?"

Louis shot him a skeptical look. "That's not going to work, Abe. None of the servants, including the security guards, at this house have gotten the disease. Only Hernández and Romero are sick. If we try to escape, we'll get stopped, maybe even shot, by the guards. You remember their automatic weapons, right?"

Abe sighed. "Fair enough," he muttered. "But there has to be some explanation for it all. Why would every household in Hernández's organization get the same sickness except for this one?"

A thought hit me like a bolt of lightning. "Wait a minute," I said. "What if the servants here aren't getting sick because they're waiting on us? If they get sick, we aren't taken care of. They're the ones who have to be healthy to keep things running."

Abe's eyes widened, looking hopeful again. "If this is Jehovah's doing," he said slowly, "that makes perfect sense."

The idea that we might be spared sent a strange shiver down my spine. It felt like a twisted miracle, and I didn't know if I should be grateful or terrified. But something was happening, and it was bigger than any of us could fully understand. It seemed we were at the center of it all.

***

The first light of the morning filtered through my window, casting warm, golden streaks across the room. I stretched out, feeling the soft, luxurious Egyptian cotton sheets wrap around me like a cloud. The king-sized bed felt perfect. For the first time in what seemed like forever, I had slept through the night without waking up once. I felt refreshed, like I could take on the world.

Outside, the storm had quieted down for now. It had been rolling through all night—those outer bands whipping around and stirring up the air. I didn't know if we were in the clear yet, but for now, it seemed calm.

Hernández had stayed in his room, still sick. I had checked on him before I went to bed. He was covered with angry red sores on his stomach, his palms, his feet, even around his mouth. He still had the high fever, and his throat was so sore he could barely talk. His muscles ached, and he was barely conscious. It was hard to believe this man, this intimidating figure I had been terrified of a day ago, had been neutralized by whatever sickness was plaguing his people.

As I moved around the room, I heard the soft shuffle of footsteps behind me. Honey appeared in the doorway, her face lighting up when she saw me. She pointed to the bathtub and said, "Bath?" Her English was still rough, but I felt a little burst of excitement that she remembered the word I had used yesterday.

I had planned on taking a quick shower, but I smiled at her suggestion. It was a small thing, but it meant she'd been paying attention, and that made me feel a little better about the situation.

I pulled out my phone and opened the translator app. "Did anyone get sick last night?" I typed, watching as the app translated the words into Spanish. "¿Alguien se enfermó anoche?"

Honey shook her head, her dark eyes bright with reassurance. "No," she answered softly. I smiled again, clapping my hands lightly in front of me, relieved.

Honey set about preparing the bath for me. I sank into the warm water, letting the bubbles rise up around me, the heat of the water soothing my tense muscles. I closed my eyes as she gently massaged shampoo into my hair, and my thoughts drifted like the steam curling up into the air.

I couldn't deny the comfort of La Mansión de Tampico. The luxury, the space, and the food were all so different from any place I had ever known. But as nice as it was, I didn't like being separated from Abe. I didn't like the feeling of being treated like a possession.

And there was always the constant fear. Fear of Hernández and the danger that came with being part of his world. Fear of the business he ran, the operations that seemed to stretch far beyond what anyone could see. Fear that, one day, the darkness he carried with him would catch up to me, too.

As Honey finished washing my hair, I let the warm water pull me back into the moment, knowing that for now, at least, it was quiet. But I also knew this calm wouldn't last as long as I was tied to Hernández.

After Honey helped me get ready for the day, I made my way downstairs to the dining room. The smell of the rich and savory breakfast hit me as soon as I stepped into the room. The long dining table was already set with plates of food—steaming guayin, sweet pastries, and egg tacos piled high with salsa and melted cheese. The servants stood nearby, waiting patiently with fresh coffee. As soon as I sat, they filled my cup without a word.

Some of the others were already at the table, enjoying their breakfast. Louis was poking at his eggs while Emma passed around the tacos for Ellie and Harper. The atmosphere was relaxed, almost peaceful, despite the tension that had been hanging over us for days.

Abe came in a few moments later, his tall frame filling the doorway, followed by Liam with Luna and William Junior, who was bouncing around like he always was. The kids scampered to their seats, and the servants quickly swapped their china plates for the plastic ones they'd used the day before. Once they were settled, they dug into their food like they hadn't eaten in days. It was a rare moment of normalcy in a world that felt strange and foreign.

As I was about to take a bite of my taco, the doctor stepped into the room. He didn't waste any time getting to the point. "Hernández's fever has broken," he said, his voice low but clear. "He's feeling a little better. He's conscious now, able to think and reason."

Everyone looked up from their plates, a small ripple of relief spreading through the room. But the doctor wasn't finished. His eyes were darkened with concern.

"Unfortunately," he continued, "the disease has spread to all of Hernández's people. The other households, his tenientes, halcones, mulas, everyone in his organization is now infected. But, strangely, it hasn't affected anyone in this household. No one in the country outside of his cartel has been touched by this illness. And it hasn't spread anywhere else in the world, either."

A strange silence fell over the room. The news was both good and bad, a strange mix that no one knew quite how to react to.

"The good news," the doctor added after a pause, "is that Hernández is aware of the situation. He's been briefed, and he's requesting to see his wife and her immediate family."

Abe, Louis, and I exchanged uneasy glances, our faces betraying our fear. *Is Hernández beginning to suspect what we feared? Could he be thinking that this plague, this strange disease, is somehow our fault?* The thought twisted inside me like a knife. *What would he do if he found out we might be the cause of his suffering? Could this be how it all ends for us? How did things get so out of control?*

We couldn't escape him. Hernández was a powerful man, surrounded by guards, security, and a network of loyal followers. There was no way out. The only choice we had was to face him.

In silence, we stood from the table and began walking through the house. The air felt heavy, thick with tension. It was as if we were walking toward our own execution. Each step felt slower, more uncertain. My stomach twisted with dread as we climbed the stairs toward Hernández's room.

Abe was the first to speak, his voice low and quiet. "I'm sorry, Princess. I didn't think it would go this far."

There was worry in Abe's eyes. He thought this was the end. I nodded slightly, a gesture that meant more than words could say. We were all thinking the same thing: *this might be the last thing we ever do.*

When we reached the door, I could feel my heart pounding in my chest, the sound loud in my ears. Abe gently pushed the door open, and I flinched instinctively. Nothing happened. No hitmen followed, no weapons were pointed at us. It felt too calm.

We stepped into the room. Abe entered first, I followed, and Louis closed the door behind us.

Hernández was sitting propped up in his large, luxurious bed. The sight of him was unsettling. The man who had once looked so powerful and intimidating now looked fragile, broken. His shirt was off, and I could see bandages wrapped around his torso, stained with pus that oozed through the cloth. His face was covered with sores around his mouth, along his jawline, and at his hairline. His strong, commanding presence had been replaced with a much more human vulnerability.

"Come in," he said, his voice strong; even in his weakened state, it carried an edge of menace.

We stepped forward, moving closer to the bed, unsure of what to do or say. The silence between us was thick, uncomfortable.

I swallowed hard, trying to steady myself before I spoke. "How are you feeling?" My voice was quieter than I intended, timid.

Hernández shot me a glare that sent a chill down my spine. "How do I look like I'm feeling?" he snapped. His words were sharp, full of anger and pain.

I instinctively took a step back, moving slightly behind Abe, as if his presence might offer me some protection.

"Terrible," Hernández spat. "My body's wasting away, and there's nothing I can do to stop it." He turned to Abe, his gaze hardening. "Abe, you're a smart man," he said more calmly but with lingering suspicion. "Tell me why it is that everyone in my organization is being eaten alive by this parasite while you, your family, and everyone here who serves you are unaffected." He spoke slowly, emphasizing each phrase.

The question hung heavily in the air, pressing down on all of us. I could feel the tension in the room rise. My heart skipped a beat.

Abe cleared his throat, buying himself a few extra seconds to think. "I can't be sure," he said, his voice tight. "It's certainly a very strange phenomenon."

Hernández's eyes narrowed as he leaned back in his bed. "I was with Isa the whole night before this happened to me," he said, his gaze locking onto Abe. "Close with her. Kissing. Touching. Intimate. Skin to skin." Abe shifted uncomfortably in his spot, and Hernández noticed, his lips curling into a knowing smirk. "Yet," he continued, his voice getting darker, "she hasn't been affected by this disease." He paused, letting his words sink in. "Why do you think that is?"

Abe's face twisted with discomfort. He knew exactly where this conversation was going, and so did we. It was the same conclusion we had all quietly feared. Abe cleared his throat again, trying to buy himself more time, but we all knew the answer was already hanging in the air.

"We serve a god named Jehovah," Abe started, his voice steady but strained. "Jehovah is the creator of the entire Earth. He controls the sun, the moon, the stars. He created me, and He created you. He controls the wind and the storm and every disease, including the one that's affecting you right now. Jehovah has called us to South Texas to build a new tribe, a new nation. We put that on hold because of the hurricane, which forced us to evacuate here to Mexico. But that's temporary. We'll be returning to South Texas soon to continue Jehovah's plan."

Hernández was quiet for a moment, his gaze unwavering. "And I haven't stopped you from leaving to go back, have I?" he asked. "In fact, I've even given you resources to help you succeed." Abe nodded in agreement. "So, if I've done nothing to prevent you from following your god's will, why has this disease struck my people?"

Abe's expression turned grim. "Jehovah promised to give the land of South Texas to my children," he said softly. "The children of my wife and me. The children I don't have yet."

Hernández raised an eyebrow, his curiosity piqued. "And how does this concern me?"

Abe let out a long, slow breath. None of us knew how Hernández would react to the next part. With one last look at me, Abe said, "Your wife and mine...are one and the same."

The room went still, the tension unbearable. Hernández's face went from confused to shocked in an instant, his eyes narrowing in disbelief. "What?" he rasped. "You're saying...Isa is—"

"Your wife is my wife," Abe said quietly, his voice steady despite the storm that seemed to be building in Hernández's eyes. "She is the mother of the future children Jehovah promised to me. And because of that...this disease, this plague, it's happening to you. To your organization."

The silence that followed was deafening.

TWENTY-EIGHT

Hernández's face twisted through a range of emotions—understanding, fear, and pure rage. His face turned beet red, and he shouted, his voice thick with anger and pain, "What is this you've done to me? Why didn't you tell me she was your wife? Why did you say, 'She is my sister,' and let me take her as my wife?"

He was furious, and I couldn't blame him. Abe had lied, and that lie, as small as it might've seemed at the time, had blown up into an issue far bigger than we could have ever imagined. It had hurt me, making me feel cheap and betrayed. And it had affected Hernández and his entire organization, leaving them all sick and dying from the disease.

Abe's lie had put us all in Hernández's crosshairs. He had the power to destroy us all, and in doing so, he could wipe out any chance we had to follow Jehovah's plan.

But Jehovah was stronger than Hernández. That truth gave me a flicker of hope.

Hernández's face slowly lost its red hue, though the boils and sores still marked his skin. He took a deep breath, clearly trying to control his fury. Through clenched teeth, he spat, "Now, here is your wife." He waved a hand in my direction, a gesture that felt more like a dismissal than a command. "Take her and go."

Abe nodded quickly, his expression filled with a mix of respect and relief. Without a word, he bowed slightly and began backing away from Hernández, as Maria had done when we had first arrived. It was a sign of submission.

Abe reached out, gently grabbed my arm, and guided me and Louis out of the room. We moved quickly, our footsteps echoing in the hallway. We didn't stop until we reached the room where Abe had been staying at the opposite end of the house.

"What do we do now?" I asked, trying to catch my breath.

"Get packed and get out of here," Abe answered, tossing things into a suitcase with urgency.

Eddy walked into the room, his eyes wide with surprise. "You're leaving already?"

"Yes, we're all leaving," Abe said, still focused on shoving clothes and supplies into the suitcase, moving with quick, practiced motions.

"Including Señora Isa?" Eddy asked, glancing over at me.

"Yes, including Isabelle, my Princess," Abe replied, looking into my eyes and straight into my heart.

An alarm blared through the house's intercom system, making us all jump. Abe, Louis, and I froze in fear, but Eddy shrugged it off.

"I have to go," Eddy said. "That's our cue for a house-wide servants meeting." He turned and disappeared out of the room without another word.

We stood there, the tension thick, until the sound of his footsteps faded away. We all exhaled in relief, though the feeling didn't last long.

"He said we could go, right?" I asked, my voice shaky with nerves. "You don't think he'll try to kill us now, do you?"

"I have no idea," Abe answered, his voice tight with worry. "Louis, go get packed. Princess, you, too. We need to be ready to leave as soon as possible. We're not out of danger until we're out of this country."

"What about the others?" I asked. I hadn't seen them since breakfast and didn't know if they had been impacted by our predicament.

"Yes, you're right. We need to alert the others. Text Amelia and Emma, and I'll text Henry and Theo. That should cover everyone," he said.

I nodded and headed for my room, but my nerves wouldn't stop churning in my stomach. My room was right next to Hernández's, and the thought of being anywhere near him made my skin crawl. I was afraid of him, but I also couldn't shake the pity I felt. He had been through so much in the past couple of days, much of it because of the lie Abe had told. He was another victim in all of this, like me. *But hadn't I been complicit?* I'd never corrected the lie Abe had told or the misunderstanding Hernández had about our relationship. *What if I had? Would Abe have been killed? Or would Hernández have ignored me and thought I was the liar instead?*

If there was one thing I'd learned from all of this, it was that lying only made everything worse.

I entered my room and glanced around, feeling out of place. I hadn't even bothered to get any of my things from the RV since we'd gotten here. Everything I needed had been provided for me. There was nothing I had to pack.

I texted Emma and Amelia to tell them we needed to hurry and pack and that I was available to help if they needed it. I waited to get confirmation they had gotten the text message. They were headed to their rooms with their kids to get their things together.

I walked over to the closet. The clothes were beautiful, expensive, designer things. They fit me perfectly, had maybe even been tailored specifically for me. But as I reached out to touch them, a wave of discomfort hit me. They weren't mine. They weren't me. I wasn't a person who belonged in a life like this. I had my own clothes, my own identity. They fit the "me" who was about to help Abe start a new nation. The real me.

I took one last look around the room, at the life I'd been living for the past few days, then turned and walked out.

Abe was already in the hallway, his suitcase packed and ready to go. Louis was still in his room, rushing to gather his things.

Once he was finished, we checked in on the others. I headed into Emma's room to help pack Ellie and Harper. As soon as I took over, Emma went to work on packing for her and James.

I moved quickly, tossing the kids' clothes into their tiny suitcases. I checked the washroom for toiletries and any other items. "Did you bring any toys in from the RV, kids?" I asked as I zipped up Harper's suitcase.

"I have my blankie and stuffy. They're on my bed," Harper said, her voice full of excitement as she rushed to grab her things.

"Anything else?" I asked Ellie.

She shook her head. "Nope."

"Great. I think we're all packed." I handed Ellie the handle of her suitcase. "Take this over to your mom."

Ellie nodded and carried it off while Harper returned to me, holding her blankie and stuffed animal.

"Hold on to those tightly, Harper. We don't want to lose them." I smiled, grabbing her suitcase. "I'll take this."

We were ready to go in the Williams's room, so I left Harper's suitcase with Emma and went to check on the Johnsons. They were about done, too. We all gathered in the hallway, and I did a quick headcount. Thirteen people, all accounted for. Everyone was here.

We hurried down the stairs, and to our surprise, Eddy and Honey were waiting for us at the bottom with a basket full of keys to the RVs, the Jeep, Mateo's RVs, and James's SUV.

"We're coming with you, Abe," Eddy said, his voice firm. "We've been released from our duties here. We're heading to the States with you. That's what the meeting was about. Hernández has given orders for no one to harm you as you leave, and we are to ensure all the gifts he gave you and your family go with you. Including us."

Honey beamed with excitement beside him, looking like she couldn't wait to get going.

Abe raised an eyebrow, glancing at the basket of keys. "Can you do that? Do you have the paperwork to get into the States?"

Eddy smiled proudly. "I'm an American citizen. Born in Texas. Honey has her papers, too." He paused. "Berry and Daniel are coming, too. They'll drive the horse trailer."

"I forgot about the horses," Abe muttered, running a hand through his hair. "Okay, if everyone's good to go and we can get across the border, let's get moving."

Eddy nodded. "We'll make it happen. Let's go."

With that, we all hurried to the front door, ready to leave the mansion behind and head toward whatever the next chapter would bring.

***

The three-vehicle caravan that had started our trip to Mexico had grown into a six-vehicle convoy on the way back to the United States. Louis had added to the convoy his new massive motor coach RV, Abe was driving his new Range Rover with the luxury towable RV attached, and we had the stable boys hauling the horse trailer. The rest of our group were packed into our original three RVs. Theo and Henry drove Abe's Jeep with our original RV while Eddy and Honey rode with us in the Range Rover.

Our first test was getting out of La Mansión de Tampico. Guards were standing at the gates, armed and staring us down. Even though Hernández had supposedly told his men to stand down and let us go, I couldn't shake the feeling that this was all a trap. It didn't help that the whole exiting process felt like it took an eternity. We had six vehicles now, and each one had to pass through the gates slowly. One by one, each of us made it through and got our tourist cards back without any shots being fired, and I counted every moment as a small victory.

But even after we made it through the gates and onto the highway, we weren't exactly in the clear. Fear still clawed at me. Hernández had eyes everywhere. Halcones, spies, whatever you wanted to call them. He had people watching every exit, every road, and every truck stop along the way. The rumor was that he had agents at nearly every checkpoint in the country, and with the resources he had, I didn't doubt he could send a hitman to find us even after we crossed into the States.

But, at least for now, they were all sick like Hernández too.

Still, I kept looking over my shoulder as we drove, wondering if we'd ever be safe again. *Will we make it back home without being hunted? Will we ever be free from this nightmare?*

I pulled out my phone and checked the weather app. The hurricane was out of South Texas, but it wasn't done yet. It had made a sharp turn, curving back north and east. It had weakened to a Category Three but was still powerful enough to cause serious damage. I couldn't help but think about how Midland, Texas, far from the coast and always dry, had never seen a storm like this.

My nerves tightened as I thought about what awaited us in South Texas. The storm, which had hit with Category Five strength yesterday, had left chaos in its wake. The weather app was full of videos showing flooded streets, homes with roofs ripped off or leaking, and people desperately trying to save whatever they could. As if losing their homes in the storm wasn't bad enough, now they had to face the aftermath of more rain that was expected over the next few days as Gert left Texas for good. I tried to push the worry from my mind. There was nothing I could do except keep moving forward, but I dreaded the thought of what we'd find when we got to South Texas.

Eddy said, his voice flat, "I'm sure the power's out, and the cell service is down, too. That's what usually happens after a hurricane."

I shifted uncomfortably in my seat. "We've never dealt with a hurricane. Abe, Louis, and I are from northern Minnesota. We don't get storms like this."

Eddy explained, "After a disaster like this, it sometimes takes days before they'll let you back into the area."

"So, we might have to detour around the damage to get into the country?" Abe asked, raising an eyebrow.

Eddy nodded. "I wouldn't be surprised if a lot of the roads are closed, maybe even the bridges. There's probably debris everywhere, and some roads might even be washed away."

Abe sighed, rubbing his chin. "Great. And gas might be in short supply, too."

Eddy looked over at him. "Exactly. Gas will be hard to find once we hit the worst areas, especially if the power's out. Make sure you top off before we get too close."

Abe thought for a moment. "Good point. I remember the long lines at the gas stations before we left. They might be completely out of fuel by now. At least Hernández's crew made sure we were all topped off before we left, but we should keep an eye on the gauges and make sure we're ready to fill up before we need it."

"Yeah, better safe than sorry," I muttered. I started a group chat for everyone on the drive to keep us all connected. I sent a message, *Keep an eye on your gas level. We need to fill up early and often.* A bunch of thumbs-up emojis popped up from the non-drivers in the group.

As we got closer to San Germán, we spotted a gas station that still had fuel and enough space for all our RVs to park. We all lined up to fill up, even though we could've made it the rest of the way on one tank, since we didn't know if we'd be able to find gas once we reached the storm zone.

I glanced around, and my shoulders relaxed a little. For now, it didn't look like anyone was following us. But after what we'd been through, I wasn't sure I could ever shake my fear completely.

***

We didn't have any problems at the checkpoints or with customs and immigration. Everyone traveling with us from Hernández's organization had the right paperwork to enter the States, so there were no delays or strange issues like there'd been when we'd crossed into Mexico. It felt too easy. Maybe it was because we were finally following Jehovah's plan again, and He was watching over us. It felt like another sign Abe had made the wrong choice by bringing us to Mexico instead of staying in the Promised Land even with the storm on the way.

Jehovah controlled the wind and the rain. If we'd stayed and followed His plan, He would've kept us safe and provided us with what we needed. We had to stop running away or trying to figure things out on our own when we were scared. We needed to learn to trust Him completely.

The sun was low in the sky when we crossed the border, its orange glow hanging heavy in the humid air. The asphalt felt like it had been baking under the intense heat for days, the roads cracked and uneven as Abe drove toward Brownsville, a place that last week had been home to the sounds of happy children splashing in the RV park's pool. As we got closer, the devastation started to unfold, and it hit me like a punch to the gut.

Even though Brownsville was about one hundred fifty miles south of where the center of the storm had made landfall in Corpus Christi, the eye of the record-breaking storm was nearly two hundred thirty miles wide. Brownsville had been on the south side of the storm, close enough to the southern eye wall for the winds to still be nearly one hundred fifty miles per hour. The impact was undeniable.

Buildings that had once stood tall and proud and been bustling with life were now skeletal frames, their windows blown out and roofs peeled back as though they'd been shredded by some giant hand. The streets were eerily quiet, save for the distant hum of a generator or the occasional thump of debris being moved. Power lines lay like fallen soldiers, tangled in a mess of broken concrete and twisted metal. It was as if the hurricane had come through and erased everything.

The smell was the next thing that hit me. The scents of wet earth, saltwater, and a metallic odor that made my stomach churn. There was the stench of rotting, too, as if nature itself was trying to reclaim what had been taken by the storm. Trees that had once been full of life were now partly uprooted or snapped in half, their branches scattered across the roads like forgotten limbs.

We drove slowly around fallen debris, trying to make sense of what we were seeing, but the scene was overwhelming, like a war zone. A family was sitting on the curb by what used to be their house. A mother was holding a child, wrapped in a tattered blanket, her eyes hollow, like all her hope had drained away. They didn't seem to notice us and just kept staring at the remains of their world in silence.

The city felt suspended in time, like it was holding its breath, waiting for help. I passed more wreckage: a car overturned on its side, windows shattered, tires blown out; a grocery store that was an empty shell now with its shelves stripped bare, though I wasn't sure if that was from pre-storm prep, looting, or the aftermath of nature's fury.

A group of National Guard soldiers were up ahead, their faces grim, their eyes scanning the horizon, their presence both reassuring and chilling. They were helping people, but there was a helplessness in how they moved, like they, too, were fighting a battle they couldn't win.

As we drove farther into the heart of Brownsville, the streets got narrower, the wreckage denser, and I felt a weight settle in my chest. It was as if the air itself was thick with grief. I could hardly wrap my mind around it. This wasn't just destruction. This was survival.

TWENTY-NINE

We drove through the town slowly, taking in the damage. The power was out, which meant the traffic lights, what was left of them, weren't working. Stop signs were gone, and road signs had been ripped off or bent beyond recognition. Business signs had been shattered, the broken light frames standing like skeletons. Billboards had either been knocked over or were standing half-torn and bare, their advertisements nothing but a memory of what they used to be. It was hard to tell where we were going. The streets were almost unrecognizable after the storm's fury; the town had been left in pieces.

When we pulled into Prevailing Winds RV Park, where we'd stayed before heading to Mexico, the sun had already set, and the world was wrapped in darkness. With the power still out, no streetlights shined, and no lights were coming from buildings or homes, only the headlights of our vehicles cut through the blackness. We knew there wouldn't be any hookups or amenities at the RV park, but we hoped the owner would still let us stay overnight.

The owner was standing by a small shed near the entrance. He recognized us right away and gave us a sad smile as we approached. "Our little town's looking rough tonight," he said with a sigh. "You're welcome to park here, but there's not much else I can offer you right now."

It was dark, and a curfew was in place because of the missing streetlights and signs. We paid for the night even though we wouldn't get the usual services. They were going to need every bit of help to rebuild after the storm, and we wanted to do our part. This was the land Jehovah had given us, after all. It felt like an honor to contribute to the community, to help them get back on their feet in whatever small way we could.

Once we were parked, we gathered inside Louis's RV to figure out the new sleeping arrangements and discuss what our plans for tomorrow might be. Berry and Daniel went to tend to the horses while the rest of us settled in around the small table. The air inside the RV was thick with the tiredness you only get after a long, stressful day.

"Louis, have you heard from Olivia yet?" I asked.

"I tried to call and text her, but the cell signal is out," Louis said. "I'll keep trying and let you know as soon as I hear from her."

"There's a lot of destruction across the whole area. We've only seen the beginning of it," Abe started. He leaned forward, his voice steady but urgent. "With the number of people we have and all the different skills everyone brings to the table, we could do a lot of good across South Texas. Imagine how many lives we could touch if we all put our heads and hands together."

Liam raised an eyebrow. "What are you suggesting?"

Abe took a breath, his eyes gleaming with purpose. "I'm suggesting we take a break from our regular work for the next month. We could travel from city to city, helping out wherever we can. There's so much need right now, and we have the ability to make a real difference."

He paused, letting his words settle before continuing. "When Jehovah first called me to come here from Minnesota, He told me He would bless me, so I could be a blessing." Abe emphasized his last words, making sure everyone felt their weight. "I don't have to wait until my new tribe is all set up. I can be a blessing to others right now, in the middle of all this destruction."

The others seemed to feel the same quiet admiration I did. Abe wasn't talking about what we could do for ourselves; he was thinking about how we could help the whole community. I admired his determination. It felt like he was trying his hardest to make up for the mistakes of the last few days. He was trying to get back on track with Jehovah's plan after the detour that felt like it had nearly dragged us all through hell and back.

***

Over the next week, we did exactly what Abe had suggested. We moved from one job to the next, helping wherever we could in Brownsville. We tarped roofs, cleared fallen debris, and pulled out soaked carpet padding from flooded homes. Each day was hard work, but the progress we made was rewarding.

By the end of the week, Elijah's family, Mateo and Charlotte, Lucas and Ava, and Mia had all rejoined us. Our little group, or "tribe," had grown to twenty-two people, and each of us used our skills to help the community in any way we could. Louis had finally heard from Olivia, and her family was safe. They were returning to Houston the following week, and Louis was going to drive up with his new RV and join them.

We retraced our route back to the north, slowly making our way toward the area where the eye of the storm had made landfall. We returned to Harlingen, Edinburg, Raymondville, and Encino, all places that had welcomed us when we'd passed through before. Now, it was our turn to help them.

Even though we were surrounded by the destruction of the storm, there was a quiet sense of purpose among us. Every day, we saw how much work needed to be done, but we also saw how much we could accomplish together. There was hope in the air, hope that maybe we could make things a little better for these communities, our Promised Land, one roof, one meal, and one day at a time.

***

It had been two months since the hurricane hit, and things were slowly starting to return to normal. We had finished making our rounds through the Promised Land and were now in Falfurrias, getting ready to pack up and head to Progeny Ranch RV Park near Alice for the weekend. The landscape was changing, though it would take many more months before Gert's destruction was a distant memory. Large trucks with cranes were still picking up piles of debris, like broken tree limbs and mangled fences the storm had left behind. They were hauling it all to makeshift landfills far from town. Every time a new business sign went up, covering the skeleton of light fixtures, it felt like a small victory.

Our relief efforts had been a big help, and every city we visited showed us how much they appreciated the work we were doing. Over the past couple of months, we had all learned a lot about building and repairing homes. Berry and Daniel were especially valuable with their skills in carpentry. They had learned the craft while working with horses and managing stables, and now they were teaching the men in the towns how to build structures from the ground up. Eddy, always quick with his hands, was a huge asset when it came to mechanical and electrical projects. He showed the team how to correctly wire homes and even helped fix electrical systems in a few places. Meanwhile, Honey took charge of cooking meals for everyone and keeping the RVs spotless after every day of hard work, which was no small task between the mud, dirt, and debris we tracked inside.

Emma, Liam, and Elijah had to shift back into their roles as managers in Abe's company as soon as the internet was restored. They worked hard to get the company back on track, making sure their teams met the year's goals, and the clients were taken care of. While we were unavailable, the employees who lived elsewhere had kept the company running, but they couldn't do it forever. Especially with the new influx of investment from Hernández, Abe had a lot of work to do to put that money into action. Luckily, now that everyone else was back at work, Amelia and I had Berry, Daniel, Eddy, and Honey to help us out with the day-to-day tasks and homeschooling the kids.

As for me, I was still struggling to process my feelings after what had happened in Mexico. Before Mexico, Abe had always been a stable figure in my life, someone I trusted. We had been building a life together, a life that was real, one that would last. With him, I had felt a love deep and real enough to carry me through the rest of our lives together. But after Hernández had entered my life, everything I'd known had come crashing down. It had only been for one night, but it had felt like an eternity. Even though Abe hadn't had much choice in the matter about what had happened, he had set us up for it by denying our relationship. And that left me feeling...unsettled.

I kept replaying it over and over in my head, trying to make sense of it all. *What does it mean? How am I supposed to feel?* Part of me wanted to block it out, pretend it hadn't happened, but that was impossible. The memory was there, and every time I thought about it, my chest would tighten, making it hard to breathe.

Mentally, I was a mess. My mind would race at night, running through memories of what had happened. Every part of me was torn. I wanted to shut down, close off, but I couldn't. If I wanted my relationship with Abe to work, I had to try to suppress my worries. I was constantly wrestling with the parts of me that still cared about Abe and the parts that felt violated, confused, and betrayed by what I had gone through. I had become a puzzle with pieces scattered everywhere, and no matter how hard I tried to put myself back together, I couldn't find a way to make the pieces fit. I didn't know how to heal or if I even could.

I had to keep myself busy to stay sane, and moving this weekend helped a lot. We were heading from Falfurrias to San Berry, Texas, one of the northernmost points in the Promised Land. It was also one of the towns hit hardest by the hurricane, only about forty-five miles inland from Corpus Christi. This was the place where Abe had built that altar in the woods, where he had sacrificed the animal and heard from Jehovah before we'd detoured to Mexico. It felt like forever ago yet was still fresh on my mind.

Both San Berry and Alice were still recovering, with homes damaged and lives uprooted. People there were beyond grateful for any help we could offer. With the power back on, we set up camp at the Progeny Ranch RV Park. It was familiar ground, and I appreciated the comfort of it. We spent the day in Alice offering whatever help we could—fixing roofs, clearing debris, distributing supplies. People were trying to move forward, but you could see the weight of the disaster on their faces.

That evening, Mamre Ammore, the owner of the RV park, invited us to a cookout. The park had a big double-layer grill and a firepit near the office, and the smell of food drifting through the air made my stomach growl. Mamre was one of those people who made you feel like family the minute you met him. His hospitality reminded me a lot of Abe's; they were both warm, welcoming, and generous. The two of them hit it off instantly. Mamre was thrilled to see our group had grown, and he was more than happy to make room for our horses, too. They could roam freely in a big fenced area near the railroad tracks, by far the best setup we'd had so far. The horses were happy, and we were able to focus on what needed to be done without worrying about them too much. It felt like we had peace here, even if it was only for a short while.

As night fell, we gathered around the firepit with Mamre, grilling hamburgers and hot dogs on his massive grill. The sound of the sizzling meat and the crackling of the fire was almost enough to make me forget the tension in my shoulders.

We told Mamre about our journey—how we'd traveled through South Texas helping people recover from the hurricane's destruction, building whatever we could to make life a little easier. He listened closely, nodding along, clearly moved by the stories.

"So, what's next for y'all?" Mamre asked Abe.

Abe looked up at the night sky, the stars bright above us. "I don't know yet. All I know is we're supposed to stay here, in South Texas, to build our family...somewhere."

Mamre nodded. "Well, I have a lot of open land here, if you'd like to set up camp. There are fields of oak trees south of the highway between Benavides and Alice. It's all owned by my family. There are some roads cut into the fields, but no homes yet. If you're interested, I'd be honored if you'd build your family there."

We all went quiet for a moment, letting his words sink in. The offer took us by surprise. The idea of settling down felt so foreign, but here it was, laid out in front of us. Mamre was offering us a chance to plant roots, to make a real future in a place Jehovah had promised to our offspring.

Mamre added, "I can see you're a man of God, Abe. And I know you're doing good for the people around you. I would be honored if you'd consider building your family on my land."

I could hardly believe what he was saying. For over a year, we'd been living out of our RVs, moving from town to town. The RVs were great for getting by, but they weren't a home. The thought of having a permanent place, a piece of land where we could settle in and build our tribe—it felt like a dream.

Abe spoke, "Thank you, Mamre. We'll think about it. But it means more than you know."

Mamre smiled at Abe, his eyes full of sincerity. "Take your time to think about it. You're welcome here for as long as you need."

We spent the rest of the evening around the fire, talking about the possibilities. The idea of a permanent home seemed crazy after all the moving, but it also felt right. We didn't have all the answers yet, but for the first time in a long time, it felt like we were getting close to Jehovah's promise. After Mamre's offer, it was like the universe was telling us it was time to focus on ourselves, for once.

The next day, Abe and the guys took the Jeep and Range Rover out to the land Mamre had talked about to see if it was as perfect as he had said. Abe hadn't made up his mind yet, but it seemed like, unless there was a major problem with the land, he was ready to go for it.

I couldn't help but feel a surge of excitement about having my own place again. A real home, with walls, a roof, and a foundation instead of wheels. A real kitchen where I could cook meals for our growing group. Maybe a place where I could raise a child one day. The idea of it made my heart beat faster. It felt like my dreams were within reach.

When Abe came back, he was grinning from ear to ear. His eyes were bright, like he had a secret to share. I already had a pretty good idea of what his answer was going to be.

"Princess," he said, his voice bubbling with excitement, "I'm not going to make any more big decisions without talking to

Jehovah first. The land looks amazing. Perfect for us to build a real home, somewhere we can stay forever."

I smiled, my heart lifting. Hope swirled inside me like a whirlwind, growing stronger by the second.

"But," he continued, his voice turning more serious, "the last big decision I made, the one to go to Mexico when the storm was coming, I thought it was the right call. It seemed obvious at the time. But...it was a huge mistake."

The light in his eyes flickered with fresh tears that threatened to fall. His face was a mix of pain, regret, and love, a combination that broke the walls deep inside me. "I'm sorry, Princess," he whispered, his voice thick with emotion. "I'm sorry for everything that happened in Mexico. I shouldn't have lied. That one lie...it set off a chain of events that spiraled out of control. It almost cost me you. You're the most important person in my life."

He gently took my hands in his, looking at me like he was seeing straight into my soul. His gaze felt like it was pulling all the truth and love from deep inside of him. "I won't make that mistake again," he promised, his voice raw. "I won't make any more decisions that could hurt you or our relationship. I love you so much."

The words hung in the air between us, and my chest tightened then slowly loosened. There it was, the truth, all of it. His fears, his regrets, his love. It was real.

For the first time, I felt like we were in sync. Like we were on the same page, fighting for the same thing.

"I'm going back to the altar I built in the woods," he said quietly, his voice steady and filled with determination. "I'm going to call on Jehovah's name. I need to know if this is the right thing to do, if we're meant to settle here, or if He wants us to keep moving." To my shock, he asked, "Will you come with me?"

For a moment, I was frozen, the words catching in my throat. Abe had always made the big decisions alone. He didn't need anyone else, not even me. I had been there, yes, but only in the background, following his lead. Now, he was asking me to step into his world, to share in a relationship so deeply personal to him, his connection with Jehovah.

It felt like he was letting me in in a way he never had before.

I smiled, my heart so full it ached. After what we had been through, the chaos in Mexico, the uncertainty that had gnawed at me about our future, my own fears about being enough for him, I realized he was trusting me with the most important part of his life. His faith. His heart.

That simple, powerful invitation made me believe that maybe we would be okay. This mission of his would become our mission. That thought settled like a warm light in my chest.

"Yes, Abe," I said, my voice steady but full of emotion. "I will go with you."

Associated Scripture

Chapter One

Genesis 11:27 NET: This is the account of Terah. Terah became the father of Abram, Nahor, and Haran. And Haran became the father of Lot.

Barren **Notes:** Terah is Grandad or "Terry." Abram is "Uncle Abe." Nahor is "Uncle Nate." Haran is Daddy or "Harry." Lot is "Louis."

Chapter Two

Genesis 11:28 NET: Haran died in the land of his birth, in Ur of the Chaldeans, while his father Terah was still alive.

Barren **Notes:** Abe lives on Ur Street and is a member of the Chaldean Indian tribe.

Chapter Six

Genesis 11:30 NET: But Sarai was barren; she had no children.

Barren **Notes:** The name Sarai means "princess."

Chapter Seven

Genesis 11:29 NET: And Abram and Nahor took wives for themselves. The name of Abram's wife was Sarai. And the name of Nahor's wife was Milcah; she was the daughter of Haran, who was the father of both Milcah and Iscah.

Barren **Notes:** Milcah is "Michaela" or "Mickie."

Chapter Nine

Genesis 11:31 NET: Terah took his son Abram, his grandson Lot (the son of Haran), and his daughter-in-law Sarai, his son Abram's wife, and with them he set out from Ur of the Chaldeans to go to Canaan. When they came to Haran, they settled there.

Barren **Notes:** Grandad took Abe, Louis, and Princess from Ur Street on the Chaldean Indian's reservation to go to Houston. Haran is "Houston."

Chapter Twelve

Genesis 11:32 NET: The lifetime of Terah was 205 years, and he died in Haran.

Barren **Notes:** Grandad lived to be 75 and died in Houston.

Chapter Thirteen

Genesis 12:1-3 NET: Now the Lord said to Abram,

"Go out from your country, your relatives, and your father's household to the land that I will show you. Then I will make you into a great nation, and I will bless you, and I will make your name great, so that you will exemplify divine blessing. I will bless those who bless you, but the one who treats you lightly I must curse, so that all the families of the earth may receive blessing through you."

Barren **Notes:** Jehovah calls Abe out of his reservation to go to a land He will show him.

Chapter Fourteen

Genesis 12:4-5 NET: So Abram left, just as the Lord had told him to do, and Lot went with him. (Now Abram was 75 years old when he departed from Haran.) And Abram took his wife Sarai, his nephew Lot, and all the possessions they had accumulated and the people they had acquired in Haran, and they left for the land of Canaan.

***Barren* Notes:** When Abe was 25 years old, he takes Louis and Sarai to go to the promised land in south Texas.

Chapter Sixteen

Genesis 12:5b-6 NET: They entered the land of Canaan. Abram traveled through the land as far as the oak tree of Moreh at Shechem. (At that time the Canaanites were in the land.)

***Barren* Notes:** They entered the promised land in south Texas and went to the oak tree at SeaWind RV Park.

Chapter Seventeen

Genesis 12:7 NET: The Lord appeared to Abram and said, "To your descendants I will give this land." So Abram built an altar there to the Lord, who had appeared to him.

Chapter Eighteen

Genesis 12:8-9 NET: Then he moved from there to the hill country east of Bethel and pitched his tent, with Bethel on the west and Ai on the east. There he built an altar to the Lord and worshiped the Lord. Abram continually journeyed by stages down to the Negev.

***Barren* Notes:** They went to a place with Benavides on the west and Alice on the east. Abram journeyed by stages down to the Rio Grande River.

Chapter Nineteen

Genesis 12:10-13 NET: There was a famine in the land, so Abram went down to Egypt to stay for a while because the famine was severe. As he approached Egypt, he said to his wife Sarai, "Look, I know that you are a beautiful woman. When the Egyptians see you they will say, 'This is his wife.' Then they will kill me but will keep you alive. So tell them you are my sister so that it may go well for me because of you and my life will be spared on account of you."

Barren **Notes:** There was a hurricane in the land, so Abe went down to Mexico to stay because the hurricane was severe.

Chapter Twenty

Genesis 12:14-15a NET: When Abram entered Egypt, the Egyptians saw that the woman was very beautiful. When Pharaoh's officials saw her, they praised her to Pharaoh.

Barren **Notes:** When Abe entered Mexico, the cartel saw that Princess was very beautiful and praised her to their jefe Hernández.

Chapter Twenty-Two

Genesis 12:15b-16 NET: So Abram's wife was taken into the household of Pharaoh, and he did treat Abram well on account of her. Abram received sheep and cattle, male donkeys, male servants, female servants, female donkeys, and camels.

Barren **Notes:** So Princess was taken into the household of Hernández, and Abe was treated well because of her and received RVs, SUVs, horses, male and female servants, and money.

Chapter Twenty-Six

Genesis 12:17 NET: But the Lord struck Pharaoh and his household with severe diseases because of Sarai, Abram's wife.

Barren **Notes:** Jehovah struck the cartel with syphilis, or possibly leprosy, because of Princess.

Chapter Twenty-Eight

Genesis 12:18-20 NET: So Pharaoh summoned Abram and said, "What is this you have done to me? Why didn't you tell me that she was your wife? Why did you say, 'She is my sister,' so that I took her to be my wife? Now, here is your wife. Take her and go!" Pharaoh gave his men orders about Abram, and so they expelled him, along with his wife and all his possessions.

***Barren* Notes:** Hernández sends Abe and Princess away with all of his gifts.

Chapter Twenty-Nine

Genesis 13:1-4 NET: So Abram went up from Egypt into the Negev. He took his wife and all his possessions with him, as well as Lot. (Now Abram was very wealthy in livestock, silver, and gold.)

And he journeyed from place to place from the Negev as far as Bethel. He returned to the place where he had pitched his tent at the beginning, between Bethel and Ai. This was the place where he had first built the altar, and there Abram worshiped the Lord.

***Barren* Notes:** Abe went back up from Mexico to south Texas with all his possessions, Princess, and Louis. He journeyed through the land of south Texas until he went to the place between Benavides and Alice.

CARAVAN CHARACTERS

The Johnson family driving their van: Liam (project development manager), Amelia (teacher), Luna (F, age 9), William Junior (M, age 7)

The Williams family pulling Mateo's RV with their SUV: Emma (customer service manager), James (sales), Ellie (F, age 8), Harper (F, age 7)

The Brown family driving their RV: Elijah (sales manager), Sophia (customer service), Levi (M, age 5)

The Martinez family driving their RV: Mateo (CFO), Charlotte (customer support), two dogs and a cat

The Flores family driving their car: Lucas (sales), Ava (customer service), baby on the way

Mia Garcia (customer service) driving her car and staying in the RV with the Brown family

Theo Rodriguez (product development) riding and staying in the RV with the Martinez family

Henry Lopez (product development) riding and staying in the RV with the Martinez family

Book Club and Bible Study Discussion Guide

These questions are designed to help readers reflect on the themes and characters in *Barren*. Book clubs or Bible studies may choose the questions that best fit their conversation. Some groups may prefer to discuss the questions during meetings, while others may reflect on them while reading.

First Impressions (Whole Book)

- What moment from the novel stayed with you the most after finishing the story?

- Which character did you connect with the most, and why?

- Did your understanding of any character change as the story progressed?

- What themes stood out most strongly as you read?

- How did the story affect the way you think about Sarai from Genesis?

Chapters 1–7

Scripture: Genesis 11:27–32

- What do the opening chapters reveal about Princess's personality and the way she observes the world around her?

- What details in the first chapter help establish the emotional tone of the story?

- How do the relationships introduced in chapter two influence Princess's sense of identity?

- What early signs of tension or uncertainty appear in the story?

- What emotions does Princess seem to be processing in chapter three?

- How does her perspective shape the way readers understand the events unfolding around her?

- How does the setting influence the mood of chapter four?

- What questions about the future begin to emerge for Princess?

- What does chapter five reveal about the expectations placed on women within Princess's cultural environment?

- How does Princess begin wrestling with questions about her future?

- What role does family heritage play in shaping Princess's identity?

- Genesis 11 briefly states that Sarai was barren. How does the novel begin exploring the emotional weight of that reality?

Chapters 8–14

Scripture: Genesis 12:1–5

- How do the characters react to the idea of leaving home and stepping into the unknown?

- How does the idea of leaving home affect Princess emotionally?

- What fears or uncertainties appear as the journey begins?

- What challenges appear as the journey continues?

- How does Princess view the changes happening around her?

- What themes of faith or doubt begin appearing in the story?

- Why do you think faith often requires stepping into the unknown?

- How does the journey begin to affect the relationships between the characters in chapter eleven?

- What moments reveal the emotional cost of leaving familiar places behind?

- How does the environment influence the tension of the story?

- How do the characters rely on each other during difficult moments?

- How does the novel help readers imagine Sarai's emotional experience during this time?

Chapters 15–21

Scripture: Genesis 12:6–13

- Where do you see fear influencing the characters' decisions?

- What does this part of the story reveal about vulnerability?

- How does Princess respond to the situation unfolding around her?

- How do the events of chapter seventeen increase the tension in the story?

- What does Princess reveal about her internal struggle?

- What turning points occur in chapter eighteen?

- How does chapter nineteen represent a climax in the story?

- How do the characters begin responding to the aftermath of what has happened?

- How do relationships between the characters begin to shift?

- How do the characters wrestle with trusting God

during uncertainty?

- How does this section help readers understand the tension in the Genesis story?

Chapters 22–29

Scripture: Genesis 12:14–20

- How does the story portray God's intervention in the characters' lives?

- What new understanding does Princess gain about herself in chapter twenty-three?

- How does the story begin moving toward resolution in chapter twenty-four?

- How do the characters support one another during this stage?

- How does Princess's understanding of faith develop in chapter twenty-six?

- What themes of hope appear as the story approaches its conclusion?

- What consequences remain even after the immediate danger passes?

- How does Princess reflect on the journey she has experienced?

Scripture Reflection Questions

- After reading Genesis 12:10–20, how does the novel change the way you view Sarai's experience in Egypt?

- What emotions might Sarai have felt during this event that the biblical text does not describe?

- What does this story reveal about the relationship between fear and faith?

Grief and Healing Theme Questions

- The novel begins with the devastating loss of Isabelle's parents. How does grief shape Isabelle's decisions and perspective throughout the story?

- How do Isabelle and her siblings process grief differently?

- What role does community play in helping the characters begin to heal?

Cultural Identity and Tradition Theme Questions

- Native American traditions appear throughout the novel, including powwows, community gatherings, and mourning practices. How do these traditions influence the characters' lives?

- Why might cultural rituals be especially meaningful during moments of grief or uncertainty?

- How do elders and community members help guide the younger generation in the story?

Womanhood and Fertility Theme Questions

- Isabelle begins experiencing severe medical symptoms that make her question whether she will ever be able to have children. How does this possibility affect her sense of identity?

- Why does the idea of barrenness carry such emotional weight within the story?

- In what ways does the novel challenge the idea that a woman's worth is defined by her ability to have children?

Faith During Uncertainty Theme Questions

- Throughout the novel, Isabelle wrestles with questions about faith and the future. Where do you see her struggling to trust God's plan?

- How does Isabelle's journey reflect the biblical story of Sarai in Genesis?

- What does the novel suggest about faith during seasons of waiting or uncertainty?

Final Reflection Questions

- How has Isabelle changed from the beginning of the novel to the end?

- What message do you think the author hopes readers take away from Isabelle's story?

- How did reading *Barren* influence the way you read the story of Sarai in Genesis?

If you liked BARREN, you'll love REJECTED.

Book Two in the *Margins of Genesis Series*
REJECTED
A Contemporary Story of Hagar
ELIZABETH SIMON

REJECTED

CHAPTER ONE

Puerto Cabezas, Nicaragua

My stomach growled as I dug through a heaping trash pile in desperation. I hadn't eaten in two days, and the smell of rotting vegetables and moldy banana peels attacked my nose. My long hair fell into my face. I pushed it back behind my ears as I picked through the crumpled-up food wrappers. Flies buzzed past my ears mocking me, and I swatted them away.

This cafe was my first choice for leftovers. Most nights I could find a half-eaten tamal tossed out by a tourist or sailor. Midnight approached, and the full moon cast dark shadows over the spooky alleyway. I wanted to hurry home, but I didn't want to go empty-handed.

Papá died over a year ago. Before he died, he came home in the evenings from working at the dock, his face red, and weariness showing in his eyes. He would sit down, clutching his shirt. Mamá would run to him, saying something about his health. And then one day, he never returned home. I didn't see Mamá smile again after that day. Papá's strong arms would never hold me again. Mamá said he lives in my eyes and my smile, and that my big heart held his memory. But memories don't bring home dinner like Papá used to.

Now, at nine years old, I had to find our food. I helped because Mamá took care of my baby brother, Jose, in our tiny one-room shack farther in town. Mamá needed the most, since she still fed Jose with her milk. I was too big for that now. The last two nights, I found a half-eaten quesilla in this café dumpster and brought it home. It wasn't enough for both of us, so I told Mamá I'd already eaten. That way she and Jose could have it.

I hoped today's search would be better.

A crash sounded at the far end of the alley. Fear shot through me, and I pressed my thin body against the cold concrete wall, shrinking into the shadows. A tall man dug through the heaps of trash. I assumed he was trying to find his dinner too. He was stick-thin, but his belly stuck out like the bottom of a bowl. He must have found some food to fill his belly. I would try his spot once he left.

I hid in the shadows, watching and counting the minutes to myself as I waited. It took nearly thirty minutes before he moved on. Nothing worth bringing home was left in the scattered heaps of trash strewn about, so I headed toward the motel where the tourists stayed.

I squinted through the darkness to see if the coast was clear. The dark nights could be dangerous for a girl to be alone if I wasn't careful. Last week, Mamá told me about some kids going missing near the docks. Abril from my class at school hadn't been back since that day.

I hugged the shadows and crept down the street toward the hotel, scurrying like a rat between buildings. If I didn't find food and head home soon, Mamá would be worried.

I reached the motel and headed for the back alley where a kitchen filled the back side of the motel. It was one of the biggest motels in the city, big and so close to the beach that its pretty lights shone off the waves at night.

I rounded the corner and saw a pile of garbage. It was glorious! So many bags packed with rotting food. The smell of the old fruit, moldy vegetables, and rotting meat filled the air. There would be plenty to feed me and Mamá here!

I raced to the bags and heaved them around, searching for ones with food smashed against the sheer plastic. I shoved one bag, and it rolled, knocking over a tin garbage can. It clanged as it toppled to the pavement. I jumped and grimaced, hoping it hadn't been heard.

The back door of the restaurant banged open, and a plump man ran out, yelling in Spanish. He wore an apron smattered with food stains, and it made my mouth water. "¡Sal ya de aquí, rata!" he said. "¡Sale!" He called me an animal, but he ran at me with his teeth bared like a wild boar. He screamed at me again to go away. I ran back around the corner toward the front of the motel and smacked into a woman.

The woman wore nice clothes, so different from my brown, dirt-stained rags which barely held together. Soft hands landed on my shoulders, and I looked at her. She batted her long eyelashes at me and flipped her dark hair behind her back. She didn't seem disgusted as most people did when they saw my filth. She smiled at me with pity. There was something behind her smile I couldn't quite understand.

"Hello, sweetie," she said in Spanish. Her voice dripped with sweetness, too much sweetness. "Isn't it a little late for you to be out wandering the streets?" I stared up at her. I didn't know her, and she made me feel uncomfortable.

She took a puff of a cigarette and looked me up and down with a glint in her eye. I glanced around for a way to escape her. She blocked my way, and I couldn't go back since the man was still shouting at me from behind the motel. I didn't know what to do or how to get around her, so I said, "Excuse me. I think I'll go home now."

"She speaks!" the woman said drawing her hand to her mouth with mock shock. She smiled. "Are you hungry, dear?"

I nodded. My stomach growled in response, as if it heard her speaking. She waved her hand toward the door leading me on. It might have been my tummy doing the walking when I followed her. I was so hungry.

She led the way toward the motel lobby. I paused at the door, feeling too ashamed to enter. It was much nicer than any place I had been to. "I shouldn't go in there. I'm going home."

"Nonsense," she said, turning to me. "I'll buy you a nice dinner, and you can bring the leftovers home with you." She waved at me again to follow her as she walked into the lobby. The click of her high heels echoed against the tile floor.

I hesitated, but she seemed nice enough. She must be a tourist, so maybe she felt sorry for me. I had heard of such things.

The lobby was painted in reds and yellows, and four chairs sat in a circle to the right. A simple opening in the far wall revealed an old man sleeping in a folding chair behind the counter.

"Excuse me. Is the kitchen closed?" the woman asked.

The man grunted and woke up. He was thin and looked unkept, much like the man I saw scrounging for food in the trash. He waved her off and growled, "Room service only."

"Even better!" she exclaimed to no one in particular, with glee in her voice. What was making her so happy? She turned to me and said, "You can come to my room, and I'll order some food."

It was getting late though. Mamá would start to worry if I didn't return soon. The latest I had been out was 2 a.m., and it was still a thirty-minute walk home. I bit my lip and thought about leaving, but only for a moment. My tummy won again.

I followed her up a staircase.

"The rooms aren't super nice," she said, "but they're nice enough. The food is good."

I wasn't paying much attention to what she said, as I fought inside about going with her or returning home empty-handed.

"I just came in on one of the ships yesterday, but I won't be staying long. I leave tomorrow morning," she said.

The doors to the rooms lined the outside corridor. She went down a long concrete walkway and stopped at the last door. Unlocking it with her key, she pushed it open with her bottom, leaving it wide for me to enter. She smiled and waved me in.

I inched into the room. It was bigger than our entire house! A large metal box by the window blew cool air into the heat and humidity of the night, soothing my sweaty skin.

A single table stood in between two beds with a phone sitting on top of it. The table was bigger than our only table at home. The phone was like one the principal in my school used.

A fancy bathroom appeared through another door. A bathroom, with running water! Our house didn't have any running water. I fetched water from a well down the street every morning, and we peed and pooped in a hole in the small backyard.

The two beds were so big, one of them could fit my entire family. Clean white blankets that smelled like wildflowers covered the beds, along with pillows that felt like giant clouds. We didn't even have a bed in our house. We slept on blankets on the dirt floor.

I had never seen a place so fancy in all my life. I skimmed the bedsheets with my finger. They felt so soft, so inviting. I imagined curling up and going to sleep on top of the soft mattress. I almost forgot my hunger. Almost. My tummy hadn't though, and it roared, reminding me I hadn't eaten in two days.

The strange woman picked up the phone and ordered food. "We'll have a little of everything on the menu."

The woman continued to chatter away about this and that, and waved at the bed, urging me to climb up. Feeling embarrassed and fearful, I paused and looked at her. She smiled and nodded toward the bed, inviting me on.

I climbed on the bed, leaving dirty streaks on the white cotton where my clothes touched, and propped myself up on the pillows. They were soft like a stuffed animal but for your head. I pressed my face into one of the pillows, and it didn't scratch or poke. It hugged me back. I didn't even know you could sleep with something so soft under your head. At home, I used my arm or a rolled-up shirt.

I felt like a princess. Nothing I knew was as comfortable as this bed. I closed my eyes, content and amazed at my luck. I wasn't still scrounging around in trash heaps in the heat and humidity but was comfortable in the soft, cool motel bed.

It didn't take long for the food to come. Someone rapped on the door, and the woman opened it to a young man carrying a tray. She took it from him and placed it on the table next to the phone. The smells of the earthy steamed banana leaf and smoky gallo pinto filled the room.

I rubbed my eyes and stared in awe. It was a feast! Gallo pinto, nacatamal, vigorón. The woman invited me to eat, and I dug in, stuffing food into my mouth with my hands, trying to appease my hungry belly. The flavors mixed in my mouth: salty, garlicky, tangy, nutty.

She watched me, not eating. Maybe she was waiting for me to finish before she started. I didn't know. I didn't care. I ate the fresh, delicious food, not leftover scraps from the trash.

It didn't take long for me to eat so much I almost made myself sick. There were plenty of leftovers to take home to Mamá, and she would have her fill too. But...maybe Mamá could wait a minute. I needed a little rest. My tummy was so full, I couldn't think straight.

My tired body was so heavy as I sank into the soft pillows, yawning. My eyes fluttered, shutting out the room around me. I could take the leftovers home to Mamá after a short, little nap...

***

When I woke up, I was no longer on the soft princess bed. I wasn't even on my dirt floor at home. I was on a hard surface in a dark room. The room was moving back and forth, like it was swaying in the wind...or on the sea.

Acknowledgements

Bringing this book into the hands of my wonderful readers has been an incredible journey, and I am deeply grateful to those who have helped me along the way.

First and foremost, I give all glory and honor to God—Yahweh, Yahweh, compassionate and gracious, slow to anger, and abounding in loyal love and faithfulness (Exodus 34:6). It was HE who placed the idea for *Margins of Genesis* on my heart, HE who blessed me with the talent to write, and HE who strengthened me through every draft and revision. Without HIM, I would not be here, and this book would not exist.

To my beta readers—Stephanie Weaver, Erin Levesque, Robb Bossley, Camille Elliott, and Brittany Rutherford—thank you for your patience, your thoughtful feedback, and your willingness to endure the earliest versions of this story. Your insights were invaluable in shaping it into what it is today.

To my critique groups—Suncoast Writers Guild's Long Writers group and the Women's Writers Fellowship of New Day Christian Church—I am so grateful for your encouragement, wisdom, and thoughtful critiques. Your support has made me a stronger writer, and I cherish the time we've spent together refining our craft.

To my editors, Melody Delgado and Danielle Dyal, your keen eyes and expertise have been instrumental in polishing this manuscript. Thank you for pushing me to be better with each revision.

To the Robert Herrick and the Florida Writers Association's Self-Publishing Support Group, your guidance was a beacon through the maze of publishing. Your advice and encouragement gave me the confidence to see this project through to the end.

To my inspiration for reading Genesis fifty times – Tim Mackie, Jon Collins, and The Bible Project (bibleproject.com) – and for my desire to learn more about the cultural context and authorial intent of the Bible – Marty Solomon, Brent Billings, and the BEMA podcast (https://www.bemadiscipleship.com/) – I can't thank you enough. Without you, I wouldn't have become so in love with Genesis to want to complete a project like this.

To my sister, Dr. Amy Coker—thank you for your invaluable guidance on the medical details.

To my esteemed colleague, Rachel Hruska—your insight into Minnesota lingo and Native culture brought depth and authenticity to this story. I may not have captured everything perfectly, but your support made it far more genuine than it would have been without you.

And finally, to you—my amazing readers. Your love for stories and willingness to embark on new journeys make all the hard work worthwhile. I hope this book has brought you joy, inspiration, and a fresh perspective on Genesis. May it bless you as much as writing it has blessed me.

With gratitude,

Elizabeth Simon

About the Author

Elizabeth Simon is a storyteller at heart. A native of Ohio now living in sunny southwest Florida, she began writing stories as a teenager, scribbling characters and plot lines between homework and youth group. Life took her down a different path—into the world of accounting, corporate compliance, and risk management—but the love of storytelling never left her.

For over two decades, Elizabeth built a respected career helping organizations uphold ethics and integrity. She's been a featured writer in *Compliance & Ethics Professional* and *Fraud Magazine* and has spoken across the country on doing what's right—even when it's hard. But behind the spreadsheets and boardroom presentations, a deeper calling stirred: to tell stories that wrestle with truth, faith, identity, and redemption.

Her debut novel, *Barren,* is the first in a powerful series that blends Biblical themes with timeless struggles—legacy, betrayal, love, and the search for belonging. Inspired by her deep study of Genesis and authors like Francine Rivers, John Grisham, and Karen Kingsbury, Elizabeth writes with both heart and grit, weaving suspense and spiritual insight into every chapter.

When she's not writing or leading in the corporate world, you'll find her reading, reflecting, or walking near the water, dreaming up the next story that just won't let her go.